Scratch is a hit!

"A powerful story of pain and healing, and the redemptive power of forgiveness. Every character in *Scratch* is beautifully flawed, their emotions raw and authentic. Helms's storytelling flows like beats in one of Casey's DJ mixes—fast, engaging, and addictive—and I didn't want it to end. I cried, I laughed, I *swooned*. Phenomenal!"
—Rachel Harris, *New York Times*–bestselling author of *Accidentally Married on Purpose*

"*Scratch* is at once haunting, hopeful, and heartbreakingly tender. Readers will swoon for Daniel!"
—Lexi Ryan, *New York Times* bestselling author

"Gripping new adult romance . . ."
—*Booklist*

"A refreshingly strong-willed and flawed heroine makes this layered page-turner memorable."
—*Publishers Weekly*, starred

"I cannot put into words how much I loved the depth of Casey's story and the craft in which the author weaves the story. There are a few lip-biting moments that are very exciting. But the real winner here is Casey's journey in learning to love and trust! Definitely recommending this one!"
—*Night Owl Reviews*, 5 stars top pick

"Touching . . . This one's for readers everywhere, both on and off campus."
—*RT Book Reviews*

Novels by Rhonda Helms

Scratch

Published by Kensington Publishing Corporation

Break Your Heart

RHONDA HELMS

KENSINGTON BOOKS
www.kensingtonbooks.com

KENSINGTON BOOKS are published by

Kensington Publishing Corp.
119 West 40th Street
New York, NY 10018

All Kensington titles, imprints, and distributed lines are available at special quantity discounts for bulk purchases for sales promotion, premiums, fund-raising, educational, or institutional use.

Special book excerpts or customized printings can also be created to fit specific needs. For details, write or phone the office of the Kensington Sales Manager: Kensington Publishing Corp., 119 West 40th Street, New York, NY 10018. Attn. Sales Department. Phone: 1-800-221-2647.

Kensington and the K logo Reg. U.S. Pat. & TM Off.

eISBN-13: 978-1-61773-123-5
eISBN-10: 1-61773-123-4
First Kensington Electronic Edition: August 2015

ISBN-13: 978-1-61773-122-8
ISBN-10: 1-61773-122-6
First Kensington Trade Paperback Printing: August 2015

10 9 8 7 6 5 4 3 2 1

Printed in the United States of America

To my husband, who gets me, who supports me, who shows me he loves me in a thousand ways. The journey to find you took a long time, but I can't imagine my life without you in it. Thank you for being you, and for loving me for being me.

Chapter 1

"There isn't enough coffee in the world to make a Monday morning doable," I grumbled as I reached for the coffeepot and poured. The liquid sloshed over the side of my mug.

From her open bedroom door, my roommate, Casey, laughed and ran a brush through her brown hair. "You were just like this the first day of fall semester too, remember? Completely groggy and out of it. Maybe you should have gotten some sleep last night instead of creeping in at three in the morning."

I shrugged and shot her a crooked grin. "Hey, it was a good night." I'd been invited to a last-day-of-winter-break-before-the-new-semester party off campus with a couple of fellow seniors. We'd lived it up. After all, today kicked off our final semester of undergrad.

"I'm going to meet Daniel for breakfast before my first class," Casey said. She walked over and gave me a hug. I paused, surprised, then hugged her back. She'd come a long way from the distant, awkward roommate she'd been last year.

Her boyfriend, Daniel, had changed her. No, *love* had changed her. Over time, she'd become more affectionate, more open with everyone, not just him. I liked the fact that we felt like real friends now, not just roommates.

"Tell hottie I said hi," I told her, then waggled my fingers when she grabbed her coat and books and darted out the door. I chugged my coffee and hopped in the shower. Threw on my favorite skinny jeans and bright red cashmere sweater, paired with knee-high black boots. Then I stuffed my books into my backpack, locked the door behind me and made my way down the street a few blocks toward campus.

The early January air was crisp, biting. Dark clouds hovered over my head, threatening to burst open with torrents of snow. But even the gloomy atmosphere couldn't shake me. As much as I griped about morning classes in general, I was pretty happy with this semester's schedule and even happier that I'd gotten into modern cryptography, a rarely offered course on campus.

I plodded along the snow-edged sidewalk, stomach tightening with a tension I'd been trying to ignore the last few days. Thinking about cryptography, the class I was heading toward now, made me think about the class's professor, Dr. Reynaldo, my senior thesis advisor. He should have gotten back to me about my thesis by now. I'd turned it in to him more than three weeks ago. Why hadn't I heard from him? Did he hate the paper? He was normally more responsive and prompt than this. Well, I'd just corner him either before or after class, because this not-knowing shit was driving me crazy.

Clusters of students thickened as I stepped on campus, passed rows of stately buildings. Leafless branches were coated in a thick layer of snow, a bright contrast against the red and brown brick buildings. Smythe-Davis was a gorgeous campus, no matter the season.

I loved living around here. Though this was my last semester in undergrad, I'd already been accepted into the master's program here—with a full scholarship *and* a TA position. It was both a relief to have my plans right on track and a thrill to get to stay at the school for two more years. But first I had to graduate.

Which meant speeding up and getting to class on time. Dr. Reynaldo hated stragglers, and I didn't want to piss him off the first day.

I hustled and made it to the large brick building with a full wall of windows facing the center of campus. Our math department—my home on campus.

"Hey, Megan!" a male voice said from my right. Patrick took a drag from his cigarette and shoved away from the stone half wall where he was leaning.

"Hey, yourself!" I said with a saucy wink.

He gave me a broad smile in response and eyed me up and down. "Looking *good*, baby." Patrick, one of our school's top basketball players, had been on my radar for a while. He was a tall, gorgeous dark-skinned man with huge muscles, sexy tattoos and thighs as big as tree trunks. We flirted off and on whenever we saw each other on campus, but it never got beyond that.

I glanced at my phone. Crud, no time to chat him up. "I gotta run," I said apologetically. "I work at Stackers. Come see me there sometime, and I'll hook you up."

His smile grew wider, and his bright teeth flashed. "It's a date."

I walked into the building, a smug grin on my face. The semester had just begun and was already off to a good start. I went up the stairs and made it to my classroom two minutes before the start of the class.

As I wove my way toward a chair in the back row, I waved at various fellow math majors I recognized. We'd been in many of the same classes together, had done overnight study sessions and last-minute cramming.

I settled in, got out my notebook and cryptography textbook. Huh. Dr. Reynaldo wasn't here yet. That uneasy flutter in my stomach returned. I'd taken two other classes with him before, and the man was always the first in the room and the last to leave.

By a few minutes past eight, the whispers started.

"Excuse me. Am I in the right room? This is cryptography, right?" the brunette beside me asked.

I nodded. "Yeah, this is it."

The door opened then, and the noise quieted down a bit . . . then turned silent as an attractive Asian man walked to the front of the room and dropped his books on the desk in front. His shock of black hair was sculpted in a trendy style, short on the sides and longer on the top.

My heart throbbed in a vivid reaction to him. Who was he? Dr. Reynaldo's TA or something?

The man cleared his throat and turned to face us. I could see he was maybe ten years older than me. His eyes were dark, his cheekbones defined, his lips full and slightly turned up in the corners. He slipped off his coat and draped it over his chair. His form-fitting blue dress shirt showed off his lean muscles.

"Hello, everyone," he said in a low, rumbling voice. His gaze slid over all of us, and when his eyes hit mine, I swear my skin did a strange shivery thing. He rolled up his shirt sleeves, revealing toned forearms. "I'm Dr. Muramoto. Unfortunately, I have some bad news for you. Dr. Reynaldo suffered a heart attack a couple of weeks ago, and he's unable to teach his courses this semester."

A few students gasped in surprise. I bit my lip. No wonder I hadn't heard anything from him.

"Is Dr. Reynaldo okay?" the girl at my side asked.

Dr. Muramoto nodded. "He had to have bypass surgery, but he's finally home recuperating. In the meantime, the faculty is splitting his coursework, and I'm going to be teaching your class." He shot us a crooked grin, which made my heart stutter. "I hope that's okay."

I dropped my gaze down to my blank notebook paper to cover the flush crawling up my cheeks. *He's only a professor, Megan. No biggie. You've had attractive teachers before.*

Okay, just once—Mr. Mars, back in sixth grade—but whatever.

I heard scrawling on the chalkboard and raised my gaze to see Dr. Muramoto's hand flying across the surface as he wrote *Nick Muramoto, Modern Cryptography.* The fabric of his pants stretched across his tight ass, and I swallowed.

"Welcome to modern cryptography," Dr. Muramoto said as he turned around, a smile in his voice, in his eyes. "I'm very excited I was able to take this class on. I see a couple of familiar faces in here from other courses. They'll tell you I'm a pretty laid-back guy, but I do expect you to work hard and do your best."

Some heads nodded in the rows in front of me, and he nodded at them in response.

"Cryptography, which is the study of codes, fascinates me," he continued. "Always has. And I think by the end of the semester you'll find yourself intrigued by the subject too if you weren't already." He divvied up a stack of papers and gave them to the front row to distribute back. "Here's your syllabus. You'll see the weekly topics outlined, plus homework and paper due dates. Let's spend some time going over this before moving on, just to make sure we're all on the same page."

For the next twenty minutes, Dr. Muramoto spoke. I made myself focus on writing notes in the margins of the syllabus so as to ignore the cadence of his voice. Something about it was magnetic; I'd never quite had a reaction to a person like this before. So vivid and immediate. It was like all my senses were tuned in to him.

"Excuse me," the brunette beside me said to me in a quiet voice. "Do you have an extra pen? Mine just ran out of ink." She gave a frowny face.

"Sure." I dug into my bag and gave her one.

"Thanks. I'm Kelly. Want a piece of gum?" She held out a stick.

"No, thanks. I'm Megan. Have we been in any classes together yet?" I didn't remember her being around here, though I didn't know all of the math majors.

"No, I'm a transfer from Chicago. Just moved here last semester."

"—rest of today discussing the origins of codes," our professor was saying.

I snapped to attention, not wanting to miss the lecture portion.

Dr. Muramoto leaned back against the desk and crossed his legs at the ankles, his hands propped just behind him on the table surface. I couldn't stop staring at his long, slender form as he began delving into the ancient Egyptian and Greek use of secret codes.

He didn't look at any notes, just talked off the cuff. Obviously the guy had more than a little expertise in this field. Something about that unaffected air of confidence made him even hotter.

Kelly gave a soft sigh under her breath. "Gotta admit, I didn't expect our prof to be so . . ." She cleared her throat delicately. "Smoking hot."

I swallowed, nodded.

"And he's smart too. He's, like, perfect." She pressed a hand to her cheek and gave a quiet chuckle. "I've never understood the whole 'hot for teacher' thing, but I get it now."

For some reason, her words twisted my gut. Normally I'd just laugh and agree with her—I had no qualms about checking out hot guys on campus and enjoying the eye candy. But this felt different. My instant attraction to him was a bit stronger than I'd like it to be.

Not to mention the underlying feeling of guilt that it was

wrong for me to think about him this way. Totally the taboo factor of him being off-limits. Students and teachers didn't fraternize, period. School policy made that very clear.

The rest of class flew by. Dr. Muramoto's easygoing manner encouraged students to start speaking up about their knowledge of secret codes and ciphers in history. I was normally interactive, but today I found myself just listening, watching, absorbing the information instead of trying to prove I'd retained and could recite it back. By the end of class, I was disappointed it was over. I wanted to know more. Maybe I could do some research on ancient codes in my spare time.

That thought made me laugh at myself. Right. Because I was rolling in extra hours.

I lingered in my seat for a moment as I tucked away my books.

Kelly ripped off a corner of her paper and scrawled her name and number on it. "So, Megan . . . if you need a study buddy this semester, I'd love to get together." She flushed, her cheeks turning a dainty pink. "Well, if that works for you. I don't wanna be pushy or anything."

With a smile, I took the paper, then gave her my own number. "Sounds good." It didn't hurt to have more friends or connections in mathematics. As my dad had taught me, you never knew when a beneficial networking opportunity could crop up.

The class was almost empty when I stood to go, backpack slung over my shoulder. Dr. Muramoto was behind his desk, gathering up his papers and the leftover syllabi. When I walked past him, I heard him say, "Are you Megan Porter?"

My lungs tightened in surprise at the sound of my name on his lips. I paused and turned to him. "Um, yes."

"Sorry, I meant to talk to you before class, but I was running late." Up close I could see tiny stubble along his jaw. I had this crazy impulse to touch it. I crammed my hands in my coat pockets instead. His cologne had a slightly spicy scent that was warm and inviting. "Since Dr. Reynaldo is out for the rest of the semester, the dean asked me to take over as your thesis advisor." He paused and gave me a polite smile. "I hope you don't mind."

My heart jumped in my throat. Thesis advisor. That meant not just seeing him in class. That meant conversations. In his office.

Alone.

I could feel my cheeks burn as I said, "Uh, no, that's fine. I look forward to hearing your thoughts."

He nodded. His eyes lingered for a long moment on mine before he turned his attention to straightening the papers on his desk. His jaw ticked, and I saw his Adam's apple bob. "I'll have my feedback to you in a week or two," he said, his voice gruff. "I'm taking over a couple of his classes, so I'm playing catch-up. Thank you, Miss Porter." He grabbed his pen and started writing notes on the top paper.

My flush grew almost painfully hot at the blatant dismissal, and I lifted my chin and shifted my bag on my shoulder. "That sounds fine," I said. "See you Wednesday, Dr. Muramoto."

With that, I left the classroom, went down the stairs and thrust the building doors open. The brisk wind, stirring snow in the air, cooled my face instantly. I welcomed the cold as I headed down the sidewalk toward the coffee shop.

What the hell was up with me? Maybe it was the fact that I was running on fumes, since I'd gotten practically no sleep last night. It was messing with my brain, making me hallucinate. I totally must have imagined that brief flare of interest in his eyes.

Sixteen weeks to go until graduation, I told myself to help me refocus. I wasn't going to let this . . . stupid and weird attraction to him get in the way of my plans, which were (a) kick ass on all my classes and keep up my honors record, (b) flirt with Patrick shamelessly, (c) complete my senior thesis with a high score and (d) sweet-talk Stackers into giving me more hours this semester and during summer break.

Being attracted to my prof didn't factor into that plan.

Coffee Baby was packed—no big surprise there. They had amazing coffee, plus their pastries were decadent and inexpensive. Not to mention it was cold outside and most students were dragging ass like me. I got in line, waited patiently, then ordered my coffee and cream cheese pastry and hovered by the wall as my order was filled.

When I got my stuff, I spotted a lone seat at a table and darted toward it—I'd learned as a kid that being shy got you nowhere. "Excuse me," I told the people at the table as I gave them a charming smile. "Is this seat taken? Do you mind if I sit here?"

"Not at all," a girl replied. She gave me a polite nod, then went back to her conversation with her friend.

I sipped my coffee and nibbled on my pastry. It was delicious, and the caffeine gave me that needed jolt to go to psychology of stress next. Ugh, I was dreading that one. Why had I put that general ed requirement off for so long? Oh, right— because I'd been too busy focusing on taking my major classes.

Hopefully it wouldn't be a bunch of "breathe deeply and meditate to get rid of stress" crap. That advice never helped me much. Where was the practicality in telling someone to just breathe through difficult situations?

Breathing, meditating, praying hadn't helped me at all when dealing with my mom's accident a few years ago, the most difficult situation I'd encountered so far. Those weeks she'd spent in the hospital, suffering with broken bones and crying out in pain for hours when the meds wore off way too fast. The subsequent intense months of physical therapy. It had been exhausting for all of us.

But she'd picked herself up by sheer strength and gone back to work, despite the fact that it had happened on a job site. She wouldn't let the accident get in the way of doing what she loved.

The woman had courage and strength I could only dream of. A real hero to me.

Her and Dad's jobs were intertwined, and in fact they often did a lot of work together. My mom was a well-respected engineer, and my dad owned a thriving construction company. From what Dad said, it had been love at first sight. He'd seen her in a hard hat, bossing around a bunch of men who were doing a reconstruction on a historical building in downtown Cleveland, and he'd fallen head over heels.

I took out my cryptography syllabus and scanned it again. Attractive professor aside, it promised to be an interesting course I could look forward to. I had to admit, as a kid I'd always been curious about messages and codes. My mom and I had watched a special on code breakers in World War II, and I'd been riveted by the idea that people were paid to break messages about top secret war strategies.

Honestly, I'd never made the connection between cryptography and math, so when I'd seen this course crop up last semester, I was beyond excited and had signed up immediately.

I chugged more of my coffee, stuffed the papers back in my bag and left the coffee shop, hot cup in hand. I had to brave the crowds and hit the bookstore before they ran out of the last textbook I needed. Then on to psychology to learn all about stress.

Fun, indeed.

Chapter 2

"I can't believe they made an entire class out of this topic," I said as I rubbed a knot on the back of my neck. "Only one week under my belt, and I already want to choke myself." I was tucked in the corner of the couch, hunched over my psychology of stress book, eyes glazed from boredom. It was so hard to focus on the introduction and opening chapter, which were filled with dull, obvious commentary.

Gee, you mean stress impacts your physical and *mental health? You don't say.*

My phone buzzed with a text: *Come out with us 2nite!*

It was Nadia, one of my party friends. An evening out with her was guaranteed to go into the wee hours of the morning. The girl knew everyone on campus and went to all the parties.

So tempting, especially since I couldn't get enthused about what I was reading. I could take a nap right now, before my work shift, so I could stay up later tonight. But I made myself type, *Can't. Drowning in psych. If I don't resurface soon, send beer and hot guys.*

Then I shoved my phone away so I wouldn't be tempted to

cave. My classes were a bit more challenging this semester; I had to focus, which meant staying at home more instead of chugging beer and dancing.

Casey, who sat on the couch beside me, was busy highlighting something in her business book. "I hear ya on hating your class. I felt that way about philosophy last semester. I barely passed it—it was only Daniel's tutoring that got me through it." Though she didn't stall in her task, she gave a small, secret smile, and I found myself smiling in response.

Casey in love was a sight to see . . . like watching the underdog finally win the big fight. All the stress and tension that had weighed her down for so long was gone. She'd even started letting me hear her compose music on her computer, an activity she'd previously confined to late nights when no one was up. Made me wish I'd kept up with music after middle school, because her passion for it inspired me. Maybe I needed a new hobby.

Not gonna lie, I loved dating around, having fun with guys, no pressure. But I was kinda envious of the easy familiarity she had with her boyfriend. Casey had had a traumatic childhood experience, which had caused her to be closed off and cautious for many years. Daniel's steady love had broken down those walls, opened her up.

"So how's Daniel today?" I asked her with a sly grin. "When's he coming by to get you?" It was Sunday, which they usually spent together doing . . . well, whatever people in love did, I guessed. Probably involving lots of bed squeaking.

Casey put down her highlighter and looked up at me, her eyes suddenly serious.

My heart thudded. "Everything okay?"

She bit her lower lip and reached up to play with a strand of her hair. "So . . . I've been meaning to talk to you about something." Her eyes met mine. "Things have been going really well with me and Daniel. As you know. And we've been doing a lot of talking about where we're going and what we want. I mean, out of life. In the future."

"Are you pregnant, Casey?" I teased.

Her face flamed. "Oh God. No. No, there's no baby—"

"I'm kidding. I think I get where this convo is going. Are you two moving in together?"

Her eyes lit in excitement, and she nodded. "But not until the end of the semester. I didn't want to leave you in a lurch. And frankly, I'm still a little scared to take that leap and need more time to prepare for it." Her throat bobbed with her visible swallow.

I reached over and rubbed her upper arm. Tears came to my eyes, and I blinked. "I'm happy for you," I said in a quiet voice. "Really happy. You deserve it. And I'm proud of you for taking this chance. All the good things come with a risk. But I know it'll be worth it."

She moved her books onto the coffee table, then reached over and hugged me. I wrapped my arms around her and we sat like that for a moment.

"Thank you for your support," she said as she pulled back and sniffled. I saw small tears in the corners of her eyes, and we both gave goofy laughs at how emotional we'd gotten. People who hadn't watched her uphill battle wouldn't understand why.

Hell, I barely did. My childhood had been wonderful. Two doting parents with strong work ethics who encouraged me to follow my dreams. Casey hadn't had that—she'd lived with her grandparents since she was a young teen.

I felt like I had a part in helping her, which humbled me.

Time to lighten the mood a bit. "Soooo," I said in a slow drawl, "there's a party next weekend." Surely a hardworking student like myself deserved the occasional break, right?

Her lips quirked. "There's also an eighties movie marathon on one of the movie channels."

"Free beer."

"Chocolate ice cream."

Damn. She had me there. Sugar and caffeine were my mortal weaknesses. Still, I was hoping Patrick might come to this particular party, since he hadn't dropped by Stackers yet like I'd invited him to. Maybe he just needed to see me in a social environment, hanging out and looking good and having fun.

My brain suddenly went to Dr. Muramoto, a jarring image of him sipping on a beer at a frat party. Which was utterly crazy, because what prof would ever do that? Hang with students and have drinks with them? I couldn't help my flushed reaction to the idea though.

Casey gave me a knowing look. "Hm. Is there some guy at the party you're hoping to attract?"

I licked my lips. "No. I mean, yeah." In that moment, I'd completely forgotten about Patrick. Whoops.

She cocked her head and eyed me. Crossed her arms over her chest. "Okay. Here's the deal. I'll come with you to the party."

I clapped.

"If," she continued, holding up a hand, "before the party, you come with me to my grandparents' house for dinner."

I stilled. She'd never invited me to meet her grandparents before. My chest tightened, and I gave a wordless nod.

"Okay. Good." She sniffled again and swiped a hand under her nose. "Now we have to get back to studying before I end up girl crying all afternoon. Daniel's going to see my eyes and wonder what's wrong."

I laughed and turned my attention back to my psych text. But it was kinda hard focusing when I felt like I'd broken past another one of Casey's walls, had been invited even deeper into her life.

I had friends on campus. Lots of friends, in fact. If I was bored, my phone had a dozen people I could call up to hang with on a moment's notice. I was a math nerd, but I didn't have to succumb to the stereotypes. I could be smart *and* fun. I made an effort to reach out to people because every connection mattered, either in the present or in the future. My parents' words always stuck with me.

But few of my friendships were as genuine as the connection I was building with Casey. She'd taught me a lot since we'd become roommates last year—about trust, about hope and love. It had me craving more of that sincerity in my life, those quiet moments when you connected with others.

Being around Casey put that in perspective for me. Made me hold the mirror up and examine myself with full honesty. Yeah, I could probably find my own guy like Daniel if I stopped seeking out hot athletes . . . the type I was usually physically attracted to. But there was a lot less pressure when you knew it wasn't going to be permanent with a guy; long-term dating was never on the table. Not with them.

I wasn't going to settle down with a guy like Patrick. He was safe and fun and *now*. He didn't challenge me mentally or emotionally. He didn't rock my boat. It was easy to fit guys like him into my busy life because they weren't needy—and they didn't make me needy or weak or vulnerable. If we hooked up now and then, awesome. When we broke up or stopped dating, it sucked but it didn't crush me. I could pick myself up and keep going.

All good things come with a risk, I'd told Casey. I glanced over at her and watched her scrawling mad notes on her paper, chewing on the end of her pen. She'd taken a chance, had jumped off the cliff and had Daniel as her reward for her efforts.

I hadn't yet met anyone who was worth that risk.

"—and I want extra cheese on that," the woman barked at me. "Oh, and more sauerkraut." Her brow rose as she looked from her date, a portly man in his fifties, to me. Her lips pursed in derision. "You didn't write any of that down. Are you sure you remembered what we ordered?"

I sighed. "Two double stackers, both with extra mayo and extra onions. Large cheesy fries. One Reuben, light on the corned beef, extra cheese and extra sauerkraut. Salad, no tomatoes, extra cucumbers."

Her face twitched, but she shut up after that.

"I'll be back with your drink refills—Diet Coke and unsweetened ice tea," I added as I picked up their almost-empty cups, then gave her a polite smile and walked back to the cook station to give him the order.

I shouldn't get frustrated that people had certain preconceived notions of me—for being decent looking. For being a woman. For being black. My mom always taught me to be proud, to stand up for myself and not let anyone make me feel like less of a person for anything about me. Some days were easier than others though.

I relayed the order to the fry cook, who gave me a gruff nod and went back to flipping burgers. Then I reloaded their drinks and brought the cups back to their table. I busied myself with rolling napkins and cleaning up the countertop. The crowd usually thinned out this late on a Sunday.

One more hour, and I could go home and relax. Eat some ice cream and veg out to mindless TV. This first week of school had been harder than I'd envisioned. Hard and challenging in a way I hadn't expected.

A group of college jocks came in with rippling muscles in tight T-shirts and arrogant grins. They sat in the corner booth, a loud stirring of elbowing and jostling their way into the stretch seat. My section. Of course.

I chuckled under my breath. I had all the luck. While I definitely liked checking out athletes for their prowess, they were shit tippers for the most part.

"Order up," the fry cook hollered.

I grabbed the picky woman's plates, dropped their food off, then went over to the college guys.

When they saw me, they straightened in their seats, their smiles spreading wider. They picked up the menus and eyed them. A couple of their gazes slid over to me, raking me from head to toe.

"What can I get you guys? Want anything to drink?" I asked them with a flirty wink.

The one in the middle, a guy with a neck almost as thick as his head, lifted his chin at me in a *'sup* way. "Got anything hot and juicy?"

The other guys laughed.

It was so hard to not sigh out loud. Waitressing could be a drinking game. Dirty innuendo—drink. Guy touches your butt "on accident" as you walk by—drink. And none of them were that original in their come-ons, either, which made it worse. My kingdom for someone with half a brain for once.

"We have some great burgers on special today. Check them out on the big board behind me," I said smoothly. "How about you take a few minutes to read over the menu and I'll come back to get your orders?"

I walked away, then stalled when I saw Dr. Muramoto sitting at a table by himself, a paperback in hand, sipping a cup of coffee. He had on a long-sleeved black sweater, and his hair was relaxed today, not carefully styled.

Somehow the casualness made him look even more attractive.

He put his mug down and scrubbed a hand over that scruff on his face. So far this week, I'd noticed that he occasionally had a little stubble, though it never got out of control. That his fingers were long and strong. That he had a dimple in his right cheek, and the crow's-feet around his eyes when he laughed made my stomach tighten in awareness.

Before I realized what I was doing, I picked up the coffeepot and walked over to his table. He was flipping a page of the thick book—an epic fantasy, from what I could tell. Looked like he was totally into it. When was the last time I'd been able to sit down and read fiction? I made a mental note to do so.

"More coffee?" I murmured.

He nodded absently, saying, "Yes, caffeinated please," then looked up. When our eyes locked, there was a crackle of energy between us that was almost physical. I felt like every nerve ending in my body woke up and jumped to attention.

Something about the weight of that gaze hit me right in the chest.

Then he blinked, and I saw the moment he realized who I was—a student. He pulled back into himself and offered me a courteous nod. "Megan Porter, right?"

"Yes," I repeated dumbly. My brain scrambled for something to say. I shifted the coffee into my other hand, just for something to do. "Can I get you anything else?"

"I'm good, thanks."

I was glad we'd moved back into the student-teacher zone, because this attraction I had for him was wrong. A hundred times wrong. Not only was he a prof, he was *my* prof. And my advisor. Still, I couldn't help but feel conflicted over what definitely had seemed like interest in his eyes.

A loud roar of voices at the front door had me turning around. I saw Patrick stroll in . . . along with my ex, Bobby.

My heart sank. Ugh, wonderful. I watched as they squeezed into the end of the booth with the other jocks. Of course they were at my table. Because I was having that kind of luck, apparently.

It took all my skills to paste a fake smile on my face, drop off the coffeepot and go over to their table. When Bobby saw me, he stopped talking, and his cheeks flushed red. Apparently he'd forgotten I worked here.

He and I dated last semester for a little while. We weren't

super serious, but I thought he had more respect for me than he did. One evening, I'd shown up at a party he knew I was coming to and found him drunk and in bed with two girls.

And that had been the end of that.

He'd blown up my phone for weeks afterward, giving me all the "Babe, I'm soooo sorry" apologies he could type out. Then total silence. I figured he'd moved on to someone who gave a shit about his words. I'd also made sure to stay away from parties where I knew he'd be.

"Hey, Megan," Bobby said.

"Have you guys decided on what you'd like to drink?" I asked them with as much casualness as I could muster.

They gave me their drink orders. I walked off to fill them and almost made it to the soda fountain when a large hand on my shoulder stopped me.

"You've been avoiding me," a familiar voice said. Bobby. "Haven't seen you around any."

I shook his hand off and turned around to shoot him a glare. "Don't touch me, please."

His brow furrowed in a frown. "God, lighten up. I just wanted to talk to you."

"You talk without touching. Hands to yourself." I started pouring drinks.

"Babe—"

"Don't 'babe' me, Bobby. I'm not interested in talking to you." I was proud of how even I sounded. Like I didn't give a shit about him.

Honestly? I didn't. Well, okay, I was still a little mad. But I wasn't hurt anymore. That feeling had gone away pretty fast when I'd started really thinking about him—how all he would call me for was a hookup. How we'd rarely gone on real dates, mostly to parties or whatever. I'd been convenient for him. And that arrangement between us had been fine until he'd embarrassed me by sleeping around without caring about being caught.

There had been nothing of substance between us, nothing to talk about. He was an attractive guy with no depth or resonance who barely skated by in his classes because he just didn't give a shit or put effort into them. No character.

His lips thinned. He looked like he wanted to say more.

"Go back to your seat," I said to cut him off. "I'm at work, and I'm not talking about anything with you here. I'll bring your drink over in a minute." He didn't move, so I said, "Go," a little louder.

When he did, I felt the tension in my back ease up a touch. I finished filling the cups and loaded up a tray. I distributed the drinks and took their orders, noting with a small bit of pleasure that Bobby wouldn't look at me.

What did he think, he could come here and touch me and I'd melt in his hands? Hell no. Gotta love the arrogance of guys like that.

As I walked away, I felt another gaze. Dr. Muramoto's book was still in his hands, but his eyes, so enigmatic, were right on me. I couldn't tell what he saw when he looked into my eyes— did he think I was just a party girl? Then he turned his attention back to his book, sipped his coffee in silence, the moment gone.

Chapter 3

When I exited my ordinary differential equations class on Tuesday morning, I felt my phone buzz in my pocket. I looked at the caller ID. "Hey, Mom. Good timing—I'm just leaving a class."

"Morning, sunshine," she said in a soft, sleepy-sounding voice. "How's school going so far?"

I stepped to the side of the hallway, right in front of the classroom door. "It's good. What, did you sleep in today? You sound groggy."

Mom was a morning person, normally up at five-thirty daily on the dot. When I'd lived at home, there were many mornings she'd push my tired ass out of bed with a not-so-gentle shove.

There was a pause. "Oh, I woke up with a bad backache, so I took some pain meds. They make me a little fuzzy."

My heart rate picked up a bit. "You okay? When did the backache start? Have you talked to the doctor about it?" Mom hadn't indicated any pain from her injury in a long time, so naturally I was alarmed. Hopefully this wouldn't turn out to be something chronic for her.

"No, no, it's fine, I'm sure," she said. "I probably just slept weird or something. But if it keeps up I'll call the doc. Anyway, that wasn't what I was calling about." Her voice threaded with excitement. "Something awesome happened, and I wanted to ask you to come to dinner tomorrow so we could talk about it and celebrate. You free?"

I quickly scanned my mental calendar. "Yeah, that should be fine. Can I bring anything with me?"

"Just yourself. And anyone you might be dating . . ." She stalled off with a meaningful pause.

I tried not to groan. It was no secret my mom wished I'd settle down a bit. Whenever I brought a guy over, she was always excited and enthusiastic, but I could tell it disappointed her that I hadn't had a serious boyfriend in a couple of years. "I'm not dating anyone, but thanks for the offer."

"Just checking," she said lightly. "Okay, I'll let you go. Study hard."

"See ya Wednesday," I said right before we hung up. Wonder what it was she wanted to tell me about? Surely there wasn't a baby on the horizon or anything crazy like that. My mom and dad were great, loving parents, but they'd been happy with just one kid. Not to mention that both of them were devoted to long work hours, with little free time to spare. Probably something job related then.

I tucked my phone back in my pocket and headed outside. The sun shone, so snow sparkled on the ground, on the trees. I tugged my scarf a little closer around my neck, since the light didn't have much effect on the piercing cold.

Still, at least the sun was out. In Cleveland, you learned to take whatever you could get. Winters were brutal.

We were going to have a quiz in ordinary differential equations on Thursday, so I decided to go to the commons to study, while it was fresh in my mind. The class was a little more challenging than I'd expected, but I was still confident I'd do okay.

I'd maintained a solid A and B average every semester. Surely I wouldn't crap up everything during my last chunk of undergrad.

The commons was in the middle of campus, a large glass-walled building that let in light and made the interior warm and welcoming. On the first floor were clusters of chairs and couches, designed to encourage students to relax, linger, study, talk.

As I walked toward the center of the room, I saw a familiar person alone, near the group of chairs by the fireplace. Kelly, from my cryptography class. I changed direction and headed to her.

"Mind if I sit here?" I asked her.

She gave me a wide smile. "No, please! Have a seat."

The fire was warm and took away the slight cold sting in my fingertips and nose. "This is cozy," I said, stripping off my coat and settling into the plush tan chair.

She nodded. "I come here between classes a lot. It's warmer than the dorms."

"I've heard that," I said with a laugh. I had some friends who lived on campus. The rooms were nice and decent sized, but sometimes the heat went a bit wonky in the older dorms. "Whatcha studying?" I nodded at the open book in her lap.

She held up the cover—a thick collection of short stories. "I put off English as long as I could," she said with a grimace. "So I had to take 102 this year in order to graduate."

"Yup. Psychology of stress for me," I said as I shook my head, chuckling. "I feel your pain." I dug my notes for the previous class out of my bag and grabbed a pen. "Sorry, I won't bug you while you're studying."

"You're not bugging me at all." She sighed and gave a sad, shy smile. "I don't really know many people on campus, so it's kinda nice to have someone else to talk to." With that, she turned her attention to her book. A courtesy so I could study, I was sure.

But my heart ached for her loneliness. Eh, I could go over my notes later, right? "What are you going to do after you graduate?" I asked. "If you don't mind me being nosy."

She looked up at me and dropped her pen in the seam of her text, closing it with a decisive thud. "I'm going to teach," she said. "I'm a math ed major. After this semester, I do my student teaching in the fall. Shoulda done it this semester, but with the transfer, everything got thrown off a bit."

"What made you move here, of all places? Surely it wasn't our majestic weather," I said with a pointed look outside.

She huffed a laugh. "Not quite." Her eyes turned serious, and she ran a hand along the back of her neck. "Things went . . . a bit bad at my old campus. So I moved here for a fresh start. My aunt used to live in Cleveland and loved the area. This school has a great academic reputation. So here I am."

I was so curious and wanted to ask more, but I remembered how Casey would shut off when I'd push her to talk to me. Trust was important to establish before trying to pry into such personal matters. And the stiffness in her body language gave away that she was uncomfortable, didn't want to reveal too much right now. So I gave her a warm smile and pushed back the questions I wanted to ask. "Well, we should try to hang out sometime then. Without books involved," I added.

Her responding grin was warm and appreciative. "Really? I'd like that."

"My roommate deejays at a dance club nearby—The Mask. It's great. Or we can hit a party on campus or something. Lots to do around here." Kelly seemed like a nice person; maybe a little nudge would help her expand her social circle.

We made small talk for a few more minutes, about the weather, about our other classes, then slid into an easy silence as we worked. Students milled and talked around us, the fire crackled between us, but we studied for another hour on our notes and such.

My back was getting cramped, so I stood and stretched. Gathered my stuff up and put it in my bag. I needed coffee and a bagel before my next class. After class I had a work shift—it was gonna be a long day. "I'm heading out," I told Kelly. "But I'll text you when I find out what's going on. Maybe we can do something soon?"

She nodded. "I'd like that. A lot. See ya tomorrow morning."

I left, and as I walked to the coffee shop, I tried not to think about the sheen of tears in her eyes. How hard it must be to feel that lonely, to wander around school and have few familiar faces. Whatever Kelly went through must have been pretty awful if it had made her pick up her whole life and re-locate.

As I shifted in my seat in cryptography on Wednesday morning, I realized my pulse had begun to flutter, and my pen was tapping on the corner of my paper without me realizing it. I was nervous. How crazy was that? Nervous and full of antic-ipation to see my prof again. Only a few class sessions in and the guy had somehow begun to worm his way under my skin. I looked forward to hearing the vivid excitement in his voice as he spoke about the day's topic. Watching how his hands waved in the air to punctuate his words. The way his gaze was so pen-etrating when he locked eyes with students. Like he was seri-ously interested in our opinion. Like he found us to be his equal.

I'd never been drawn to a teacher like this before. Then again, I'd never had a teacher like him before.

Dr. Muramoto walked in with a broad smile. "Morning, class. Glad to see I didn't scare you away with Monday's lesson."

There were a few chuckles. It had been an intense session, but he'd gone over the material thoroughly, asking questions to make sure we all understood.

Kelly sighed and leaned closer to me. "I wish he taught all my classes."

I nodded. "He's something else, isn't he." For some reason, I was hesitant to let anyone know how much I was attracted to him. It was goofy—why should I care if Kelly or Casey or anyone else knew I thought he was hot?

But I knew why. Because it was more than just his looks. His brain was hot. His intensity was hot. And those things made me think about him far, far more than I should have. Which was so embarrassing. I was a cliché—girl with a huge crush on her teacher. Ridiculous.

"Megan?" Dr. Muramoto said with a brow raised, which jarred me out of my thoughts.

My heart pounded. Shit. What were we talking about? "Um, yes?"

"Do you know the answer?"

My brain scrabbled with desperation as I eyed the chalkboard, the room, trying to figure out what we were talking about.

His brow quirked. "I was asking what the two types of symmetric key ciphers are. It was part of your reading from last class."

Shit. My brain was totally blank, caught off guard. I took a second to close my eyes, regather myself. "Stream ciphers and . . . block ciphers," I finally said.

He gave me a nod, and his gaze moved away from mine to slide over the faces of other students in the rows in front of me. Once he stopped looking at me, I found I was able to breathe again. "These two types of ciphers use one key to both encrypt and decrypt a message. As the text explained, that might seem handy, but the sender and receiver need a secure way to send that key." He talked on, and my pulse finally dropped down from the danger zone.

"Good save," Kelly said to me. "I hate being called on."

I chuckled under my breath. "My brain just died, I guess."

The brown-haired guy in the seat in front of me turned around and said in a low voice, "Where did you find that, by the way? I don't remember reading it in the chapter."

"Oh. Um, hold on." I turned my attention to the text and flipped through the pages until I saw where I'd highlighted about symmetric key ciphers. "Top of this page." I turned the open book around so he could see.

His green eyes flashed a thanks. "Got it." His gaze lingered on my face for a moment, and then he faced forward again.

Hm. I looked at Kelly with a raised eyebrow, one she met back. She scrawled on the corner of her notebook, then showed me what she'd written.

He likes you.

That was totally the vibe I'd been getting too. I nodded with wide eyes at her, then checked him out. I'd seen him around in the building, of course, because the guy was my usual type—athletic build, attractive. And he was in an upper-level math course, so he must be pretty intelligent too.

Maybe the thing to snap me out of this lame-o teacher crush was to foster interest in another guy. One who was my age. One who wouldn't get in trouble if we ever were to date.

Not that Dr. Muramoto was ever going to date me anyway, of course.

I took notes during the lecture, making sure to pay attention so I wouldn't get caught unaware again, but he didn't call on me. When we were dismissed, the guy in front of me stood and faced me again.

"Thanks again for showing me where that was," he said. His eyes twinkled.

"It really wasn't a big deal," I protested.

I heard Kelly smother a laugh beside me. I shot her a mock glare, and she shrugged and gathered her stuff.

"Um. I'm Dallas," he offered to me.

"I'm Megan. Hi." I nodded my head at him in a greeting.

"Okay. Well, I'll see you next Monday." He scratched the back of his head, a light flush crawling up his cheeks as he got his stuff together and practically ran out the door.

"That was so cute," Kelly said as she burst into giggles. "You had him *crazy* nervous."

"I just have that effect on men. Or maybe he was nervous because of *you*," I teased her back.

She rolled her eyes. "That guy didn't notice anyone else in this room. But that's fine. I don't want a math major anyway. We're all way too stuffy and practical for my tastes."

I donned my coat and followed Kelly toward the door, when Dr. Muramoto waved me over. "I'll catch you later," I told her, then tried to ignore the stutter in my heart rate as I reached his desk.

He handed me a stack of paper—my thesis. "I have to say, Megan, I found this a really good and engaging read. Your ideas on how to stimulate math interest in gamer kids were intriguing. I offered some commentary in the margins, but I think you're on the right track."

The warmth and approval in his voice made me flush. I glanced at the paper and saw block script notes in the margins. I was dying to read what he'd written. "Thank you," I told him. "I appreciate your squeezing me in. I know you've been busy."

His eyes flashed with something, and he paused in his gathering of papers. "It wasn't a problem at all," he said. "Drop me an email if you have questions about my feedback. My address is on the syllabus."

I left and headed to a student lounge area in the corner of the building. Flipped through each page and read his margin notes. His feedback was in the form of probing questions, challenges to push me harder. He offered thoughts on stuff I hadn't considered, stuff Dr. Reynaldo hadn't brought up either.

I stared blankly at the paper as my mind wandered to thinking about Dr. Muramoto. He was a smart, savvy man. Who was he outside of school? Was he married? I hadn't seen a ring on his finger, but that wasn't always an indicator of solo status. Besides, he could have a girlfriend or fiancée. What kinds of things did he do in his spare time? And how did he get to this level of professorhood at such a young age?

Something about him intrigued me, against my better judgment. Something in me wanted to know more. And in that moment, I had a sudden, real discomfort that distracting myself with other guys wouldn't satisfy that itch right below my skin. The itch to understand who my professor was and what made him tick.

Chapter 4

The waves of Lake Erie slapped the shores of our beach as I stared at the waterfront from my parents' patio. There was nothing quite like seeing a sunset on the water, even in the wintertime. The sky, which had cleared up this afternoon, was awash in brilliant ribbons of pinks and purples. To my right, the sun dipped in the western horizon. To my left, darkness edged in with a blanket of star-pierced navy blue.

I sat in silence, sipping a glass of my mom's favorite white wine and relaxing. No matter how stressed I'd gotten as a kid, my refuge had been the water. I kinda missed being so close to it, having it right there whenever I needed it. I missed falling asleep with my window open, listening to the waves lap at the sand.

Mom and Dad were inside, making dinner. I'd asked if I could help, but they'd shooed me away, telling me to relax. So I'd wrapped up in a thick blanket—the way I had countless times growing up—and perched on a patio chair.

My cheeks were cold, but it was well worth the sight.

After a few more minutes, I heard my mom's call for dinner.

I came inside and helped set plates. She'd made chicken with asparagus, mashed potatoes and parsnips. My mouth was already watering—I missed home-cooked food.

"Casey and I don't eat like this," I said with a mournful sigh as I settled into my seat.

Dad laughed. "Guess you guys should come over more often," he teased.

"I would if I weren't so busy acing my classes," I lobbed back with a wink. My parents knew my schedule was crazy, but I also knew that they missed me. We got together when we could.

Mom moved toward the dining room table, then paused, turned around and left the room. A moment later, she returned with a smile. As she settled into her chair, she said, "Okay, the big news." She reached over and squeezed Dad's hand. "Your father and I got a lucrative contract to renovate the dorms on your campus."

I blinked, my jaw dropping open. "Seriously? That's awesome. Congrats to you guys! When did all of this go down? How did it happen?"

"I have a contact at Smythe-Davis in the maintenance department. When the bid opened up due to some immediate issues that happened in one of the dorms, he told me about it. The project manager chose our company to handle the restoration." He glanced at Mom and smiled. "This is going to be a big opportunity for us. We've never had a project of this size and scope before. It will push us into the big leagues."

I speared a stalk of asparagus and chewed. I was glad for my parents, but I had to admit it'd be a little strange having them on campus. The independence I'd experienced the last three and a half years was probably going to be impacted by this. I shoved that uncomfortable thought aside. "Is business okay otherwise?"

Mom's smile stiffened just a fraction of a second before she said, "It's good. Just a little . . . slow. Winter months are always like that though. Nothing to worry about." She waved her hand at me to keep eating.

My parents hadn't struggled with money in quite a while. They'd bought this house when I was in elementary school, and it had seemed like their business was steady. Still, I was sure it was a relief to have a big project lined up. I felt a little bad for my earlier discomfort. It wasn't like they were going to be up my ass, checking on me every five minutes to make sure I was doing homework or whatever. My parents were supportive and pushed me hard to do my best, but they'd never been controlling. Surely they'd respect my space, right?

"How are classes going?" Dad asked in between bites.

I filled them in on what I was taking this semester and some of the people I'd met so far. Of course, I carefully regulated my voice when it came to discussing cryptography . . . and my intriguing teacher.

"I think my hardest class is going to be psychology of stress," I admitted. "Which sounds crazy, I know, but it's just so much theory being thrown at you. About how this psychologist or that theorist thinks stress originates, manifests and so on. It's not the most engaging subject matter to me."

Dad laughed. "I didn't go to college, but I'd find that stuff boring too. A little too woo-woo for my tastes."

"Exactly." I nodded.

Mom dabbed her napkin over her mouth and sighed. Her smile turned gentle and soft, her eyes a touch hazy. If I didn't know better, I'd think she was buzzed. But she'd been drinking only water since I'd gotten here.

"Your back still hurting?" I asked.

She blinked and looked at me, and I swore it took a second for her eyes to focus. "Oh, just a touch. But I think it's getting better."

I could practically feel Dad's frown aimed toward her. Obviously she hadn't told him about the recurring pain. And obviously when she'd gotten up before dinner, she'd taken another pain pill. "Mom," I said evenly, careful to keep my voice neutral, "the doctor said there was a possibility of pain returning, due to nerve damage, but there were options. Like going to the pain clinic. You should really give him a call, even if you feel like the pain is lessening." Mom was strong and independent, and she didn't like being told what to do, but I remembered all too vividly what kind of agony she was in while healing.

She hadn't complained to us, but I'd hear her quiet cries in the night as she tried to fight off the pain. Her tears had gutted me. I hated to think of her going through that again.

The sincerity in my eyes must have reached her, because she nodded. "Okay. I promise I'll talk to him. Now stop nagging me about it." The last sentence was said with a joking tone.

Dad still hadn't spoken up, had just silently watched us converse. I could tell he was bothered though; there was a big frown line between his eyebrows, and he'd stopped inhaling his dinner. I knew he wasn't going to let this go, which helped me feel a little better.

Dinner conversation flowed on after that. Mom caught me up on what my aunts and uncles were up to, who was feuding, who had gotten fired. Apparently, it had been a busy couple of weeks.

My extended family was rather large. My mom had four sisters, who each had several kids. Our small family of three was the odd one out. But reunions and get-togethers were always a blast. I loved my cousins.

We finished off dinner. Mom kept smothering yawns—obviously the meds were hitting her hard now. My heart pinched as I watched her tired eyes scan over the table. Before she could protest, I gathered up the plates, scraped them off and popped them in the dishwasher.

"I think I'm going to bed," Mom said on a low sigh. She gave me a hug, then shuffled down the hallway.

My dad and I watched her go. He put away the leftovers while I wiped down the counters.

"So, when are you guys going to be on campus?" I asked him to get my mind off my mom. "We should have lunch or something." Maybe if I scheduled get-togethers with them, it would let them feel like they're a part of my campus life while giving me some measure of control over things.

He tilted his head. "Actually, we'll be there next week to meet with the project manager. We can at least get coffee or something." He popped the last container in the fridge. "So, are you doing okay?"

I gave him a hug. "I'm good. Everything's going well so far. My senior thesis is ready for revisions. The end is in sight."

He pressed a kiss to my brow and wrapped his arms tighter around me. "I'm proud of you, you know. Never thought I'd have such a smart, beautiful daughter. I feel so lucky."

My eyes stung, and I nuzzled my face into his soft long-sleeved shirt. "Thanks, Dad." I felt lucky too.

When I got back to the apartment, Casey was already in her room. I could see light spilling out from under her bedroom door. Probably working on homework. The girl was as diligent as I was.

I heard her voice, then a low male chuckle. My grin widened. So Daniel was over here too. *Good for you, Casey,* I thought as I went to the fridge and grabbed a soda. I had to admit, the thought of her moving out made me sad, even as I was happy for her. I hoped she wasn't too freaked out about the change. Sometimes it took her a while to adjust.

I took my soda to my room and closed the door. Put on some ambient music and opened up my thesis paper again. It was pure impulse that had me firing up my laptop and logging into email.

Earlier today I'd written Dr. Muramoto's email address at the bottom of my paper, just to have it handy. I typed it into the address line, then wrote "senior thesis" in the subject line. Then stopped. The blank cursor in the message box blinked.

What should I write?

Dr. Muramoto, I started to type. *Thank you for the extensive feedback on my paper. I'm ready to work on revisions. I'll get those back to you as soon as possible.* I paused. *And I promise to not be caught like a deer in the headlights next time you call on me in class. I don't know where my brain was. Sorry about that.*

I typed my name and hit send before I could talk myself out of it. Then I hopped online to check out my social media and see what people were up to. I'd barely been on much since the semester had started.

An email popped into my in-box about five minutes later.

Megan,
You're welcome. And no worries—I had plenty of oh-crap moments in undergrad myself. You rallied nicely. ;-)
Nick

My lungs squeezed as I read the message. He'd signed his first name. Did that mean I should use it? What was protocol here? And why the hell was I stressing so much about what to call him? Ugh. I decided to skip the greeting and go right to the message.

I see you're online late too. No rest for the wicked—at least not in academia, huh? Are there other students you're advising on their thesis this semester?

This time I didn't bother to flick back over to my social media. I kept my in-box open. The single line of his reply sent a low glide of heat through my belly.

No one but you, Megan.

My skin tightened at the fantasy of his dark eyes growing darker and more hooded as they locked on mine, all that intensity he brought into the classroom solely focused on me. His lips brushing my earlobe when he leaned in close and whispered those words in my ear.

I bit my lip and willed myself to shake off this train of thought. *Be rational,* I told myself. Nothing in that reply was sexual or sensual. I was just reading into it.

But . . . what if I wasn't? That was a totally loaded response by him; surely he knew it could be interpreted in more than one way.

Suddenly I wanted to keep this conversation going, to learn more about him. The only way to find out if I was reading into his words was to write him back, draw him into a conversation.

I stared at his message for a moment, my flesh prickling with anticipation and a tinge of fear. I took a moment to wipe my damp palms on my thighs. Then I typed out a reply.

How long have you been teaching here? And where did you go to undergrad? Yes, I know I'm nosy, by the way. Let's blame it on senioritis, shall we? ;-) I'm looking forward to graduating.

The pause after I hit send was much longer. A full twenty minutes ticked by. Maybe I'd interrupted him when he was trying to get work done. Maybe he didn't want to talk to a student. Maybe I was too pushy and bugged him. After all, this was his free time.

Then again, he was the one responding to my emails. Or had been until now.

Finally, my in-box dinged. I was pretty sure my heart stopped beating for a couple of seconds. *He wrote back,* my brain yelled at me. My traitorous fingers trembled as I opened his message.

I went to undergrad and grad here, at Smythe-Davis. I graduated high school early and with several college credits under my belt, so I got my bachelor's at age 19, my master's at 21 and my PhD at 24. I taught at another college for a year, but when a position opened up in the S-D math dept, I applied.

Are you going to grad school? If not, you should think about it. I believe you'd do well in that environment.

A warm flush stole over my face, down my throat. I knew it was goofy to read into the fact that he'd been thinking about me, about my goals and future. But so be it. My hands were a bit steadier this time when I replied.

Yes, I'm actually going here in the fall—I've already been accepted. I'm looking forward to it.

My fingers hovered over the keys as I debated what to type next.

Do you like math jokes? I've been gathering them since I was a kid. Here's one: Why do they never serve beer at a math party?

I sent the message. It was another fifteen minutes or so before I got a reply. I stared at his email blankly—it was just a jumble of letters.

Uh, did he have a cat that had jumped on the keyboard or something?

I eyed it again. Wait, there was something in this. It wasn't random—it was a pattern. My brain whirred as I tried to figure it out. Was he sending me some kind of a code? A small smile broke out on my face. Interesting.

It took me a good ten minutes to identify the code. The letters he'd typed were two off from the originals, so A was C, B was D, and so on. I grabbed a piece of paper and translated.

Hah. I love that joke—because you can't drink and derive.

I couldn't help it—I burst into laughter.

Casey's voice called out from in the living room. "Hey, Megan. You want some ice cream? And we're going to watch *Teen Witch*—come join us. I'm pretty sure you could recite this movie by heart now."

"Girl, you *know* I can," I replied as I shut my email down. I joined Casey and Daniel on the couch, and we fired up the amazingly funny and bad eighties film we'd stumbled across on accident over winter break. She and I had watched it a few times already, cracking up at the horrible rapping and the eighties-tacular clothing.

Even as I laughed and talked with them, the email exchange lingered in the back of my mind. I couldn't help the faint secret grin that wouldn't leave my face.

Chapter 5

I slicked the soft pink lip gloss across my lips and eyed myself in the mirror. My hair was wild and fun tonight—I'd let it loose with a swirl of puffy curls around my head. My top was tiny, my jeans were slim and my black boots were high.

I was so looking forward to a fun night out.

Not that school was going badly or anything. It was the end of January, and my classes were moving along at a steady pace. I'd done well on the papers and assignments I'd turned in. Work had even bumped up my hours; another employee, a sophomore, had quit to move out of state.

I grabbed my clutch, tossed on my coat and left the apartment, locking it behind me. Since it was a Friday, Casey was already deejaying at The Mask. I was going to meet Kelly there.

I found a spot on the street a block from the club, pulled my car into the tiny space and parked. Crossed the street and followed the siren song of the pulsing music thrumming from the brick building. People poured in and out, smiling and laughing and talking and dancing.

I couldn't help but feel uplifted. Gotta love a good crowd.

"Megan!" I heard from my right side.

I spun to find Kelly standing against the brick wall near the corner, dragging on a cigarette.

She gave me a sheepish grin and waved the cigarette in the air. "I keep trying to quit, but old habits die hard."

"No judgment here," I told her as I gave her a quick hug. "We all have our crutches."

The warmth in her eyes was genuine. "Thanks. My parents ride me about it all the time. I had quit for a while, but . . ." Her smile cracked a little around the edges. Then she smashed out the cigarette against the wall and said with a light laugh, "Anyway, you know how stress can eat away at you."

"In fact, I do," I replied. My psych prof had talked about stress and addiction just last week—surprisingly, I was retaining information from the text. "If you ever need to talk . . ."

"I appreciate it," she said in a light tone that didn't quite match the look in her eyes. "It's not a big deal. Just some shit from my past that won't get out of my head, that's all."

My heart dipped in sympathy for her. This close, I could see the stress lines between her brows, around her eyes. She didn't seem to be getting much sleep. I wanted to ask her more questions, but I was afraid of making tonight too depressing for her.

"Is there anything I can do?" I asked.

Her smile was a bit sad. "No, but thank you. I'll get back to my normal self again soon enough. I just need a distraction right now."

"Well, if tonight doesn't work, I know a few hot football guys," I said, only half joking.

She squeezed my upper arm, and this time her smile was real. "I might take you up on that."

"Let's go inside," I said, and we headed into the building.

The music throbbed, almost like a second heartbeat in my chest.

Kelly clapped in anticipation, the shadows gone from her

face now, and eyed the dance floor. "That looks awesome!" she shouted. "And I love this song—I've never heard this mix before though."

"Casey probably created it," I said proudly. "She's amazing."

We peeled our coats off and hung them on nearby racks.

I grabbed her hand and led her into the middle of the crowd. Bodies swayed around us. We thrust our hands in the air and shook our asses, laughing and bouncing along with the music. Casey kept the jams going, sliding one song effortlessly into another.

A hot Latino guy sidled up to Kelly and shot her a crooked grin. She blinked, then gave him a tentative smile in response as she tossed me a quick look.

I waved her off with a laugh and did my own thing for a while. Closed my eyes and let myself just . . . feel. There was something so awesome about getting out of your head and living in the moment. People bumped into my sides, but we didn't care. We simply kept moving. A light sheen of sweat glistened on my skin.

When the song changed, I checked on Kelly, who was grinding against the guy, his hands sliding down to her ass. *Go get 'em, honey.* Nothing like new eye candy to get your mind off old troubles. I bit back a chuckle and left the floor to get something to drink. My throat felt dry, and I needed a moment to cool off.

A pair of guys at the bar saw me behind them and moved out of the way so I could lean between them. I murmured a thanks. I could feel their eyes on me as I waved at the bartender. What was his name? Casey had told me before.

Oh, that's right.

"Justin, hey!" I said with a toothy grin.

He came over. "Megan, looking good! What can I get ya?"

"How about a beer?" I waved my hand in front of my face; droplets of water slid down the back of my neck, down my spine. "I'm roasting." I eyed what was on tap and pointed to a local brewery's beer. It was strong but full of flavor.

"Good crowd," he said as he poured me a cup.

I gave him a few bucks from my clutch, strung around my wrist, and thanked him, backing out of the way so the guys could go back to their conversation.

"Hey, wait," the one on the left said to me. "Megan, right? That's what the bartender said." When he grinned at me, I saw a huge gap between his front teeth. "You here by yourself?"

Ugh. "My friend's out on the floor." I tried to keep my tone polite. "Have a good evening!" I moved away before he could keep talking to me. As I took a deep swig of my drink, I stopped in shock.

Near the end of the bar was Dr. Muramoto.

Nick.

I couldn't help but check him out. He took a draw from his beer, and his Adam's apple bobbed as he swallowed. His hair was styled, his white dress shirt casually rolled up at the sleeves, opened at his throat. I could see his gaze roaming the dance floor, head bobbing in time to the bass.

My body hummed all over at the surprise of seeing him here. He didn't look like a professor here. He looked like a very attractive man.

Apparently I wasn't the only one to think so. A pair of girls just a couple of years older than me popped on either side of him and struck up a conversation. My heart pinched in response. I chugged a good portion of my beer to give myself time to cool down. Wiped my suddenly damp palms on my thighs.

Nick threw his head back and laughed at something one of the girls said. His lips were parted, and I could see his bright teeth in the open-mouthed smile.

I remembered the email he'd sent me last week with the

coded response to my joke. Had I made him laugh like that? I wanted to.

Before I realized it, I had finished my beer. A light buzz stole over me, flushed my cheeks. It didn't take away my nervousness though. So I slid up to the bar and ordered another. I tried to keep my attention off him, to just listen to the music and the conversations around me, but he was like a magnet.

I eyed him again. He still hadn't seen me.

The next beer went down just as fast. I sat at the bar, torn between staying the hell away from him and wanting to go over and talk. But talking would probably be a bad idea, one part of my brain argued. Part of me knew I didn't want to just talk. I wanted to lean close and smell him, wanted to see the flecks of colors in his eyes up close. Wanted to make him laugh, find out more about him. Pick his brain.

Kiss him.

My cheeks flared at that thought. My head felt all light and floaty from the beers. They'd been stronger than I'd realized. Maybe I should have eaten more than just a salad for dinner.

I needed to get away from this dangerous train of thought about my teacher for a moment. It was a good time to go say hi to Casey.

I pushed through the crowd and got up to the DJ booth.

"Megan!" Casey cried out in pleasure as she came over and hugged me. Her headphones were draped around her neck. "You made it. Is Kelly here? I wanted to meet her."

I laughed and turned to eye the crowd from up here. "I think she already found a date." I spotted Kelly, still dancing with the guy, their mouths so close they were almost kissing. "I'll tell her to come by and say hi if she detaches herself from him."

Casey darted over to the system and fiddled with a few switches. She pressed one of the headphone cups to her ear. A new song transitioned in. She beamed at me. "So, how's your evening going? Any requests?"

I shrugged. "No requests I can think of. Just keep doing what you're doing. The crowd is loving it."

A shy smile stole across her cheeks. Casey was so confident behind the DJ booth, but she was rather unassuming in real life. She shrugged. "So have *you* seen anyone hot out there?" Apparently, she read the answer on my face, because one brow shot up. "Where is he? I wanna see. Tell me everything. Do you already know him? And why aren't you out there dancing with him?"

Oh, man. Do-or-die time. Should I keep bottling up this secret, or should I spill the beans and see what she thought? I thought about all the ways Casey opened up to me, how she'd trusted me with her secrets. Friends did that for each other. And frankly, maybe she had an idea on how I could handle this.

"Actually," I started, then made myself say, "my cryptography professor is here."

Her eyes grew wide. "Wow, that's awkward." Then she paused, and a knowing look flashed across her eyes. "Wait a minute. Are you attracted to him?" She looked toward the crowd. "Where is he?"

I groaned and leaned closer, telling her where he was sitting at the bar.

"Oh, he *is* cute," she said in a rush. "I can see why you like him."

I wrapped my arms in front of me. "It would be okay if I just found him hot. But . . . I don't know. There's something about him that sticks with me. He's smart. Funny. And this is totally stupid and I can't believe I actually have a crush on a teacher." I dropped my attention to her DJ equipment. "What do I do here? I just don't know. It's not like I can avoid him, either—he's my thesis advisor, so I have to talk to him. And I'm in his class." I paused. "And frankly, I don't want to avoid him."

"Oh, honey." The sympathy in her voice drew my gaze to her concerned eyes. "I want to tell you screw it, to explore whatever is going on here, if anything. But there are huge things at stake here. His career. Your schooling. If you get caught . . ."

I knew what she was going to say. "Of course, this is even assuming he has any interest in me. And given the way he's talking to that redhead at the bar, that's a big negative."

"Well, he'd have to be a blind idiot not to notice you," she said hotly. There was a fierceness in her gaze I rarely saw. "Anyone with two brain cells can see how amazing you are. You're smart, beautiful, witty, caring . . . you have everything going for you. If he doesn't see that, he isn't worth your time or effort." Her voice turned gentler. "I just don't want you to get hurt. Or in trouble."

"I know. Me neither." I huffed a sigh. "Actually, it helped to get that out. I'd been keeping it inside me since the first week of school."

She quirked a brow. "I'm pretty sure a certain someone here told me it was unhealthy to bottle your feelings."

"And that certain someone was right . . . and doesn't always follow her own advice," I replied in a droll tone.

Casey laughed. "Well, here's my advice for you. Take it or leave it. If at the end of the semester it seems like he's into you, see what happens then. That way you're not *his* student anymore. The circumstances will be different and maybe a bit more forgiving. But in the meantime . . ." She shrugged. "I guess try to keep your chin up and stay the course. We're super close to graduating."

I knew she was right. As I hugged her and stepped out of the booth, her words resonated in me. It was the logical thing to do. The smart thing.

The *right* thing.

Not to mention I was all worked up over a man who had

given me mixed messages at best. There was a big probability I was reading into it and seeing something that wasn't there.

I glanced over at the bar and saw Nick was gone. Dr. Muramoto, I reminded myself. I shouldn't think of him as Nick. That was too intimate. That crossed the line.

My mood felt dampened, so I moved right onto the dance floor and tried to fall into the music again. It took a few minutes, but I was able to shake off the slight edge of melancholy and self-doubt. Kelly wiggled her way over, her hand wrapped in her dance partner's.

"Having fun?" I asked with a wide grin.

Her eyes sparkled as she leaned close to me and said in a low voice, "I am. Just wanted to check on you—didn't want you to feel like I was ditching you."

"Not at all," I replied earnestly. "Go have fun. Seriously. Tonight is about relaxing. I'm glad you're having a good time." Not to mention that frown line between her eyes was gone. That alone made me happy.

She gave me a quick peck on the cheek. "I'll text you later, okay?" The guy's hand slid around her waist, tugging her up against him, and she laughed on a gasp. They disappeared into the crowd.

"I see you're all alone," an unfamiliar voice said from behind me. I spun to see the gap-toothed guy from the bar eyeing me. "Wanna dance?"

"I'm good, thanks." I took a step back.

"I'll bet you are." He moved toward me and reached a hand out to touch my waist. I shoved my hand on his chest to push him away.

"I said no." My bitch voice was out in full blast now. Usually I wasn't this harsh, but the combination of alcohol and frustration made me edgy.

The smile fell from his face, and I saw a flash of shock in his eyes. Before he could respond, I walked away from him and made my way to the fringe of the dancing crowd. And there was Nick—Dr. Muramoto, standing by himself, swaying in place, a water bottle in hand.

Before I knew what I was doing, I was right in front of him.

He blinked. "Megan." My name was a breath on his lips, and the sound of it set my skin tingling all over.

"Dr. Muramoto," I murmured.

He chuckled, and a dimple popped up in the corner of his mouth. "We're not in class. You can call me Nick."

I swallowed. "What are you doing here?"

"I'm a teacher, not a dead man. I love good music and dancing."

A laugh slipped from my lips. "Fair enough. My roommate is the DJ. I came with a friend."

"Where is he?" The question was light; I couldn't read into it.

"*She's* dancing with some guy she just met."

Nick took a fraction of a step toward me, and I did the same. We were only a couple of feet apart now. Music throbbed in the space between our bodies, filled my pores, made me feel light and free. I found myself moving. Our movements flowed together; his eyes were locked on mine, seeking, intense.

I couldn't look away.

When our chests brushed against each other, I realized we'd moved together again without me knowing. All the noise and anxiety and frustration fell away from my mind. My body became my focus—my body and his proximity, the weight of his gaze. He kept his hands off me, but his eyes roamed me freely.

It was a visual caress that made me throb.

Sweat slid down my skin; I barely noticed. I was in this bubble with Nick, absorbing all those small details about him I hungered to know. The light scent of his soap wrapped around me. His lips were parted ever so slightly, breaths coming out in small huffs to brush against my cheeks. Even in my boots, I noticed he was a few inches taller than me.

"There you are!" a giggling voice said from behind him. Redhead wrapped her arms around his torso and tugged him back, away from me. "I wondered where you went off to."

He paused and tore his gaze from mine to eye her, murmuring something in her ear as he disentangled himself from her grip. But he kept his hand in hers.

And just like that, the spell was broken. I stood in place, drowning in disappointment.

This was crazy anyway. What was I doing? Trying to hit on someone who would only ever view me as a student? This was far too desperate for me.

I needed to go home. Right now. Frustration tightened my chest. I turned away from them, dug into my purse and grabbed my keys. Snagged my coat off the rack and thrust my arms into it, then stepped out into the cold night. The wind stole my breath, slapped my cheeks.

I crammed my hands in the coat pockets and tucked my neck deeper in the collar as I made my way to my car. A hand on my upper arm stopped me.

It was Nick—*Dr. Muramoto . . . stop that, Megan!*—concern flooding his eyes. "Hey, wait. Where are you going?"

"I'm driving home," I said, unable to keep the petulance out of my tone. I hated that he made me feel this unsure of myself, this unsteady. I'd never experienced that with a person before.

His lips thinned. "How much have you had to drink?"

"I'm fine," I shot back as I removed my arm from his grasp. Even as I said it, I could feel myself sway a bit. Okay, "fine" was a little off the mark. Maybe I could walk home then.

"No, you're not." His voice was low and soothing. The music from the club was less intense from here, and we were alone at the corner. A soft light from a nearby street lamp cast us in a golden glow. "Let me take you." I opened my mouth to protest, and he said, "Either me or your DJ friend. But you shouldn't drive, and she's working." He paused. "Unless there's someone else you want to call."

I didn't want him to feel like he was obligated to take care of me. But I knew he was right. I found myself shaking my head and following him to his car.

Chapter 6

We pulled into the parking lot of my apartment complex. Nick let the car idle in the spot. Neither of us had spoken on the ride back. All of my emotions had been overwhelming me, probably not helped by the beer I'd chugged.

Nick raked fingers through his hair, mussing it up. He turned to look at me. I could see the highlights of his face through the streetlights in the parking lot. "Megan . . ." He stopped, closed his eyes for a moment. Rubbed his brow.

I lifted my chin. "Thanks for the ride," I managed to say. I put my hand on the door handle to open it.

"Wait. Shit. This is going badly." He huffed a sigh and looked at me. I felt pinned to my seat. "I wasn't expecting to see you at the club tonight, so I'm a little thrown off. My academic realm is usually separate from my private life. I'm afraid of crossing a line I can't uncross. There's a lot on the line for me right now." There was a tinge of vulnerability in his voice that made my heart squeeze in sympathy.

He sounded so conflicted. Could I be upset at him about that when I was too?

"What's on the line for you right now?" I asked in a tentative voice.

He blinked. One hand dropped to his lap, the other toying with the ball of the stick shift. "I just got accepted for tenure track. I applied back in the fall, but I didn't think I had a chance."

"Wow, that's great. You must be thrilled."

"I am . . . It comes with a lot of pressure. Meetings. I'm being scrutinized in a way I never have been before. My workload has doubled." His eyes raked over mine, then drifted. He gave an awkward laugh. "I feel like I'm whining. I'm not, really. I'm in a job I love, and they're basically offering me job security. Can't get any better than that."

He was open and talking to me right now, and my curiosity flamed. I wanted to know more. "What do you do when you're not working? How do you de-stress?"

"I work on home renovation—just bought an old house last year. And I have an antique car I'm restoring."

"And create your own coded messages," I added lightly.

His lips quirked, and for the first time since we'd left the club, he seemed to relax. "Yeah, I've always been fascinated by codes. My dad used to write them in Japanese for me, and I'd spend hours trying to crack them."

"So are your parents Japanese?"

"My dad is from Japan—he moved here with his parents when he was a kid. My mom's relatives are from Hong Kong, though she grew up in Ohio." His lips curved into a soft smile. "Our family reunions are crazy fun."

"I can just imagine. Do you have any siblings?"

He shook his head.

"Me neither. But I have a bunch of cousins. They felt like siblings growing up."

"Can I ask you a question?"

I nodded. It was funny how comfortable I was feeling around him now. The anxiety from earlier had seeped away. In its place was a glow in my chest that made the car seem intimate and cozy.

"Why math? You seem like you could be good at anything. What made you choose this field?"

I laughed. "If you met my parents, you'd understand." I explained how both of my folks worked together in a very math-driven industry—construction. How my mom had reared me on blueprints. How Dad took me to work with a little hard hat and explained the math and physics behind renovation. "They taught me a love of precision," I said, smiling. "Math is constant. It's ordered. It's comforting. And, frankly, it gets a bad rap. I think we need more women in math. We need more people of color in math." With that, I gave him a knowing look. "Haven't we had enough of old white men in the industry?"

He tipped his head, a hint of amusement in his eyes. "You make good points."

The easiness of conversation between us, plus the alcohol still lingering in my system, made me brave. I leaned forward a touch. "Tell me something no one else knows about you."

He paused at that and seemed to consider my request. I was afraid he was going to say no, he was silent for so long. I bit my lower lip as I waited.

"I hate pretzels." He blanched. "God, that was lame, wasn't it? Not exactly earth-shattering conversational skills here." His chuckle was awkward.

"I'm not a big fan of them either, unless they're smothered in chocolate," I said in an effort to ease his discomfort. "I'm also picky about wine. I find it pretentious and overly sweet. I never told anyone that before. My parents always drink wine, so I have it with them, but . . . I prefer beer."

"Maybe you just haven't had the right kind," he said, the corner of his mouth turning up. "There are a lot of sweet types, but you might enjoy a drier wine."

"You're probably right." I snorted. "But in the meantime, I just smile and sip."

The heat kicked up, probably in response to the dropping temps outside. I tugged my zipped coat away from my neckline, then unzipped it. As my zipper moved down, his eyes followed the path.

My pulse throbbed in my throat and my lips parted. With the renewed surge of heat was another whiff of his soap. Clean and fresh. I wanted to bury my mouth along the pulse at the base of his throat. Taste his skin.

"Megan," he said in a low groan. His eyes looked tortured.

In a rush, I leaned forward and pressed my mouth to his. He froze and I heard his rapid inhale. Then he opened his mouth and we fused together in a rush of heat and desire. My skin tingled all over as I swept my tongue along his.

He deepened the kiss, slanted his lips over mine. Devoured me, set me on fire. My nipples hardened, and my body reacted with a vivid slam of lust.

Then he was pushing me away, his breath coming out in ragged pants. "No. Absolutely not. This cannot happen."

It was a bucket of cold water over my head. Mortification swept over me, hard and fast. Oh God, I'd thrown myself at him. I scrabbled for my zipper and tugged it all the way up. "I'm sorry. I just . . . I'm going now."

With that, I ripped the door open and left his car like the devil was on my heels.

I keyed the door of my apartment and went in, leaned back against the door. Hot tears burned the backs of my eyes. Idiot! I smacked my forehead. What was I thinking, kissing him like that?

I'd never had a guy physically push me away before, like he'd been repelled by me.

My head swam. I stumbled into the kitchen and chugged a glass of water. There were two beers inside the door of the fridge. I was tempted to chug them down, but I'd probably had enough at this point. So I went into the bathroom, stripped off my clothes and took a long, hot shower instead.

Tried to not think about how good he had tasted. How he'd made me feel alive with that kiss. The sound of his breath hitching in his throat as he'd kissed me back for one glorious minute.

I toweled off, slipped into pajama pants and a tank top and flopped in bed.

The next morning, my head wouldn't stop screaming at me. Probably didn't help that two little kids were running around like idiots in the sandwich shop while their parents completely ignored them. Morning crowds were hit and miss most of the time.

I tightened my apron around my waist and grabbed the drinks for the table in the corner. "Here ya go," I said to the couple with a forced smile. "I'll be back in a minute to get your order."

Stupid hangover. I could feel my brain throbbing inside my skull. At least I'd slept it off instead of drinking away my embarrassment, the way I'd been tempted to. My stomach was still a little uneasy, so I'd eaten only toast and had a little coffee. Caffeine had a way of helping these things fade away faster.

I took the corner table's order, relayed it to the cook, then began to roll silverware in napkins. It was brainless work, not enough to distract me from the heavy guilt in my heart.

I'd made so many mistakes last night. I was going to drive home drunk. I had kissed my professor. And then, when he'd tried to push me away, I'd run off like a kid.

Way to handle it like a grown-up, Megan, I chastised myself. I could hardly believe how things had gone down. Yeah, he'd kissed me back . . . but probably out of shock or something. Not because there was anything there. Otherwise, he wouldn't have shoved me away like that. I wasn't sure how I'd live this down.

The food order came up. I served it. Fetched ketchup, poured more coffee. I was basically on autopilot. My mind was plagued with what to do now.

Only one idea came to mind.

I was going to have to quit cryptography. There was no way on God's green earth I could face Nick—Dr. Muramoto— again. Not after I'd thrown myself on him. Not after he'd had to remind me what a bad idea that had been. The look in his eyes, the tightness of his face, had been difficult to see.

Shit. This was going to ruin my plans. Anxiety wrapped around my gut and squeezed. I was supposed to graduate in the spring. I'd already put my application in. What could I do now? All my major classes were closed at this point.

I ducked behind the counter, stopped and drew in a steadying breath. There was always a solution. My parents had told me that time and again. Life might not work out the way I wanted it to, but that didn't mean I was stuck.

No, I couldn't replace the class this semester. But I could take one in the summer and still start grad school in the fall. I just had to pray that there was a suitable one to fulfill my major requirement. Yeah, it would mean no graduation this spring, but what choice did I have?

Then I remembered that he was my thesis advisor. Double shit.

That couldn't be helped. He was already my second in that position. I couldn't see the dean assigning me a third. But I could limit our interactions to email only. He'd given me the feedback, and I was working on it now. If he was a gentleman, maybe he'd just leave it at that and not mention any of that . . . thing between us. Or my dropping his class.

The faster I finished the paper, the faster I'd be done dealing with him. I could move past this awful stage.

Even though I'd still see him around campus. Ugh. But maybe with time, the pain would lessen. It had to.

Yeah, I had a lot to do when I got off work.

The door dinged, and in came Patrick, alone. He sat at my table, so I pushed aside my stresses, walked over and gave him a big smile as I handed him the breakfast menu. "Hey, how's it going?"

He groaned and gave me a weak smile. "Hangover."

"I feel ya." I chuckled. "Good night?"

"Could have been better." There was a meaningful look in his eyes that should have made my body react. But I didn't feel anything. It was either because I felt all busted or because of that kiss.

"What can I get ya?" I asked him smoothly. "Coffee?"

He flipped his mug over. "Yes, please."

I came back and poured coffee in the mug.

"I know what else I want," he said, then paused. "Your number." He pushed the napkin over toward me as he eyed me up and down.

I bit my lip and tried to not roll my eyes at the lack of finesse in his approach. Then I grabbed my pen from my apron and scrawled my name and number down. As I walked away, I realized the enthusiasm over Patrick wasn't there anymore. But I also knew I couldn't sit here and think about something that was never going to happen.

The best way to move on was to move on. And that was exactly what I was determined to do.

Chapter 7

I exited my ordinary differential equations classroom on Tuesday morning, clutching my quiz in my hand and grinning like an idiot. Aced it—as well I should. I'd studied hard last night. I stuck the paper in my bag and went into the student lounge area, coffee in my other hand.

I dropped in a seat near the corner, out of the path of people walking, and eyed clusters of students wandering through the math building. My next class, algebraic number theory, wasn't for a couple of hours. So I sipped my coffee and rolled my tight shoulders. The tension in my body hadn't gone away when I'd sent in my class drop request yesterday. If anything, it had gotten bigger.

I wasn't guaranteed there'd be a suitable class this summer. That was a *huge* gamble. Plus, I hadn't heard a peep from Nick yet. Yeah, I'd totally given up on trying to think of him as Dr. Muramoto. The kiss had knocked down that wall for me.

I reviewed the test to check out the two problems I'd missed. At first it wasn't apparent what I'd done wrong, but when I'd found my error, I wrote notes in the margin to help me remember for next time.

"Hey, Megan!" The voice jarred me from my review. Dallas stood there, beaming widely as he peered down at me. His hair was tousled and his cheeks tinged pink, like he'd just come inside. He unwound his scarf. "Missed you in class. You feeling okay? Wanna see my notes on what we discussed?"

I squirmed. I hadn't had a chance to tell Kelly or anyone else in there that I was dropping. I figured I'd shoot her a text in a bit. She'd sent me one yesterday asking if I was coming to class, but I hadn't responded. "Um, I'm good, thanks. I'm going to drop the class, actually."

His brow knitted. "Really? Why?" He took the seat across from me. His eyes flashed with concern. "Are you doing badly in there or something? You seemed on top of everything so far." The flush on his face grew bolder and he swallowed. "Sorry. I'm being really nosy and overwhelming you with questions."

He was a sweet guy. I found myself softening a bit toward him. It was obvious he liked me—and that I made him nervous. I had to admit, it was flattering. "It's not that. It's just . . . not working out. I think I'm going to try another class in the summer."

"Miss Porter," I heard from beside me.

My whole body flushed all over in a flare of heat, and I swallowed hard. I looked up to see Nick's eyes hard on mine. I couldn't read the expression on his face. "Good morning, Dr. Muramoto," I murmured.

"Do you mind if we talk for a moment in my office?" He sounded so professional and unemotional. I wished I could turn my feelings off like that. My heart was thrashing around in my chest.

I guessed he wanted to talk to me about the drop request. Unfortunately, I'd found out yesterday morning from the registrar that at this point in the semester, we had to get them signed by the prof. School policy—something about classroom quotas and wanting profs to be more involved in student academics. I'd figured that given what had gone down between the two of us, Nick would be all too glad to have me gone. So I'd just slid it into his mailbox.

Nick stepped away, giving me space and time to gather my stuff.

Dallas stood, and with a wink he whispered to me, "Good luck. And I hope you don't quit. I'd like to see you stick around." He walked off, holding his bag dangling from his hand.

I steadied myself and followed Nick down the hall to the second-to-last door on the right. His door was plain, with only a piece of paper taped on the window announcing his name. He opened it and ushered me inside, then closed it behind him.

As he moved toward his desk, I looked around. The room was pristine, with books tucked neatly into the large shelves. His desk was tidy, similar to mine—everything had its own pile. It wasn't impersonal; I could see a photo of an older Asian couple on the edge of the desk, plus a small pile of seashells right in front. Must be his parents in the picture. He looked just like his father. Same eyes, same hairline, same strong jaw. But the softness of his mouth came from his mother.

I sat in the chair opposite his desk and rested my hands in my lap. My pulse thrummed so hard I could hear it rushing in my ears. It was hard keeping my trembling fingers still. I knew I shouldn't be nervous, but I was. Nervous and afraid. And still crazy embarrassed.

"Megan, look at me," he said, a quiet heat in his voice.

I lifted my gaze, saw a bunch of emotions in his eyes, most prominently concern. "I know what you want to talk about, and I think this is best. I shouldn't be in your class anymore."

He shook his head, frowning. "I want you to rethink this. I know you're upset—"

"You have no idea how I'm feeling," I shot out, then bit my

lip. I wasn't going to open myself up to him and let him see how I felt. Not when I was still stinging from his rejection.

I was a rational person, but something about him made me irrational. Impulsive. This wasn't like me. I was fun, yes, but not unstable. Nick was mixing me all up inside, and my attraction to him was making me react in ways unlike me. I prided myself on being in control, having a good time with guys on my terms.

Nothing about this situation gave me any control.

"I'm sorry. You're right," he conceded. He sighed and scrubbed the back of his neck as he leaned back in his chair. "I feel bad about this, Megan. I don't want you messing up your plans over this."

"I'll figure it out," I managed to say. Why did the sound of my name on his lips make me glow, despite my best efforts? "I'm gonna see what's available in the summer. That way I can still graduate and go to grad school in the fall."

He was quiet for a moment. Tension thickened between us. I shifted in my chair.

"There's no reason why you need to get off track because of . . ." He swallowed and looked down at his desk, then up at me. Regret shone in his eyes. "I don't want that on my conscience. I know how important this is to you. Look, we're both adults. We can be totally fine and make it through this semester."

Seeing the sheer honesty in his eyes made me forget he was nine years older than me. Funny how that didn't seem to factor in to how I viewed him. Maybe because that just didn't matter to me. After all, he was right—we were both adults.

Yet I was running away, the way a kid would, not an adult who was confident with her life. Unease worked its way into my chest. I wasn't a coward normally. I faced adversity head-on. Except now.

Could he be right? Could we put aside Friday's disaster and push through anyway?

He leaned forward and rested his forearms on his desk. "I know you're uncomfortable. I'm deeply sorry about that. And if you want to leave the class, I'll sign the paper." He nodded toward the end of his desk, and there it was. My drop request. "But if you stay, I promise to be professional and do my best to help you succeed." He swallowed. "You're one of the most intelligent and promising students I've come across in a while. Don't let this knock you off your goals."

The sincerity in his eyes ate away at me. "I'm not sure I can get past throwing myself at you," I admitted, knowing my mortification was thick in my voice. I looked down at my lap, trying to regain my cool. "That was so not like me. I feel terrible. I put *you* in a bad position, and I'm very sorry about that. I can't tell you enough how sorry."

"Megan." My name was a whispered caress that made me look up. The warmth in his eyes startled me, and I couldn't look away. "That wasn't your fault. You weren't the one in the wrong here."

"But I misread—"

"No, you didn't." The admission seemed to tear out of him. He sucked in a deep breath and continued, "I wanted to kiss you. I wanted to *keep* kissing you, actually. But I had to stop because I can't let myself be attracted to you. Not when we both have so much at stake."

All the air whooshed out of my lungs. I stared at him for a moment in shock. His words echoed in my head.

He was attracted to me too.

He wanted to kiss me.

I was no longer embarrassed. It hadn't been all in my imagination.

"Stopping that kiss was one of the hardest things I've ever done," he admitted. There was a molten heat in his eyes that reinforced his words. "But it was the right thing."

My lips parted, and I found my gaze drawn to his mouth.

Remembering how good he tasted. I blinked and shook it off. If I was going to stay in his class, I had to keep these feelings to myself.

I straightened my back. Nodded. As strange as it sounded, knowing I wasn't alone in this attraction somehow made it easier. I didn't have to feel awkward. I hadn't just thrown myself at him—okay, yeah, I kinda had, but it hadn't been unwelcome.

I could be the adult I professed myself to be. I could shelve this. As my mom and dad told me, when I got out there in the "real world," I'd be forced to deal with situations that were difficult. Surely this qualified as one of those times.

"Okay. If you're sure you're fine with this, I won't quit," I said.

His body seemed to relax with my words, and he gave me a grateful smile. It made me realize that as much guilt as I'd been carrying around, he probably had too. Feeling like it was his fault that I wanted to change my plans. That understanding softened my heart some. I appreciated his not taking the easy, convenient path—he could have signed the slip and not had to deal with me anymore.

But he hadn't.

"So what now?" I asked him.

"Now you find the lecture notes from another student and get caught up. You have an assignment due tomorrow." Dr. Muramoto was back, but his smile and wink put me at ease.

"I appreciate your giving me another chance," I told him. I tossed my bag over my shoulder and grabbed my forgotten cup of coffee, probably now long cold.

"I'm glad you're not going," he said in a husky tone. "And if you need any help getting caught up, just let me know. We'll figure something out." He paused, seemed to want to say something else but shook his head instead. "Anyway. I'd better go too. I have a class in a few minutes."

I nodded and left his office. The walk back to the lounge

was light. Students passed me, but I barely noticed. I couldn't stop thinking about what he'd told me. That I was smart and promising.

And that he'd wanted to keep kissing me.

Suddenly I was glad he'd had better willpower than I'd had, given my new understanding of the situation. Was Casey's advice right—should I just give it the semester and see what happened after that? We'd both be in different spots at that point. He wouldn't be my prof. The line would be a lot less fuzzy.

It would be so hard sitting in his class, remembering how he tasted, how turned on he'd made me. But I would do it. I had to do it; after all, there was no guarantee I'd find another suitable class in the summer.

Surely I could keep this attraction on the back burner until then. No one else would have to know. I'd never told Kelly that Nick had been at the dance club, nor had I told her about my crush. And I knew Casey would take it to the grave if I asked her to.

This would be our secret, his and mine. And if he was adult enough to put aside his attraction and do the right thing, I could be too. I *would* be.

I dumped my coffee in the garbage and stopped at a vending machine, deciding what I should get to fuel my way through more studying and my next class. Soda? Juice?

My phone buzzed. I took it out of my jeans pocket. It was a text.

Watcha doin?

I didn't recognize the number. I stared at it for a minute, wondering how to ask who it was, when it buzzed again.

This is Patrick. Im at studnt center. LOL. Where R U? Cum ovr? Winkwink

He was texting me, asking me to hang out. Something I'd wanted for a while. But it didn't give me the thrill in my heart the way it should. It had to be because his typing was horrendous. I tried to not groan at the blatant, awkward come-on.

Not overly suave was he.

I bought a Diet Coke and took a seat back in the lounge area. Then I typed back, *Waiting for my next class to start soon.* Okay, kind of a lie, but I wasn't quite ready to see him yet. Not with thoughts of Nick still filling my head.

Wat classes R U takin?

Three math classes and psychology of stress. ;-P You? I replied.

Im takin a math class 2. U shld tuter me. Free this wk?

God, his typing was awful. Like, really awful. What were we, twelve? Then I felt bad for judging him. He didn't seem like a dumb guy in person, but here I was, making assumptions. Just because he wasn't as intelligent as Nick—

Nope. Stop that right there, I ordered myself. That was a dangerous road to start going down. I wasn't going to compare Nick to other guys. Frankly, because what was the point? He and I weren't going to date—at least, not for the foreseeable future. All it would do was frustrate me. And it wasn't fair to others either.

I refused to sit here and put my life on hold the whole semester. Especially since I had no idea what was going to happen when class was over. If he'd try to approach me or not. I was going to make myself keep on keeping on. Having fun, going out. Studying hard and spending time with friends and family. This . . . crush on Nick shouldn't change that.

Sure, I'd be happy to help you study sometime. Gotta go— talk to you later! I typed back. Vague-enough answer. Should buy me some time until we could talk in person and I could get a better feel for him then.

I popped open my Diet Coke, took a swig and cracked open my notebook. Study time.

Chapter 8

Kelly groaned and dropped her head on her open book. "Remind me why I'm taking this class again," she said in a miserable tone.

I gave a soft laugh and leaned toward her, careful to keep my voice low so as not to disturb anyone else in the library. "Hang in there. Midterm is just three weeks away." I peered down at my book to our current chapter on stream ciphers. "Okay, let's quiz each other on what we've discussed so far before we keep going."

Nick had warned us that the cryptography midterm was worth a big portion of our grade, so Kelly and I had started meeting Tuesdays and Thursdays to study. This wasn't a class we wanted to get behind on.

She looked up at me and gave a crooked grin. "You're so responsible."

I snorted. "I'm just determined to not flunk out of school my last semester. My parents would never let me live it down."

She and I spent the next half hour going back and forth, quizzing each other on the topic. We both fumbled a few times, but we worked our way through the problems and scrawled out detailed notes as we did.

Not studying alone was pretty nice. I didn't do this enough—pair up with other people to work together. Wasn't sure why, actually. I guessed it was because I tended to compartmentalize everything. I usually studied on my own or with someone else if I had to for a class assignment; I chilled with my casual party friends, who hated math and were quite vocal about it; I visited my family on the weekends for dinner. Everything had its separate space.

But this semester, it seemed like all my spaces were bleeding together, mixing with each other. Kelly and I were study buddies, plus we'd hung out socially again since The Night at the club. Through my network, she was even starting to make a couple of friends on campus.

My parents' dorm room renovation project on campus was now under way, those students relocated to special off-campus housing, and we'd had lunch a couple of times. I found myself avoiding the area they were working in unless I purposefully intended to see them. I told myself it was so they could focus on work, but I knew it was more than that. I was uncomfortable with the thought of them here. In my world, where they'd never been before.

Not to mention I struggled with how to deal with Nick too. He was my professor, but I had very un-studentlike feelings about him, reinforced more and more with each class. He and I hadn't been alone since our talk in his office, nor had we emailed. We were just kind of circling each other, not making much eye contact or initiating a lot of interaction.

Part of me was glad. The other part was disappointed. When I was alone in bed at night, staring at the ceiling, I let myself miss what could have been, had circumstances been different.

Oh well. I shoved those thoughts out of my head and made myself focus on the here and now.

"So," I asked Kelly, "have you seen that one guy from The Mask again? The hottie you danced with?" I hadn't asked her about him yet because I still felt a little awkward over what had happened that night with Nick. But since that issue seemed resolved, insofar as it could be, I guess, I wanted to know.

She rolled her eyes. "Oh, I didn't tell ya? Total dud. We went back to his car and kissed some, and then he kept trying to push for sex in the backseat. When I said no, that pretty much cooled that down. I left shortly after and I haven't heard from him since. I'd given him my number earlier that night, since he'd said he wanted to see me."

"I'm sorry," I said. I gave her a sympathetic smile and shook my head. "That wasn't cool of him." What a douche. Gotta love the guy who was only out for tail.

"I mean, I admit—there are times I've had sex on a first date. But . . . I dunno. For some reason, I thought he was into me for more than just that. I thought the situation was different." She shrugged, then looked up at my face with a touch of vulnerability in her eyes.

I hoped she didn't think I was gonna slut-shame her or anything. Hell, I had no problem with people doing what felt good for them. I sure tried to. Life was too short to walk around with a stick up my ass, worrying what people did in their bedrooms. And I didn't want them worrying about what I did in mine.

"Well, good for you for sticking to your guns and doing what felt right. And for not letting yourself feel pressured. No one wants to feel used, and if you're not into it, you shouldn't do it just to make him happy."

Her responding smile was heartfelt, even if a little shy. "Thanks. I'm so glad we started talking."

"Me too."

"Hey, guys—mind if I join you?" Dallas stood at the end of the table, a nervous smile on his face. "I saw you together and figured you might be studying for cryptography."

"You figured right," Kelly said. She shot me a quick glance, one brow raised.

"Um, sure, have a seat." I waved at the table to invite him to sit with us.

Dallas took the seat beside me. His thigh brushed mine and he paused, then shifted his leg slightly away. I saw a dark red stain crawl along the back of his neck.

Wow, this guy wore his feelings all over his face. There was no mistaking anything he felt or thought. It made me wonder if he'd ever had a real girlfriend, had ever gone on a date. His nervousness put me a little on edge, wondering what was going to happen. Somehow I had a gut feeling he'd ask me out, probably soon.

If he did, should I say yes?

Dallas opened his book and notebook, then grabbed a pen from his backpack. He nibbled on the end as he flipped with his free hand to the page we were on. He was cute, even if painfully shy. There was something endearing about him. No, he didn't set me on fire or anything, but that was okay.

Probably better that way, actually. I felt less out of control. With him, I knew what to expect. I knew it could be casual and fun and no pressure—well, I hoped anyway. After all, he seemed to like me, but it wasn't like it was love or anything.

We spent a little more time going back over our notes and quizzing Dallas on the chapter. He was a smart guy, and my respect for him went up a notch.

"So, Dallas, tell us all about you," Kelly said with a wide grin.

I kicked her under the table. To her credit, she didn't flinch, though she shot me a sidelong glance, keeping her gaze on Dallas.

"What do you want to know?"

"What do you do for fun? Let's start with that."

He slanted a peek at me, so quick I almost missed it. Swallowed. "Well, I like to ride my bike when it's nice out. I also collect old coins."

"What kind of motorcycle do you have?" I asked with a polite smile.

"Oh, it's not that kind of bike. I meant a bicycle."

Kelly smothered a laugh. My polite smile stretched at the edges, and I gave an inane nod to cover up my real feelings. Oh God, he sounded like my grandpa, who was an avid stamp collector. How dull.

He chuckled. "Yes, I'm aware this sounds totally nerdy. But the coin thing I started doing with my dad before he died, and I just kept it up because it was his passion."

My heart lurched at that, and I felt guilty for being so judgmental. What was with me lately? Apparently, hanging around the snarky guys I usually dated had rubbed off on me. I was ashamed of myself for being so dismissive.

"That's sweet," I offered in a sincere tone. "I'm sure he enjoyed spending that time with you."

Silence thickened at the table. Dallas cleared his throat, looked at Kelly, then looked at me again.

Kelly stood and glanced at her watch in an obvious move of leaving us alone. "Crap. I gotta run. You two finish up without me. I'll see you on Monday!" She gave me a quick, knowing look that said *tell me* everything *that happens,* and then she gathered her stuff and took off.

Another minute passed in awkward quiet. Okay, then.

"Well. I guess I should get rolling too," I told him, and began to put my stuff away.

"Hey, wait. Um." He cleared his throat. "Are you busy tomorrow night? Do you want to get together?"

I paused. My first reaction was to say no. But with that reaction warred a surge of guilt—my hesitation at accepting was due to it being Dallas asking me, not Nick. Not to mention the guilt I already had for judging him about collecting coins.

I owed him a fair chance. I'd given chances to far less worthwhile guys than him in the past. Who knew—he might turn out to surprise me. And I needed to stop thinking about Nick anyway. Dating other guys was the best way to do so.

"Sure, that sounds fun," I said lightly.

The smile on his face was so bright it almost made me feel bad I wasn't more enthusiastic about the date. "Perfect. Dinner? Six-thirty?" He named an Italian restaurant a few blocks from campus.

"Sounds great. I'll meet you there."

He leaned toward me. I could see the pulse fluttering at the base of his neck. "Looking forward to it." His eyes dropped to my lips, and I had a moment of real conflict about what to do if he tried to kiss me. Then he moved back, gathered his stuff and left.

I stared blankly at my book for several minutes, willing myself to feel more excited about tomorrow night. A glance at the calendar portion of my cryptography syllabus made me realize tomorrow was the day before Valentine's Day. Ugh. I hadn't had a boyfriend or significant other on that day in a couple of years.

Maybe after the date, I could run to the store and stock up on pampering supplies—chocolate, ice cream, pretty flowers—and just hole up in the apartment for the weekend. I was off work on Saturday. I knew Casey would be busy doing romantic stuff with Daniel. Oh, wait, maybe Kelly would want to hang out. I was really enjoying spending time with her, and it was nice having a single friend too.

I typed in a text to her, *Dallas asked me on a date for tmrw. Will let you know how it goes. Also, you busy Saturday? It's V-Day. Up for a foxy date with me? ;-)*

With a grin, I tucked my phone away, gathered my stuff and headed to my next class.

* * *

I headed to Bertheimer Dorms, where my parents' project was currently under way, slogging through snow as I cut across the courtyard. The snow was damp and mud tinged; I was glad I'd worn sensible boots to school today.

The air picked up and made the bare tree branches rattle and clack. I shivered in my coat. February was just as cold as January. I was so looking forward to spring, and to regular sunshine.

I shoved my hands in my coat pockets and made it to the sidewalk, stomping the snow off my boots. There was a small trailer set up on the side of the dorm, where my parents were running their operations. Contractors moved in and out between the dorm and the trailer, wearing hard hats.

I knocked on the door and heard my mom call, "Come in!"

"Hey!" I said. "Just wanted to drop by and say hi." Last night I'd lain in bed feeling guilty about avoiding them so much, so I'd decided to come by today and visit a bit. "Where's Dad?" I looked around the small trailer, which held a large table covered with blueprint drawings, a table bearing coffeepots and snacks, and a few scattered folding chairs.

"He had to run a few errands, but he'll be back later. How are you? Come in!" Mom tugged a chair up beside the one she'd been sitting in, in front of the blueprints. "Hungry? Want some coffee?"

I took a seat. "Coffee would be amazing, thanks."

She poured me some into a paper cup, dumped in several sugar packets—did the woman know me or what?—then handed it to me. "Been a busy one," she declared as she dropped into her seat and sipped her own coffee from a black mug.

"What are you guys doing right now? Isn't it hard working in the snow?"

"We're working on some interior issues at the moment. Moisture leaking through walls and so on."

I nodded. I remembered a few of my resident friends complaining about water dripping on their beds. "I'm glad you guys are fixing it up."

"Me too. Both for them and for us." She winked and tucked an errant strand of hair back in her twisted bun. I was relieved to see she looked and sounded much better than she had the last time I'd seen her.

"You seem like you're feeling okay," I ventured. "Your back doing good?"

"Definitely," she said with a relieved sigh as she pressed her hand to her lower spine. "I don't know how I tweaked it, but I'm not having any pain today. I'll take it."

"You're still going to call your doctor, right?" I pressed.

She gave me that Mom look. "If the pain comes back, I will. I already told you I would." In other words, don't nag her.

"I just worry," I said in a softer tone. "I want you to feel good." Mom didn't like to be pushed. She and I had butted heads more than once when I was growing up. We were both pretty stubborn.

This wasn't something I was going to back down on though. I'd read online about how sometimes old injury pains came back, which could be devastating for those who'd thought that period was over.

Her face lost its tension, and she sighed, cupped my hand. "I know. That time wasn't just hard on me. It was hard on you and your father too. But I really think this was a one-off. Not an indicator of the pain returning."

Nothing in her body language indicated any aches or tenderness in her back, so I had to take her at her word.

I nodded.

"Hey, will you watch the trailer for a few minutes? I'm going to run to the restroom."

"Sure."

Mom took another chug of her coffee, then darted out of the trailer. I eyed the blueprints, her familiar block script with notes written around the edges, lines pointing to areas on the walls that had leaks or damage. I couldn't help but smile. How many hours had she and I spent poring over blueprints, discussing building structure integrity?

Engineering wasn't necessarily my thing, but I respected her passion for it. It had fed into my own passion for math.

As I shifted in my chair, I kicked my foot under the table and connected with her purse. The rattle of something falling on the floor drew my attention. I ducked my head down to see what I'd knocked out of her bag. It was a bottle of pills.

I picked them up and saw her name wasn't on them. It was another woman's, a person I didn't know.

My heart gave a strange thud. Why would she have someone else's prescription? What was this medication? I read the label a few times.

Inside her purse were two other bottles, half empty. These had her name on them.

The trailer door opened, and I dropped the bottle I held into the purse, then sat up with a smile plastered on my face.

Mom came in with a relieved sigh. "Thank you! Okay, what we were talking about?"

I could barely get the words out. "You were telling me your back was feeling better."

"Yeah, it is." She even stretched and turned to show me.

Was there a way to ask her what was up with the bottles of pills without pissing her off? I struggled with it for a moment.

"Oh, but I did get a minor ear infection," she added, her face blanching. "I have some antibiotics for that."

Ah. What was *wrong* with me? Was I really suspecting my mom had a pill problem? She'd had back pain and an ear infection. Maybe she'd borrowed pills from a friend when she'd complained about not feeling well from the earache and she was going to return the rest of them. Guilt swam through me.

I offered a shaky smile. "Well, I'm glad you're doing okay.

I'll head out now—gotta figure out what I'm making for dinner tonight, so I'm going to stop at the store."

"Good thinking. Maybe you can come over this weekend? Your aunt Kaye's bringing the baby." Dad's youngest sister had just had a baby a few months ago.

"I'll try." I kissed her cheek and stood to go. Suddenly I needed to get out of there. Get away from this shame eating away at my chest. I couldn't believe what a path my mind had gone down. About my own mother too. The woman who had raised me to be strong and self-sufficient.

I left the trailer and walked down the sidewalk in a much more somber mood than before. The problem was, as much as I was beating myself up for having those thoughts . . . there was still a teeny, tiny chance it could be true. And I had no idea what to think about that.

Chapter 9

I smoothed the soft, buttery fabric of my skirt over my thighs and struggled to maintain an even smile over the candlelight glow on our table. It didn't help that I felt crazy awkward right now.

I should have realized that tonight's dinner date with Dallas wouldn't be the easiest ever. After all, he had never quite seemed comfortable around me. But what had seemed cute and endearing at first was now starting to frustrate me.

Dallas sipped his beer and gave a stiff smile. We hadn't been served appetizers yet, but he was already on his second drink. Not to mention he'd barely said ten words to me the whole evening.

I cleared my throat and scrambled for something to talk about. Anything. Other than class, that was. "Um. So how was your week?" *Well done, Megan,* I thought as I mentally rolled my eyes at myself. Scintillating conversation, indeed.

"Oh, it was fine." He swallowed the rest of his beer, and I noticed his cheeks were flushed and his eyes a bit larger. Obviously the alcohol was kicking in. I could see the tension in his shoulders relaxing. "Just studying and stuff. You?"

My heart pinched. Why did he have to drink so much to be able to talk and relax around me? I wasn't intimidating or anything, was I? I shrugged my shoulders. "I worked earlier today."

"You have a job at that sandwich place, right?" His eyes roamed around as he looked for our waiter. Probably to order another beer. Fabulous.

A dull heat flooded my face. "He'll be here soon," I said flatly.

"What?" His gaze ripped back to me.

"Our waiter. He'll bring you another drink."

He must have read the look on my face, because he turned red to the tips of his ears. "Oh. No, I'm fine. I don't normally drink like this, sorry. I'm just really nervous."

"Why?" I asked him bluntly. "I said yes. What's there to be nervous about?"

"Because . . ." He waved a hand at me. "You're beautiful. I didn't think you'd even agree to a date. And I don't want to screw it up."

My heart softened a touch at that. Okay, that was kinda sweet.

The waiter appeared then, bearing a plate of bruschetta. "Here you go. May I get you anything else?" He saw the empty beer and picked up the bottle. "Another for you?"

Dallas shook his head woodenly. "No, just water please."

Great. I fought against the urge to grab my phone and text someone to get me out of this. The night was going downhill, fast—Mayday, Mayday! I smothered a laugh.

Luckily, food was a good distraction, and the bruschetta was delicious. I savored the tangy bites and sipped my water.

"So, what do you want to do when you graduate?" I asked. "Any plans?"

"My cousin works for a company that gathers and analyzes

statistical data for businesses. He says there's a job for me if I want it."

"That sounds neat. Are you into statistics?"

"Yeah, I like data."

I waited for him to expand on that, but he just sat there and ate another piece of bruschetta. Okay then.

Time ticked on. It was painful—Dallas didn't ask me any questions about myself, nor did he offer up much commentary on anything other than how good the appetizer was. When the waiter brought our dinner, I ordered another glass of wine, and he must have figured it was okay to drink again, because he got a fresh beer.

I was halfway through my fettuccine Alfredo when he said, "So I hear you date a lot of athletes."

I froze midbite. Put my fork down and eyed him. He was staring right back at me. Apparently Lightweight's alcohol had kicked in hard-core. "And?"

He blinked. "Um. Well, I'm not an athlete."

I just stared. What the hell point was he getting at here?

"You look really pretty tonight." His eyes dipped to my cleavage, lingered, then swept back up to my face and my wild curls. "I've wanted to touch your hair since the first time I saw you."

I couldn't help the shocked laugh that barked out of me. "Have you ever been on a date before, Dallas?"

"What?"

"Never mind." Oh Lord. I just turned my attention to my plate. Shovel fast, I told myself. I'd be home soon enough, enjoying ice cream and pretending this never happened. Hopefully he'd get too drunk tonight to remember how awful this was so class on Monday wouldn't be crazy awkward.

Dallas tried to throw out a few inane comments about the people around us as he downed his fourth beer. I noticed his speech was getting a bit slurred and his gaze kept dipping to my breasts. He was no longer making any pretense of subtlety about it. Normally I didn't care if a guy checked me out. I felt good about myself—I wasn't embarrassed or modest, and so long as they didn't get creepy about it, all was fine. But for some reason, he was putting me off tonight. Maybe because this date had been a total flop, nothing like I'd thought it would be.

Dallas had turned out to be like every other guy, after all. Interested not in the space between my ears but in what he could touch and see. That was disappointing. Unsatisfying. Which both surprised and unsettled me. Maybe I was just burned out on casual dating. Maybe I was ready for something more substantial.

I didn't even bother finishing my second glass of wine. He paid for the meal—at least he did something right tonight. I tugged on my coat and followed him out the door.

"So, what now?" he asked as we approached my car. Thank God I'd driven separately. I just wanted to leave.

"Now it's time for me to go home," I said in an upbeat tone. It was so hard to maintain my manners, but I tried. I thrust out my hand. "Thanks for asking me out, Dallas. Hope you have a good evening."

He took my fingers in his and squeezed them, then stroked my hand with his thumb. His palm was super sweaty. I could hear his breath coming out in a rush. He stepped closer, peered down at me. His mouth was inches from mine. "So, can I get a good night kiss?"

My jaw dropped. Seriously? I just stared at him. He stared back.

"No, I don't think so." I removed my hand, dug into my purse and got my keys. As subtly as I could, I swiped my now sweat-slicked palm across the inner lining of my coat. Gross. "Good night." I ducked into my car before he could say anything else.

As I drove home, I called up Kelly and bitched to her about how badly the date went. She laughed so hard she snorted, which actually helped lighten my mood and made me laugh too.

"You just don't even know, girl," I said with a groan. "It was awful. I was probably his first date ever, I swear."

"I can't believe he got drunk. You must have looked really hot."

I rolled my eyes. "I could have looked like a yeti and he still would have been awkward. It was just never gonna be amazing. So, you still in for tomorrow night?" We'd firmed up plans to spend Valentine's Day evening eating Chinese takeout and watching *Kill Bill 1* and *2*—the least romantic movies ever. It was going to be awesome.

"All over it."

I pulled into my complex and parked. "Okay, I'm home. Thanks for listening to me whine. I'll see ya tomorrow!"

We hung up. I went right into the apartment, into my room and stripped off my clothes, tossing on comfy jeans and a sweater. I was tempted to drink more wine, but I decided on a soda instead.

I hopped online and checked out my social media. Since it was a Friday night, I saw a bunch of pics of people going out and drinking, partying. Blech. I was so not in the mood for that right now. I checked email and saw one from Nick.

Dear students,
Attached you'll find a supplementary article for Monday's discussion. Please read it before class. If you have any questions or are unable to download it, let me know ASAP.

For some reason, I wanted to talk to him. I told myself it was because he was an intelligent man who saw more to me than just a pair of boobs. He valued my smarts. And if I closed my eyes, I could still taste his kiss on my mouth. That conversation in his office had haunted me more than I wanted to admit.

I was weak, I knew. But I couldn't resist.

> *Dear Professor Nick,*
> *Thank you for the document. I'll be sure to read it—probably right now, in fact. As you can tell, I'm at home on a Friday night. Obviously you should envy my social life. :-P*
> *Megan*

My email chimed a few minutes later.

> *Since I'm responding to you on a Friday night, you should envy my social life as well. Or maybe we can just call it a draw. :-) Kinda surprised you're not at The Mask or somewhere else . . . ? Didn't you say your roommate is the DJ?*

Another email came right on the heels of that one.

> *How have you been?*

Oh, how to answer that question. Should I be truthful? Or should I be socially polite? I couldn't tell which one he wanted from me. I spent a few minutes waffling. Then I typed,

> *I've been busy, studying and working and stuff. Nothing crazy going on.*
> *Yes, Casey is the DJ. I was out earlier, but . . . let's just say it didn't go well. So I'm in and relaxing now.*
> *Some things have been on my mind all week.*

I hit send, my hands shaking and my stomach flipping over itself. That was forward of me, to hint that I'd been unable to stop thinking about him and our kiss, and I had no idea how he'd respond. But he'd asked, so I'd answered. The temptation had been too great to not see what would happen.

He wrote back:

I'm grading papers and listening to my old record player right now—parents gave it to me a few years ago when they complained about the "crap" I listened to. It's funny how they don't realize you can get some new releases on vinyl. haha

I hadn't planned on staying in tonight. I was going to go out with some friends of mine. But I wasn't in the mood.

And some things have been on my mind all week too.

My heart leaped to my throat. I stared at his email for several minutes until I almost had the words memorized. When I finally wrote him back, I asked what albums he had, said that I was interested in buying a record player too (plus, Casey was a huge fan of vinyl) and I'd love recommendations.

I wasn't sure how much time passed as we talked. And I didn't care. Our messages went back and forth, the trail of our conversation growing longer. I learned he was a fan of old metal, like Metallica, but also of the Beastie Boys and old hip-hop. I confessed I had a soft spot for eighties groups like Hall & Oates, and he addressed the next email to "Maneater."

Our messages weren't overtly flirty at first, but there was an undertone that vibrated with awareness. I couldn't help but think about his fingers typing away on his laptop or desktop. Those intense eyes locked on the screen. Our words grew more intimate as we shared favorite music memories. He told me about going to classical concerts with his dad. I wrote back how my dad's love of the Beatles had grown on me, and I owned all of their CDs.

Since my bedroom door was open, I heard a key scrape the lock, and then Casey walked in. She paused in surprise as she eyed me.

"Wow, you're up late," she murmured as she dropped her bag on the couch.

I glanced at the time—it was well after two. I'd long since finished my soda and had moved on to drinking coffee, not wanting to grow tired or end the conversation. "Yeah, just talking."

"How did your date go? Obviously not *that* great," she said in a teasing voice, "since you're on the computer and not with him."

I groaned and rolled my eyes. "It was a total dud. He got drunk and ogled me, then tried to press me for a kiss at the end of the night. Uh, no."

"Oh, that sucks. I'm sorry." Casey stretched and yawned. She took off her boots and padded across the floor to give me a hug. Her warmth enveloped me, and I smiled. It still seemed so crazy to have her reach over and touch me like this. She was growing more natural at it now. "I'm exhausted. Going to bed—let's chat more about it tomorrow. Night!"

I heard her door close behind her and turned my attention back to the computer. Nick's latest message was facing me, waiting for a response. I wrote:

I had no idea it had gotten so late. I'm sorry for keeping you up this long. I know you were going to do some grading.

His reply came a few minutes later:

I'm a late-night guy by nature, so I would have been up anyway. No big deal—and nothing to apologize for. I've enjoyed our conversation, Megan. Far more entertaining than grading freshman math tests. As you can imagine, lol.

The lightness in my chest dampened, and my old friend embarrassment came sweeping back in. I'd inflated this conversation beyond what it actually had meant. Had given it more meaning, more intimacy, because I'd wanted to believe those feelings were there. I'd needed it, actually, especially after that crappy date.

I started composing an email telling him good night when he followed up his message with a new one.

I don't know about you, but the coffee in my house is crappy. I know a great diner open 24 hours where we can get good, hot java. It would give us a chance to discuss your thesis revisions as well . . . ? No pressure. Just figured if we were both awake, we could be awake together.

That buoyancy came back in a rush that made me almost dizzy. From the wording of his request, we both knew we were crossing a line here with definite intent. No alcohol involved, nothing else to blame it on.

And yet there was no way I could say no. Every molecule in my body ached to see him. Hours of typing had built this need in me to be with him, only him. No other man had stimulated my mind or my body this fast before. Not even close. I wanted to know everything about him. I wanted to smell that soap scent and pretend I had a chance at him being mine.

I dragged in a shaky breath and wrote back, *Tell me where to meet you.*

Chapter 10

"This place is awesome," I declared as I looked around.

We had just gotten nestled in a back booth at an old-fashioned diner on the east side of Cleveland, a good half hour from campus. The place was filled with a variety of people buzzing in and out, talking about politics and books and celebrities and breakups and every topic under the sun. On the walls were black-and-white photographs of people I didn't know. Probably old celebrities. I thought I recognized a 1950s actor though.

Our table was lacquered and gleaming, and the puffy black booth was comfortable. This was a place made for lingering, for conversation. The scent of frying meat and French fries made my mouth water. I bet their burgers were to die for.

Across the table from me, Nick grinned. He had on a gray long-sleeved T-shirt; his coat and scarf were discarded beside him. With cheeks flushed from the cold and a bright smile, he looked disarming. I could scarcely catch my breath. "I grew up around the corner from here. My folks and I ate at this place all the time."

My hands shook a little as I picked up the menu and attempted to focus on it. I was trying so hard to be cool and self-assured. Nick, however, was completely at ease, not unnerved by me at all.

Was this how Dallas had felt earlier tonight with me? I suddenly felt a little bad over how I'd judged him about his nervousness. No, it didn't make me like him or want to date him again—it was vastly apparent he and I were incompatible. But maybe I could do with a bit more empathy in general. I had picked up a bad habit of judging people before thinking things through.

There was no alcohol in this diner, so I had to make do with faking confidence tonight. I didn't want to drink anyway. I loved beer, but sometimes it played wonky with my emotions. I said things I didn't mean to say, did things I shouldn't. I needed all of my senses to get through this experience without doing something I'd regret later.

"So what do you recommend I try?" I asked him evenly, studying the burger selection. When I didn't get an answer, I looked up and saw him staring at me. "What?"

His lips curved at the edges of his mouth. "Nothing." He paused. "Okay, it's kinda weird, being here in person with you after we just spent hours talking in email," he admitted with a faint shrug. "Through email, it's easier to talk in a way, because of the faceless aspect. And now I feel goofy for having admitted that." He chuckled.

The fact that he confessed that took away some of my unease. So his confidence was a front too. We were both nervous.

"It's not goofy. I totally get it. You know, I haven't done that in ages—just talked with someone that way. Usually I have a quick text or phone conversation. Get right to the point and move on with my day." There was something much more intimate about how we'd shared our thoughts, in a way that couldn't be attained in texts.

"Me too." He cleared his throat and dug into the leather satchel he'd brought, whipping out my thesis paper. "Um, so here. I have a few last thoughts on passages that could be tighter, but you did a great job with your revisions. One last cleanup should have you ready to go."

I took a few minutes to scan it over. He was right; his feedback had made the paper stronger. I had a feeling I was going to do well—there was hardly any revision left to do at all. I peered up at him as I folded the paper in half and stuck it in my bag. "Thank you again. I really appreciate all your help."

"No problem. It was my pleasure." I could tell by the earnestness in his tone that he really did enjoy it.

The waitress came by with our coffee, then took our food orders. I loaded mine with sugar, and we sipped and sat in silence for a few minutes. It wasn't awkward though. Just a comfortable lull in the conversation, filled by the hum of voices around us. I furtively studied his face over my drink. I could see faint laugh lines around his eyes. The stubble on his chin and jaw. The flare of his thick eyelashes. His face was striking.

I remembered that mouth on mine, and my cheeks burned. I looked away. "So did you grow up in the Cleveland area?"

He nodded. "Local all my life. You?"

"Same. I love it here. Can't see myself living anywhere else. My favorite thing when I was a kid was going downtown during the holidays and seeing Terminal Tower lit up in red and green."

"I used to go ice skating downtown," he said with a soft laugh. "On the outdoor rink in Public Square. My mom would freak out because I'd fly on the ice. She was sure I was going to break my neck with my daredevil antics."

"Are you a speed demon?"

He gave a wicked laugh that shot straight to my lower belly. "Let's just say I've gotten a few tickets in my time."

"I drive like a grandma," I replied primly to cover up my

very vivid sexual reaction to his laugh. "And I've never gotten a ticket."

He raised a brow. "Interesting. For some reason, I would have pegged you for a risk taker."

"Oh, I am," I agreed with a laugh. "But not in something that could kill me."

"So what do you take risks in?" He leaned forward, gaze hot and hard on mine.

My pulse picked up. My lips parted and I licked them. He dropped his eyes to look at my mouth, and his pupils flared.

We were both thinking about that kiss, I knew it. That damn kiss that haunted me. All. The. Time. That had been a *huge* risk.

"Well, I've dated some douche bags I really shouldn't have," I said breathlessly, making him bark out a laugh the way I'd hoped it would. That eased the sexual tension a touch. I swallowed. "Um, plus I learned how to shoot a gun when I was sixteen."

That made him blink. "Why?"

"Dad wanted me to know. He likes to hunt occasionally. When I was a kid I begged him to take me, but he made me wait." I paused. "I'm an excellent shot, if you can believe it." I hadn't been to the range with Dad since I'd started college, actually. I made a mental note to hit him up for another trip. I didn't want my shooting to grow rusty.

"I do." There was more than a little admiration in his dark eyes. "I bet those math skills come in handy."

"Surprisingly, it's more intuition than math. You learn how to feel the shot. I'll take you to a range sometime." When I realized what I said, I stopped. Gave an awkward laugh and waved my hand in the air, rolling my eyes at myself. "I mean, you know, if that was something you wanted to do. I don't want to assume anything—"

"It sounds like fun, Megan," he interrupted with a toothy grin.

Our food came out. I thanked the waitress warmly—I knew how difficult her job was—and started chewing on a fry. The conversation fell quiet again, leaving me alone with the loud thoughts in my head.

What were we doing here, really? After our talk in his office, I thought that would be it. That I'd let go of this silly crush at some point and move on. But we'd spent hours talking in email, getting to know each other. And now we were here . . . because he'd asked me. Those weren't the actions of an uninterested man.

It made it harder for me to think about him as just my professor. I didn't think there was any way for me to go back now.

I inhaled my burger; the pasta earlier hadn't filled me up. It was good, as was the coffee. I could see why he'd suggested coming here. In between bites, I peered into the inky blackness outside, punctuated by streetlights and the occasional car sweeping by on the street.

A few snowflakes started to fall. It was quiet, picturesque. What a lovely night. I realized it was the early hours of Valentine's Day. I hadn't expected to start it off like this—sitting across from Nick after spending hours talking. My heartbeat kicked up a notch.

"You're not exactly what I thought you'd be," he said, drawing my attention back to him and off my musings.

"What did you think I'd be?" I wasn't sure what to make of that statement, but I wasn't mad or anything. Mostly curious.

"You're mature for your age. You have fun, but there's a deep, resonant side to you I hadn't expected."

"We aren't that far apart," I pointed out. "And I am twenty-one. I'll be twenty-two this summer, actually."

He dropped his gaze to his plate and chewed on a fry. I sipped my coffee and wondered if it was immature for me to point it out. Ugh. My usual self-confidence was all but gone around him.

"Do you like teaching?" I asked randomly.

"Love it." His answer was immediate. "It was my calling."

"I don't know what I'm going to do with my master's degree," I told him. I dipped a fry in ketchup and ate it. "I've been hoping something will come to me this semester. I mean, I have options. I just don't know what *my* calling is." I paused. I hadn't admitted that out loud to anyone, even to myself.

Math interested me. I was good at it. But I didn't know what would make me passionate. What industry or job I could get into that would satisfy me. Sometimes having so many options could be overwhelming.

"There's nothing wrong with that. I changed my major in undergrad—was going to go into psychology, actually." He shook his head. The light above caught in his black hair and cast it in a golden glow. He was so effortlessly handsome that it took my breath away. Everything he did, from the way he stroked his perspiring cup to the easy smile he bore, was magnetic. I'd never seen a man so comfortable in his own skin.

No wonder I was drawn to him like this. He was what I aspired to be. What I *thought* I'd been until I'd met him. It was easy to be carefree and relaxed around people who didn't have a deep impact on you.

Something told me he was going to have an impact on me, whether I liked it or not. He already was starting to.

I snapped my mind back to attention on the topic at hand. "Then you can help me with my psychology of stress homework," I said with a light laugh. "That class is killing me."

"I took that. It was several years ago, obviously. But I might still have my notes. Want me to find them for you?"

"Really?" I gave him a gratified smile. "I was kidding, but I'd love some help. It feels too abstract for me to really get into it. I keep zoning out and missing things. Which is unlike me."

Our conversation moved to other topics, flitting here and there. What movies we'd seen recently and loved. What books moved us. Our favorite local restaurants. I quickly realized the impact of his being older than me—older and more well rounded. He'd tried a lot of food I'd never tasted before. He'd read authors I'd never heard of.

I found myself taking out my phone and typing book titles in my notes app. Hearing him speak so passionately about these authors moved me. I wanted to read them and find that passion too. Give us something more to talk about next time.

I wanted there to be a next time. Actually, I wanted tonight to just keep going. I could feel the edges of fatigue slipping in, but I stubbornly fought it back.

When the waitress came by and cleared our plates, then left the bill, he insisted on paying. I tried to not read into it, to just think of it as a friendly gesture. To help reinforce that in my mind, I paid the tip, and we donned our coats and left the diner. Snow came down in huge, puffy flakes, coating the tops of our hair and shoulders. It was still dark out, though the darkness had taken on a soft gray edge.

I glanced at my phone. It was five in the morning. I could hardly believe it. We'd sat up all night talking. And I still felt like I hadn't reached the depths of his intellect, his knowledge. I craved more.

One night wasn't going to satisfy this itch.

He tightened his scarf, and we walked toward my car. My heart sank, and I scrambled for an excuse to not go yet. Just a little more time. I saw a park right down the street.

"Wanna walk for a little bit?" I asked with a nod in that direction.

I saw the hesitation in his eyes. Was it because he was tired? Or because he was afraid of being alone with me, especially on a day that was laden with romantic expectations? Disappointment tightened my chest, and I felt my mouth turn down.

"You know, that's okay. I've already taken up enough of your evening," I said in a quiet tone. I leaned back against my car door and stared at the ground, coated in a thick dusting of snow.

"That's not it," he told me. His voice was rough, and I looked up to see his eyes hooded, staring over my shoulder. "I'm just questioning how smart it would be. I've already pushed the limits by asking you out tonight."

My breath came in small pants that puffed in the air between us. His gaze turned to mine, and I felt myself sinking into his eyes. "I'm sorry," I whispered. "About that kiss. I should never have done that. I crossed a line, and it put something awkward here. I wish I could take it back." The lie bit at me. "Actually, no, I'm not sorry," I amended with brutal honesty, "even though I probably should be."

A slow smile spread across his face, and he took a step closer to me. "I love how you just say what's on your mind. Your candidness is refreshing, Megan. And so rare." His gaze dipped to my mouth, and I found myself trembling with a hunger that spread through me like warm honey.

Kiss me, kiss me, I silently begged.

He took my hand in his, wrapped my fingers in the heat of his palm and drew me across the street. We were silent, making our way down the sidewalk into the park. The hush of snow filled my ears. I felt like all my senses were hyperaware, tuned in to his frequency.

I heard the soft rasps of his breath, caught light whiffs of his scent. His thumb stroked my skin and sent spirals of pleasure coursing through my lower belly, to my core.

We padded through the snow to an overhang of trees above us, a perfect canopy that protected us from the falling flakes.

Nick turned me to face him, cupped my face in his hands and drew me forward, a breath away from his mouth. "God, I shouldn't want you," he said, and the rawness in his voice nearly undid me. He was as hungry as I was, his anguish clear in the lines on his face, the near anger in his eyes. "I shouldn't, but I do."

I stood there, body shaking with the agony of my feelings. "I want you too," I said on an exhale. "So much. I can't stop thinking about you." My heart hurt because of how hard it was throbbing beneath my rib cage.

Then his mouth was on mine, and my fingers were twined behind his neck. He pressed his body against me, and I went up in flames. I couldn't get close enough. His tongue plunged into my mouth, taking, seeking.

His kiss owned me.

I gasped and breathed him deeper. His hands slid down to cup my waist, bringing me flush against his arousal. He was hard. My nipples tightened as my breasts swelled. His mouth slid down to nibble at my jaw, suck the tender flesh at the base of my neck. I groaned, arched into him. I was dizzy, aching, throbbing all over.

"Nick," I said as I rubbed against him. I wanted those hands all over me.

One hand cupped my ass and squeezed; I sighed in pleasure and let my fingers explore the contours of his neck, his jaw. I sucked his chin, his Adam's apple, and I heard him give a loud moan. I was so wet now, my panties drenched. My body screamed my arousal.

We kissed for I wasn't sure how long, lost in each other, all that pent-up hunger spilling out with our tongues, our hands. Just kissing, but it was enough to drive me insane.

Finally we parted, chests heaving. My face was flushed, my body burning, my mind floating. He reached a hand up and stroked my cheek with his thumb.

"I know we shouldn't have done that," he said. "But I couldn't go another ten minutes without tasting your mouth."

I sucked in a shaky breath and nodded. His words did something wicked to me.

Nick seemed to gather himself then. He dropped his hand, stepped back. Smoothed his hair and offered me his hand. "Ready to head out of here? I'm sure you're tired."

He escorted me to my car. Pressed another sweet, small kiss to my lips before standing back and watching me pull out of the diner's parking lot. I drove home on autopilot. I felt like he'd invaded every part of me, even though we'd only kissed.

When I made it home, I quietly slipped inside, stripped off my clothes and slid naked under my sheets. My last thought before falling asleep was of his smile when we'd pulled apart, beneath the trees.

That hadn't been the smile of a man who felt guilty or ashamed. Of a man who regretted his actions. No, it was the smile of a man who wanted to do it again.

God, I wanted it too.

Chapter 11

Cryptography on Monday was a bit awkward. No way to get around that. Throughout class, Dallas had turned around and shot me a few looks that I could feel, though I'd kept my gaze locked on my open textbook. I had no idea what to say to him. He'd sent me a text on Valentine's Day asking me what I was doing, but I hadn't responded.

Nick had sent me a few texts too, that same evening, to say hi and wish me a happy Valentine's Day. I was so lucky Kelly hadn't noticed my giddiness over it, or the way I'd ducked into the bathroom several times to send him replies. She must have thought I had a tiny bladder.

"Dallas keeps looking at you," Kelly whispered under her breath. "Want me to say something to him for you?"

I shook my head. "No, I'll handle it, but thanks." I'd gone into more detail about the terrible date on Saturday while we were hanging out. But we'd actually spent most of the time just talking, eating ice cream and drinking wine, getting to know each other.

Well, except for my occasional texts with Nick. Those had

felt so deliciously bad. I wasn't sure how to describe it except that he felt like forbidden fruit I couldn't resist tasting. Even though I knew it was wrong to do so.

"Maybe he wants to apologize," she mused, talking out of the corner of her mouth as she looked straight ahead.

Nick was discussing something, but truth be told, I wasn't quite listening the way I should. I kept fixating on the curves of his mouth, trying to not burst into flames each time our eyes connected. I could tell he was thinking about me too. It was right there in his eyes. If we hadn't spent the whole evening together talking, I might not have noticed it. He was good, professional.

But I noted the way his gaze lingered on me. How his mouth turned up in the corners just a fraction. His words drawling off for a second or two, the air crackling between us despite the thirty feet or so separating us.

Which drove me even crazier. Made every cell, every organ, every bone and vein and muscle on high alert for him.

"—should give him a chance to," Kelly was saying, and I snapped my attention to her words. The last thing I needed right now was to get busted checking out Nick.

I looked at her, and she nodded toward Dallas.

"Oh. Uh, yeah, I'll talk to him later," I promised.

The rest of class flew by. Nick talked, and eventually the lecture drew me in. I didn't know how he did it, but he made everything sound fascinating. His passion rang true. He wandered across the front of the room, hands waving in the air to punctuate his words. This was definitely a man who had teaching in his blood.

"So I have your papers graded," Nick was saying, and he started to chuckle when a few students groaned. "They're not that bad, actually." He paused. "They're not all that good either." His eyes twinkled as laughter burst out in the room. "I kid, I kid. On the whole, I'm quite happy with the effort you guys put into these. But if you don't like your grade, don't forget, you get one paper this semester to rewrite and turn in for a better score."

He turned around, scooped papers off his desk and wandered up and down the aisles to hand them out.

When Kelly got hers, her face screwed up tight until she flipped to the last page to see her score. The tension leaked from her body. "B-plus. I'll totally take it," she said on a heavy, happy sigh.

Dallas got his paper, and his back tightened when he eyed his last page. Obviously not a good sign.

When my paper was handed to me, Nick's fingers brushed mine. My nerves jumped in response, and I fumbled. But he moved back down the aisle away from me, cool as could be. I turned to my last page and saw my score.

A-minus, with a paragraph of feedback.

And a tiny line of coded text right beneath. I scanned it, trying to find the key to unlocking what he said—looked like it could be the same code he'd used that first time in email. My heart hammered in excitement. What did he write?

"Hey, what's that?" Kelly asked as she peered over my shoulder.

Shit. My hand shook and I dropped the papers closed. "Oh. It's nothing."

"Looked like a code to me."

I waved my hand in an attempt to look casual. "In my . . . feedback, he said I was too narrow and simple with my coding examples, so I guess he gave me one to show me how complex they can be."

She looked at me for a moment, brow furrowed. Her eyes seemed hesitant. "Well, that was kinda weird."

I tried to give an easy shrug, though I was very nervous. Shit, I was blowing this. *Think smarter,* I ordered myself. "Yeah, he's not your typical teacher. Maybe he was just showing off how smart he is or something." My chest stung as I said this, but the statement worked.

She nodded and rolled her eyes. "Totally. Sometimes they do that kind of crap. To prove why they have their jobs or whatever. Ugh, I hate that."

Relief whooshed through me. I tucked the paper underneath my notebook and turned all my attention to taking notes for our homework. I was going to have to be careful. I couldn't give away what had happened between us. And crazy or not, I didn't want it to stop.

I wanted to look at the note again, but I knew that would be dumb. The anticipation was killing me though. When he dismissed us, I noticed his eyes raked over mine once before he got his stuff together and left the room.

The tension in my back unknotted a touch. I tucked my stuff in my backpack.

"Okay, I'll talk to you later!" Kelly said. She gave me a quick hug, then left.

I was all set to escape myself when Dallas suddenly stepped in my path. Frustration made me dance from foot to foot. I so didn't want to do this right now—I wanted to find a private corner to read Nick's secret message.

"Megan," he said in a gruff voice. His cheeks grew red. "How was your weekend? I sent you a couple of texts but didn't hear from you."

"Sorry, I was hanging out with Kelly," I offered. "I gotta go. Maybe I can catch you another time—"

"I just needed to say something," he persisted, not moving away.

I sighed and stood in place. Apparently it wasn't going to be an easy escape. "Okay, what?"

"I . . . feel like things didn't go that well on Friday," he started. Cleared his throat and played with the neckline of his sweater. "I had a good time, but I don't drink a lot and I know it made me a bit awkward. But I was just so nervous. . . ."

"It's fine, I get it," I said, knowing I sounded abrupt but unable to be more patient. I was frustrated that he was forcing this on me right now when I didn't want to talk about it. On *his* terms, not on mine. Kinda made it hard to warm up to his words.

"Oh. Okay." His shoulders loosened. "So I was thinking I could take you out again, to make it up to you."

My stomach sank. "That's not necessary," I said slowly, "but thanks for the offer."

"I mean, it's not just out of obligation. I'd like a do-over." Sincerity poured from his eyes.

I drew in a slow breath. Exhaled. "Dallas."

"Just one more chance," he pressed. "I know I messed it up."

I rested a hand on his upper arm. "I'm sorry. I just don't think this is a good idea. But thank you for talking to me. And for the date Friday." That was as gentle as I could be. Hopefully he would get the point without me having to be a jerk.

No, I didn't like Dallas. I didn't want to hurt his feelings though. It was obvious he was on edge, from the tips of his red ears to the way he kept swallowing.

"Oh. I see." He stepped away out of my reach, and my hand dropped. His face stiffened and he turned away from me. "I'll see you later then." His movements were mechanical as he gathered his belongings and went right out the door without looking back.

I tried to not feel bad for stinging his pride, hurting his feelings. I was alone in the room now, and the matter of the code was gnawing away at the back of my head. So I took the paper out and flipped to the last page.

It was the same code Nick had used before. I quickly translated.

Meet me at five pm, 9th street pier downtown.

I worried my lower lip between my teeth to bite back the sigh of happiness that threatened to escape. He wanted to hang out again. Excitement slid along my veins and sped my pulse. I tucked the paper in my bag and left the room, floating on air. An off-campus meeting. It made sense—right now wasn't the best time to flaunt . . . whatever it was that was happening between us. Especially since my parents were on campus. I needed time to explore this thing between us before worrying about other people getting entangled in it. God only knew what they'd think. Frankly, I didn't care right now.

I couldn't get Nick off my mind.

Focusing on my next class was so hard. I couldn't concentrate much, so all my notes were probably pointless, but I wrote them anyway. When it was done, I rushed back to the apartment to freshen up. Then I left a note for Casey letting her know I was going out for the evening, hopped in my car and drove toward downtown.

This time of the day, in mid-February, the sky was close to sunset. It would be gorgeous to see on the water. Had I mentioned my love of the lake to Nick in our exchanges? I couldn't remember, but it was the perfect meeting place.

I made it—thankfully, rush hour traffic was moving opposite me as commuters left their offices for the day—and found a spot to park. I wrapped my scarf tighter around my neck, popped on a knit cap and slipped on my favorite warm leather gloves. Then I strolled toward the pier facing Lake Erie.

I rarely came downtown by myself. I wasn't sure why, since I loved it around here. The pier had only a few people milling around, including a police officer who strolled along the sidewalk. I gave him a friendly nod and made it to the end of the pier. The wind rushed off the lake and froze my cheeks. But that salty tinge in the air wrapped around me, filled me. I closed my eyes and breathed it in.

This—being on the water, hearing the waves smack against the rocks below—was beautiful.

The sun began its descent in the western sky. Bright splashes of pinks, purples and oranges smeared above me, bringing the darker shades of night right on their tails.

"Stunning, isn't it," a warm voice said right behind me.

I turned to see Nick grinning, the breeze whipping the top of his hair around. His cheeks were pink from the air, and his brown eyes were brilliant, reflecting the sunset in their depths. "I'm glad I interpreted your message right," I said with a laugh.

He stepped beside me. "Me too. Otherwise, that could have been really embarrassing."

We gripped the massive chains on the end of the pier and just stood there in the quiet for a few minutes, watching as the sun dipped behind the watery horizon. When the sky darkened to a rich purple, he faced me and took my hand.

"I can't stop thinking about you, Megan," he said huskily. He drew closer, his heat pouring onto me. His breath puffed across my cheeks. "I know it's crazy and probably wrong, but it's true."

"Same for me," I confessed. I felt overheated by the look in his eyes and was tempted to unzip my coat for a moment to let in a gush of cooler air.

His eyes flashed with an emotion I couldn't identify. Then he said, "I noticed that Dallas can't seem to stop thinking about you either. He looked over his shoulder at you the whole class period."

Was that a hint of jealousy in his voice? It amazed me that Nick could even feel the slightest bit threatened by Dallas. Nick was the sun, brilliant and bright and blinding. Dallas was a pale sliver of a moon at best.

Something utterly feminine coiled through me, and I found

my body responding with another flare of heat. I turned my face up to Nick, locked eyes with him. "There's only one person who has my attention in our class, and it isn't him."

His eyes narrowed, and he gave a growl before cupping the back of my neck and taking my mouth in a hot kiss. I opened to him willingly, readily, clutching his shoulders as his tongue stroked and dove and danced in my mouth. My pelvis throbbed in response to the sheer sexuality rolling off him.

Nick's hands came to my hips and he gripped them. Then his gloved thumbs brushed under my coat, stroked my bare flesh in seductive swirls that made me dizzy. I wanted those hands everywhere. It felt so damn good, him touching my bare skin.

I tugged him closer, gripped his head and deepened our kiss more. He tasted minty and warm. The chilly wind from Lake Erie sent wafts of his soap scent to my nostrils, and I breathed him in, mingled with the salt-tinged air.

When we finally parted, we were both breathing hard, mouths swollen. I bit my lower lip.

He groaned. "God, when you do that, it makes me want to suck on that lower lip. Your mouth is so sexy."

I swallowed and grinned, flustered yet flattered beyond belief. "Thank you."

He finally released my hips, taking my hand in his. "I thought we could wander around here, then grab some food."

"That sounds perfect." Frankly, I needed something to distract me from this sexual hunger he lit in me. It was going to overwhelm me if I didn't try to keep it under control.

I'd had sex before, of course. I liked it, found it enjoyable and fun. But with Nick . . . I wanted to savor every step of this. Not just rush into it because we were both horny. He felt different to me, special.

We walked along the pier, listening to the wind and the water. There were sounds of laughter off in the distance, but we were the only ones in this area. I felt like we were all alone, in a cocoon.

"What's your favorite season?" I found myself asking him.

"Summer. I love being warm. Yours?"

"Fall. Watching leaves turn in Ohio is one of life's greatest pleasures."

He shrugged. "They don't impact me the way I think they do most people, since I'm red-green color-blind."

"Whoa, really? Has that been hard for you?"

He shook his head. "Not really. My parents discovered it early on, so we made accommodations for it as I grew up. It's never inhibited me from doing what I want."

Even through our gloves, I could feel his thumb caressing my hand. Like it moved of its own volition. Like he couldn't bear to stop touching me. Something in my chest chipped away at that thought. It was hard to concentrate on the conversation when I wanted to sink into his touch, feel it all over. "I knew a guy in school who was fully color-blind," I said. "He saw everything in shades of gray."

He paused, deep in thought. "I can't imagine how that would be. Even if I can't tell reds and greens apart, I can still see all the other colors."

"He used to wear crazy color combinations at school. People teased him until they realized he couldn't differentiate them." I smiled at the memory. "He was my first boyfriend, actually."

We turned back toward East 9th Street, leaving the pier behind. The cityscape glowed with lights. Not a lot of foot traffic around since it was brisk outside.

"I bet you were cute as a kid," he said thoughtfully.

"I had a big mouth," I said, and Nick laughed hard. "It's true. It was always getting me into trouble with other kids. But I was never good at swallowing down how I felt or what I thought."

"It's one of the things I like about you." He sounded so sincere, it made my heart swell. "You're . . . you. You don't pretend to be anything or anyone else. Your sincerity and honesty is refreshing. I think I told you that before."

"You did." I squeezed his hand. "But it doesn't hurt to hear it again."

For some reason, I thought of my mom. The pills I'd seen in her purse. I had a fleeting thought of asking Nick his opinion on the situation. He seemed pretty sensible. But I didn't want to taint his view of my family, make him think something negative about her as his first impression.

Understanding hit me hard then, and everything stilled in my head. I was thinking about a future where I could introduce him to my parents. That both scared and elated me. Nick was crazy smart, clever, fun. I knew they'd like him, if they didn't get hung up on the age difference.

Or the fact that he was my professor. At least, for this semester.

The hurdles were big, but every moment with Nick was proving he was worth the risk. Did the fact that he was here now mean he felt the same about me?

Chapter 12

"How do you feel about Vietnamese food?" he asked me. "There's this great place several blocks up on East 4th. It's a bit of a hike, though—we can take my car if you want."

"Let's keep walking," I said impulsively.

"Aren't you cold?"

I shook my head and squeezed his hand. I didn't hide my feelings when I looked at him. I wanted him to know I was warm because of his being nearby. His answering smile said he got it.

As we neared Prospect, he stiffened a bit. I saw clusters of people around my age, walking and talking. And here it was— the problem we were going to face, assuming he wanted to keep seeing me.

The fear of getting caught.

He released my hand and gave me a sad smile. "Sorry. It's not that I don't want to . . . but I'm afraid if we run into some-one we know . . ."

"I get it. It's okay." Though there was a pang of sadness in my chest. To battle off that feeling, I told myself this was just temporary. Once I graduated, things could be different.

But I knew without a shadow of a doubt that I couldn't wait that long to be with him, no matter what I'd told myself before. And it seemed he couldn't either.

So we would be patient, careful. Quiet. The price we paid to be together.

Nick and I made small talk as we wove down the sidewalk through the large buildings on our way to 4th Street, a popular hangout with restaurants and bars galore. When we turned into the blocked-off district, I smiled at the bright lights strung in front of the buildings.

"Here it is," Nick said, waving toward the right side. Saigon. The warm glow inside looked inviting.

"I've heard of this place but haven't been here," I said excitedly.

"I think you'll like it."

We walked inside. He held the door open for me and ushered me in. I felt his hand ghost along my lower back for just a second, and then the contact was gone before I could savor it. Our booth was near the back, giving us privacy to talk.

I slipped my coat off, slid into my side of the booth and felt a bit of nervous tension loosen in my muscles. I hadn't realized I'd tensed up in concern over someone we knew spotting us.

Yeah, if we met again, we'd have to make sure it was in a low-populated area. Which led me to a random question I'd been wanting to ask.

"You said before that you just bought a house, right? Where is it? Tell me all about it."

Nick unwound his scarf, stripped off his coat and took the seat across from me. With his hair sexily mussed and his eyes bright from the winter cold, he looked unbearably hot. I wanted to reach over and lick his neck, bite his jaw. Feel him shudder and tighten in arousal, the way I did whenever he touched me.

Or even when he looked at me sometimes.

"It's in Parma, so it isn't far from campus. It's a small bungalow, big enough for me and my dog."

"You have a pet? What kind? Boy or girl? What's its name?"

He laughed at my exuberance. "I have a golden retriever. Her name is Gloria, and she's my old doggie—at least ten years old. I got her from the pound while I was in grad school. She was this dopey, slobbering pup who whimpered every time I passed by her, and I knew she was the one for me."

The waitress came by and took our drink and appetizer orders. We decided to split a bottle of white wine. A totally unpretentious label, according to Nick.

"I always wanted a pet," I told him with a sigh when our waitress left. "My dad is allergic to dogs, and my mom was too uptight about having pet hair all over the place."

"Can't you have pets in your apartment?"

"I can have a cat . . . but with a roommate, I didn't want to assume someone else would be okay with it." Although since Casey was moving out soon, maybe I could get a cat. Might keep me from being lonely. Because I wasn't so sure I wanted to have another roommate come in there. No other person was going to fill her space—either in my house or in my heart.

"Your eyes just got sad," he murmured.

Without going into too many details, I mentioned how Casey's struggle to open up to others and let people into her life had moved me, changed me. How she'd fallen in love and they were serious.

"I'm going to miss her." I was surprised to find my throat closing up. Thankfully, the waitress brought our wine then, so I was able to nip from the glass. He was right—it wasn't that bad. Not as sweet as the wine my mom usually bought. "The place won't be the same when she leaves."

"She's lucky to have you," he said. Sipped his wine and tilted his head to look at me.

I shook my head. "I think we're lucky to have each other. I just hope her moving out doesn't change things between us."

"I get that. I mean, it's likely going to, to some degree—your relationship will evolve since you won't be living together. But it doesn't sound like it'll fade away. She obviously cares about you, and I doubt she'll let you go. If she has that hard of a time opening up, I imagine she makes friends for life when she does."

His words soothed my heart. He was right; it was going to change. But that didn't have to be bad.

"Thank you," I said. "I hadn't realized that was bothering me so much until I just now started talking about it with you. You're very easy to talk to."

He made a face. "I don't think most people would say that about me."

"Why not?" The idea baffled me.

"Because I'm nerdy and talk too much about my job."

"So am I. Math is amazing—why wouldn't you want to gush about it?"

He narrowed his eyes. "Also, I'm the youngest tenure-track professor on campus, so most of the professors think I'm a student."

"I'm young too. And obviously the other profs are idiots," I stated.

He grinned. "I need to keep you around."

Yes, you do. The thought flew right into my mind. Our appetizers came to the table, and I nibbled on a crispy spring roll dipped in sweet sauce.

With a moan, I licked a bit of sauce that had dribbled onto my finger. "God, that is amazing."

His eyes darkened and he fixed his gaze on my finger, sliding out of my mouth. I could practically feel the heat radiating off him. "You're driving me crazy, Megan," he whispered.

That got my pulse flying. My lips parted of their own volition, and my chest rose and fell with my shallow breaths. I took a big swig of wine in an effort to assuage my sudden thirst.

His foot bumped mine under the table. I stretched my leg out and rubbed my calf against his. The vein at his temple throbbed, and he kept those hot eyes locked on me.

"I want you," I told him in a breathy voice just over a whisper. I'd told myself I wasn't going to rush into this with him. That I was going to go slow and steady.

But my body was screaming for him to touch me, lick me. Right. Now.

"You're killing me," he said with a groan. The heat from his leg burned into me. I nudged my other leg over to pin his between mine, and he sucked in a deep breath. "I didn't ask you to meet me for this, you know. I just wanted to be around you."

That admission made my body flame with even more desire, as crazy as it sounded. To know he didn't just see me as a booty call . . . to know he was just as affected by this thing between us as I was.

"Let's get out of here," I said on impulse. "Go somewhere quiet." Where we could be alone to explore this thing between us.

He stilled. I could see the anguish on his face, his desire warring with indecision about this being a bad idea. But I didn't want him to think. I wanted him to *feel*.

I reached across the table and stroked his fingers. A long, deliberate motion so I could feel the knuckle, the bone, the skin. He just sat there, his only movement the slight rise and fall of his chest.

Then he flipped his hand over and his middle finger caressed my palm. I shivered at the delicate sensation as my nerves danced to life.

"Megan," he began in a rough voice.

When I lifted his hand and sucked that middle finger into my wet mouth, his whole face, his whole body, tensed. I swiped my tongue along the knuckle and saw his pupils flare. My core tightened in response.

"Okay, we're going. Now," he ground out. He pulled his hand back from between my lips, dug into his wallet and fished out some money. Tossed it on the table, then grabbed my hand and tugged me out of the booth. His grip was tight; I could sense need shimmering off him.

Without saying a word, I threw on my coat, grabbed my purse and followed him out of the restaurant. The cold couldn't penetrate my body, which was pulsing like an exposed nerve. He kept a firm hold on my hand, obviously not thinking about who could see us.

I didn't fight it. I was almost dizzy with relief and excitement.

The walk back to the parking lot was at a fast clip. Neither of us broke the silence until we reached the rows of parked cars, because what we were feeling went beyond words.

"My car is over here," I finally said, and pointed my free hand down the row. My voice was hoarse. "Where are you?"

He spun me toward him, took my mouth in a possessive kiss that ended way too fast, then pulled away. "I'm down the row near the end. Where is your phone?"

I pulled it out of my pocket and handed it to him.

Nick loaded up my maps app and typed in his address. "In case you lose me."

"I'm not gonna lose you," I said breathlessly. As if.

His mouth quirked. "I think we already established who the speed demon was here, didn't we?"

I raised a brow. "And yet, I have a feeling you'll be driving slower to make sure I can keep up with you."

With that, his eyes grew molten. He stroked a finger down

my cheek. "Let's see who can keep up with whom tonight, shall we?"

I shivered; it had nothing to do with the cold. My nod was my answer.

He walked me to my car and saw me safely in, then strolled to his. I warmed up my engine, waiting for him to show. Finally he was just in front of me, and I pulled out and followed him out of downtown Cleveland.

The ride to his place in Parma was torture. My whole body pulsed with this deep need for him. Everything I'd been fantasizing about for a week was about to come true. Nick would be on top of me, naked, and inside me. . . .

I gripped the steering wheel and steadied my hands. A sudden nervous fear clenched my stomach. God, what if he was talking himself out of it right now? Maybe I should have ridden with him. If I showed up there and he turned me away, I really was going to die. I couldn't face rejection from him, not now.

Not when I was feeling so much, so fast, so strong.

After twenty minutes and two highways, we headed toward his exit. My heart thudded when we turned right onto a quiet side street. A few blocks up, he turned into a driveway on his left. I followed him and turned my car off.

He hopped out of his car, so I did the same. My stomach was a painful ball in my torso as I waited to see what he would say or do. In the darkness, I couldn't see his face.

He got a foot or so away from me, peering down, his expression inscrutable.

I kept my chin high in the air. If he turned me away, I wasn't going to show him how much it would hurt—both my pride and my feelings. I'd just get in my car, drive home . . .

"Come in with me, Megan," he said, and that hard knot dissolved.

His fingers threaded through mine, and I followed him up his porch stairs into his brick bungalow.

Chapter 13

The entryway was dark, but the air inside was warm. He'd obviously left the furnace on. I heard feet trampling across the wood floors, and then Nick's low voice as he greeted his dog. "Go lie down," he urged her. The dog sniffed my legs, then ambled away.

I peeled off my coat as he flipped the light switch on, flooding the hallway with a bright light. He took my coat and hung it in the small front closet, then took off his.

I stood there, my body vibrating with everything I was feeling. My fingers clutched my bag.

Nick spun around and pressed me to the hallway wall. My breath rushed out of my lungs, and then his mouth was on mine again, his tongue exploring. I dropped my purse and threaded my fingers through his silky hair. Kept him as close to me as humanly possible. Our breaths mingled, and he sighed.

His hands snaked around my waist to pull my body flush to his. I could almost smell the heat of my arousal filling the hallway. His stubble grazed my skin as he moved his mouth to my jaw, to the sensitive flesh under my ear.

Then he bit my earlobe, and I shuddered. My nipples hardened. "Yes," I panted. "That feels so good." His mouth was wet and searing.

"I need to taste more of you," he breathed into my ear. His hands worked their way to my bare torso, fingers digging into my sides. I could feel how hard he was.

For me.

I nodded, and he pulled back. His eyes were heavy lidded, almost angry-looking with the intensity pouring off him.

"My room is upstairs." He paused. Maybe to give me a chance to back out.

"Show me." I sounded so wanton. I stepped toward him and rubbed my breasts on his chest; they felt full and heavy and reveled in the sensation of touching him. I swiped my tongue along his Adam's apple, savoring the slight salty tinge of his skin.

The little shiver he gave almost did me in. He turned and walked up the dark stairs. At the top of the stairway, moonlight spilled through horizontal blinds, providing enough light for me to make my way in.

His bedroom was the whole top floor, a large loft space with a massive bed right in the middle. I shuffled right behind him and nearly ran into his back when he suddenly stopped.

He turned. I couldn't see his face well, but all my other senses became more sensitive. The soft rasps of his breaths filled my ears. The scent of his skin filled my nostrils. I stroked my fingertips along the tiny prickles on his jaw, his chin.

He sucked in a breath, then ducked his head just slightly and licked my finger. My sex thrummed in response.

Without fumbling, his hands reached up and drew my sweater over my head. I stood there in my bra, breasts heaving with the effort it took me to drag air into my rapidly shrinking lungs. My whole body was torquing tighter, like a twisting rope. I ached for him to help me release the building need swelling in me.

"You're beautiful." The words were simple but said with so much reverence, I felt my skin flush. His fingers brushed the mounds of flesh above my bra, and goose bumps broke out in response.

I wanted him to go faster. But I shoved my impatience aside. This wasn't some drunken fumbling at a party. It wasn't a casual hookup. This was going to be intense, and I wanted to savor each second. Imprint it into my memory.

Nick wasn't a horny, buzzed college guy fumbling his way through our foreplay. Self-control oozed from him. I knew he'd have the same masterful attitude in bed that he commanded in the classroom.

The difference between sleeping with a guy and making love with a man, I supposed.

I reached a hand out and touched his bare stomach under his sweater. Felt the taut lines stiffen and jump as my fingers explored each ridge. He ripped his sweater off, and I ran both hands up his pecs, swept dancing fingers over his shoulders, down his lean, muscled upper arms.

He didn't move. Just let me touch him. His skin was scorching. I swallowed, stepped closer and pressed my open mouth to the top of his right pec. It flexed under my lips, and he sighed. His hands came up to cup my waist, then slid down to tease at the flesh just under the waistband of my jeans.

And then they were unfastened, unzipped. Being shoved down my hips. I kicked them aside, now just in a bra and panties.

A nervousness I hadn't ever felt before came over me, and I was suddenly shy. The feeling of being utterly exposed to this man—body and heart and soul—had me hunching over.

He gripped my shoulders and straightened me up. "No. I want to see you."

"You already do," I whispered. With those eyes boring into mine, visually caressing my skin in sweeping bursts, it felt as if he saw right through me. Right into the core of who I was. Reached depths I'd never let anyone find before.

His hand stroked my lower belly, and I clenched with need. My breaths came faster. Harder. His fingers teased the top of my panties.

"You should take your pants off too," I said, a little embarrassed that my voice trembled a touch.

And he did, and then we were both there in our underwear, his erection bobbing between us, the thick line discernible through his boxer briefs, even in the dark. He took my hand and led me to the bed, then laid me down. His body covered mine, head to toe, our skin sizzling where we touched.

"I'm trying to go slow," he said, "because I want to make this last. Make it feel good for you. But I feel like I'm going to explode."

His words ignited that spark in my belly, driving away the discomfort. I wasn't the only one feeling a bit off-kilter; his tone revealed a hint of vulnerability that came through loud and clear.

Even more surprising was that he wasn't trying to hide it from me. He was okay with me knowing he wasn't totally cool, totally in control, despite how things initially appeared.

Our footing was more equal than I'd realized.

I wound my arms around him and touched the muscles and planes of his back. He flexed at the contact. His mouth dropped down to my neck, and the soft kisses he pressed there were so gentle, it made my heart clench.

"You taste amazing." He sucked the flesh into his mouth, then bit down just a touch. I shuddered. His hand moved between our bodies to stroke my most tender place through my panties, and I found myself opening for him, wrapping my thighs around his.

"Yes, right there," I said. Heat curled in me, a throb that grew more insistent.

His hand slid under the fabric and touched my bare flesh,

and he groaned. "Oh God, you're so wet." His expert fingers moved faster, and I felt the orgasm coming. I'd never had a guy get me this hot this fast. My whole body was on fire, lit from the inside out. "You're close, aren't you." His mouth was at my ear, and I was writhing against his open palm, his sweeping digits. Sexy assurance poured from his voice now, his earlier vulnerability gone. This man was in control of me; I craved it. "Come for me, Megan."

"Yes," I managed to say. My eyelids fluttered closed and I dropped my head back on the pillow. Gripped his arms and pressed my shaking thighs farther apart.

He hovered just over me, stroking and kneading the flesh, and then I came in a bolt of lightning. A cry flew from my lips and my whole body stiffened.

When I sank down in a heady glow into his bed several long, delicious seconds later, I belatedly realized I'd cried out his name. Another thing I'd never done—been so far gone in the moment that I hadn't realized what I'd said until afterward.

"I'm going to take you now," he promised me with a glint in his eye. He moved away from me to rise from the bed.

He whipped off his boxer briefs, and I heard his bedside drawer open, then the telltale crinkling of a condom wrapper being opened. Then he was back on me, stripping my bra and panties off and tossing them to the side. His body was almost feverishly hot.

I gasped in pleasure when he thrust in me, then paused. His arms shook as he hovered over my body.

"Oh God, so tight," he groaned. His forehead rested on mine. Our breaths fell together. I savored the feeling of being this connected to him. The threads connecting us wound tighter, stronger.

Then he moved out, in, a slow pace that once again spoke to his control. But I ground against him, felt sweat building between our bodies, making us slide along each other. I didn't want him in control. I wanted him frantic, as crazy as I felt right now. My heart raced wildly beneath my rib cage.

His breath staggered, and I saw the control slip just a touch.

"Please," I begged. I needed him to let go. My heels dug into the backs of his thighs. "Nick, *please.*"

That snapped something in him. He took my hands and pinned them over my head. With the moonlight dappling our naked bodies, his eyes looked wild. He sucked my nipple, and I writhed from the exquisite sensation.

"Don't hold back," I said as I pushed myself toward his mouth. "I want this."

He popped his lips off my breast and took my mouth in a rough kiss. No longer was he steady and even in his thrusts—they were deep, hard, almost jarring. He filled me thoroughly, our limbs entangled. He dropped a hand down to grip my hip and tilt my pelvis up.

We slammed together, and then he arched back and yelled, his body one long, hard line. When his orgasm faded, he relaxed and rested his length against me. Removed the hand pinning my hands above and stroked the side of my cheek, a crooked grin on his face. I found my own mouth curving up in response.

I let my legs go lax from their clenched position around his thighs and cupped his body into mine. Wrapped my arms around his torso. He was still inside me.

His heartbeat knocked against my breast; I could feel its staccato rhythm, a testament to his emotions and the height of his arousal. My throat tightened, and for some reason I felt my eyes get hot. I blinked away the sensation.

Then he pressed a sweet kiss to my chin and withdrew. My body was sweat slicked, so the absence of him against me brought an instant chill. He whipped the covers down and settled me in the bed. Disposed of the condom and slid beside me.

As weird as it sounded, this actually felt even more intimate than the sex we'd just had. Lying in his bed, his arm draped over me, the warmth of his body pressed against my side. Sharing the same pillow, our breaths puffing and mingling together.

His fingers made lazy circles on my stomach, and I relaxed into the soothing touch.

"That felt really good," I told him.

"It did for me too." He paused; I could almost hear his unspoken thoughts in the silence of the room. Somewhere downstairs there was a clock ticking. The furnace kicked on again, and warm air rushed through the vents.

"I hope there's not a 'but' in there," I said in what I hoped was a teasing tone.

Nick cleared his throat. "We should talk about this, Megan. About what it means." He sounded so serious.

My heart sank. I must have clenched up my muscles without realizing it, because I felt his hand pressing against my belly, his palm keeping me in place. I forced myself to relax. It was hard keeping my brain from whirring all over the place.

I didn't want to hear him tell me this was just a regular hookup, a one-time impulsive thing. Because it sure as hell hadn't felt like one to me. All I knew was that when he'd been inside me, the connection had been intense. Our eyes on each other. Our bodies moving together. His fingers woven in mine.

It hadn't been just sex. I'd felt my heart stirring, the rush that had come from us being so exposed to each other, our needs out there in the open. The kind of emotions that came with making love.

"What are you thinking about?" he asked.

How forthright should I be? Was it too fast if I told him what I was thinking? Too honest?

"Just wondering what you're going to say," I finally told him.

He sighed, and his warm breath stirred against my cheek. "Here's what I know. This could damage my career at the college. And it could impact your future there as well. We're playing with fire."

I closed my eyes and nodded as the sick feeling in my chest grew stronger. Now I didn't want to hear the rest of what he said. I sat up and swung my legs over the side of the bed. "Yup, I get it. You're right, of course." Pride made my words clipped.

His iron grip on my forearm stopped me from rising. He sat up too; I heard the rustling right behind me. Then his legs were on either side of me and his chest pressed against my back. His hands wrapped around my stomach, and he rained soft kisses on my shoulders, my upper back.

"Right now, with you here in my arms, I can't think of anywhere else I'd want to be. I'd rather burn up in the flames than be cold without you, Megan. But I need to know if I'm reading into this . . . thing with us or if you could possibly ever feel that way about me too." I felt him swallow, heard the faint shake in his voice. "I don't want to push you or make assumptions. . . ." He trailed off, his whole body a stiff cage around me.

Without knowing any of my inner anxiety, Nick was putting himself on the line. Waiting for my response to his questions.

I sucked in a wobbly breath and let his words settle in. Bit my lower lip and felt the hot rush of relief sweep through me. He wanted me—not just for his bed, but for more.

A relationship. It was right there in his voice, in the breath he held trapped in his lungs.

"I want this too, Nick," I said quietly.

The tension leaked from his limbs, and he rested his forehead against my upper back. "We have to be careful."

I nodded. "Absolutely."

"We can't tell anyone else what's going on, at least not until you graduate." His voice grew stronger. "I don't like lying, but it's the safest option right now. The semester will be over before we know it."

"I don't want you to get in trouble," I said as I spun around and faced him, my knees on the mattress right between his thighs.

Nick didn't look at my naked body, right there in front of him, and for some reason that moved me more than I could say. Instead, he looked at me with such emotion on his face that I couldn't breathe.

He cupped my cheeks and drew my mouth to his. Gave me a soft kiss that curled my toes. "Are you hungry? Someone distracted me before we got a chance to eat." I felt the smile against my lips.

I nodded. My chest and head felt lighter than they had in ages. Everything was clear, like the blinders had fallen from my eyes. This man was unlocking feelings in me I'd never had before. It was scary, overwhelming, thrilling.

Yes, there was a danger to his job, of course. There was also a danger to my heart, because I could see myself falling headfirst into love with him so very easily.

And the most dangerous part of all was I wanted it, even knowing all these risks. I wanted to scorch in the flames right beside him.

Nick rose from the bed and dug through his dresser drawer, tossing a soft T-shirt my way. He threw on a pair of sweatpants that hung low on his hips, and it was hard to not stare at his exposed torso. God, it was ridiculous how attractive the man was.

"Here, so you don't get that delectable body of yours cold." He winked. "Now let's get you downstairs and fed."

I followed him downstairs with a face-splitting smile and a bounce in my step.

Chapter 14

The next couple of weeks went by in a mad rush. When I wasn't in class or studying, I was meeting Nick everywhere I could—off campus, of course. We had impromptu coffee dates, saw an indie band concert, even had dinner at his house a few times. I never stayed the night or hinted like I wanted to, not wishing to push things, but my evenings out with him got longer and longer.

It was so hard to leave him each night when all I wanted to do was curl up in the warmth of his arms.

True to his word, Nick kept things above board when we were on campus. He didn't treat me any differently in class, and I found myself growing accustomed to this . . . thing going on between us. Though we did leave each other small coded notes on our papers back and forth. They were the highlight of my day.

Late last week, Nick and I were talking outside the math building when I saw my dad walking by with a contractor, both of them in bright yellow hard hats, Styrofoam cups clenched in hands. My heart stopped beating in my chest, and I stuttered and struggled to keep my cool. He and I weren't technically doing anything wrong right then; there was nothing unusual about students and professors having conversations on campus. But I was certain Dad would read the truth on my face. He knew me better than almost anyone and would be able to see the emotions in my eyes clear as day.

Thankfully, he'd kept walking past, not seeing me. Crisis averted, barely. But the uneasiness had lingered with me for hours afterward. Since then, I was careful about my communication with Nick outside the math building.

I'd briefly mentioned to Nick that my parents were working on a project here, but I wasn't quite ready for them to meet. Not yet, not when we were still so new . . . and had to keep things on the down low.

This was quite possibly the biggest secret I'd ever kept. And while I savored my stolen moments with Nick, I wanted more. I grew impatient for the semester to end so I didn't have to sneak around any longer. Every day I was with him, it was more and more difficult to not vocalize that. But I'd agreed to these terms and I couldn't complain about it now.

I'd known from the start what I was getting into.

After finishing psychology of stress one afternoon, I got to the apartment complex and whipped my door open. "Honey, I'm home!" I'd seen Casey's car in the parking lot, so I figured she was here.

"Hey! How was your day?" Casey waved at me from the table. Seated beside her was a short, pretty brunette; they had textbooks spilled all over the table's surface. The girl offered me a polite smile and head nod.

"It was fabulous," I declared as I tossed my backpack on the couch. I went into the kitchen and grabbed a Diet Coke from the fridge. Took a deep swig and then sighed in pleasure.

When I turned around, Casey was eyeing me with a brow raised. "Hm. Really? Even psychology? You seem awfully chipper for coming out of a class you loathe."

I shrugged. "It's getting better." Okay, I was actually riding high from having gotten a sweet text from Nick earlier, but she didn't need to know that.

That keen, knowing look was still in Casey's eyes, but she said, "Megan, this is Amanda. We had philosophy together last semester and bonded over our misery. Amanda, this is my roommate, Megan."

I stuck out a hand and shook hers. "Nice to meet you."

"You too. We're studying for midterms—you're welcome to join us." She waved a hand at the chair across from them.

I grimaced. "I can't believe it's that time of the semester." The year had been flying by. It was already early March, and midterm week was next week.

"Graduation is just around the corner for you two, isn't it?" Amanda asked. "I thought Casey mentioned you're done at the end of this semester too . . . is that right?"

I took the chair across from them and set my soda on the table. "It is. I can hardly wrap my head around it."

In between everything else, I'd been getting my graduation details sorted out. Cap and gown orders. Announcements. Exchanging texts with my dad about the cookout he wanted to host in celebration.

Would Nick be able to come? I wanted to invite him. But some of my friends on campus would be there. Maybe I could invite a few of my other profs too, just as a courtesy. So it wouldn't look like I singled him out. Then I could suss out what my parents thought of him before telling them we were dating.

"That's awesome. You must be thrilled." She grinned, and her eyes sparkled with warmth. I could see why Casey liked hanging out with her. She was bubbly but not obnoxiously so. "Okay, I'd better get back to this. I can't bomb this class or my folks will kill me." Amanda tucked a strand of hair behind her ear and ducked her head to study more.

Casey's eyes met mine. She reached across the table and

squeezed my hand. In that moment, I wanted to confess to her. Tell her all the stuff that had been weighing on my mind, in my heart.

I was falling hard for my professor, and there was no way to stop it. Somehow, with his wide smiles and big brain and skilled hands, he'd wormed his way into my life.

Thankfully Amanda was there, or else I'd have probably spilled the beans.

I stood and gave them both a shaky smile. "I think I might take a nap," I said as I turned. I didn't want Casey to read the secret on my face. With her unassuming and gentle ways, she'd get me talking before I realized what was happening.

I retreated into my room and flopped on my bed. Stared at the ceiling, eyed the clusters of photos on my walls. Lots of party pics, me posing with other girls, with countless goofy guys. The parties were fun to go to, sure.

But those experiences didn't stick with me the way the last couple of weeks with Nick had. I'd turned down a few party invites from Nadia and a couple of other casual friends to spend more time with him. Patrick had texted me once or twice, messages filled with cringe-worthy errors, but had apparently gotten the gist of my lack of interest and left me alone. I certainly wasn't missing out; I'd deleted him from my phone.

Nick and I had spent hours just talking about everything. Discussing our thoughts on politics and which way we leaned, and why. What we thought about the turmoil in the Middle East. The rampant commercialism of holidays.

But not all of our conversations were heavy. The other day, we spent a full fifteen minutes arguing mayonnaise versus Miracle Whip. There was also some debate over the best contemporary film directors. Not to mention our epic battle about the best old-school female hip-hop artists.

He stimulated me. I found myself reading more news, listening to NPR, trying to find snippets of topics we could discuss.

My phone buzzed. I dug it out.

Where are you right now? What are you doing?

A text from Nick. That familiar buzz started low in my belly and spread outward.

I'm in my apartment, lying in bed ;-) I texted back.

Groan you're killing me. I'm in my office, working on next week's midterm exams.

Any chance I can get an advance copy of ours? I laughed to myself, then added, *That was totally a joke, btw. Don't kick me. I'll earn my good grades in your class the honest way.* I took a picture of myself lying in bed, then sent it to him.

A few minutes later, I got a picture back of him. Nick was styled to perfection, his jaw cleanly shaved, the smooth front of his dress shirt pressed. I kinda wanted to muss him up, see him the way only *I* got to—slightly scruffy with a bit of bedhead. Eyes hooded and heated, locked on mine.

Send me something a little more risqué, I teased him. What would he do in response? We hadn't progressed to sending naughty texts or anything, so I was kinda pushing the envelope here.

A moment later, my phone buzzed. He'd sent me the exact same shot, except this time the button at his collar was undone.

I laughed. Leave it to him to make a joke. Still, it was a good-looking picture. I saved both of them in my photo folder.

Good thing you stopped at one button, Mr. Edgy. Two, and I might have fainted, I typed back.

I'll save the more risqué stuff for when we're alone. ;-) See you tonight? I'm making General Tso's . . . you know you can't resist the power of my cooking.

One of my favorite dishes. He remembered. *<3 I'll be there.*

I rested my phone on my belly with a happy sigh. Nick was invading every piece of my life. Even when we weren't together, I was thinking about him. Just another two months, I told myself. Two months from now, we wouldn't have to be secret.

It was all I could do to wait.

"So, I want you to do a little self-exploration for your homework this weekend," Professor Morrow, my psychology of stress prof, said. He leaned against the front wall and crossed his skinny arms in front of him.

I heard a few smothered groans around me and bit my lower lip, suppressing an eye roll. We all knew what was coming. Morrow loved to assign us introspective reflections. He said it was his way of making the material "practical" for us. I understood it to a degree, but it was kinda awkward, knowing this man was probably drinking a glass of wine and reading the divulgences of my personal life.

I knew from listening to Nick gripe about a few papers he'd gotten in that they *did* talk about us—to their friends, significant others, even fellow professors. Dating a teacher had made me more aware than ever of that.

Morrow shoved away from the wall and paced in front of the room. "We've been discussing stressors and how they impact us both physically and psychologically. For this assignment, I want you to examine your own life. Look at the various types of stressors you're encountering right now—don't forget good stress, by the way—and write which of the categories they fall under. Then pick a coping mechanism and apply it to one of your stressors over the next few days. Tell me how it impacted your level of stress, if it even did." He scanned the room with the narrowed eyes of a well-seasoned educator. "Make this thoughtful and resonant, folks. Dig deep. But I don't want to hear about anything illegal or immoral. I'd rather not have to call the police on my students. It's been a good semester so far, so let's keep that up."

There were a few chuckles.

"And don't just give me a few sentences of halfhearted crap either," he continued in his usual droll voice. While I wasn't a fan of this class, at least our prof was entertaining in a weird, dry way. "I can tell when you guys get lazy. Okay, have a good weekend, and I'll see you next week for your midterm. Go forth and de-stress."

I got my stuff together and left the room, our homework assignment on my mind. Which stressor should I focus on? Midterms next week? Graduation in two months? I mean, it wasn't like I could write that I was seeing Nick. I could only imagine what the response to *that* would be.

Maybe I could drop by the work trailer and see my folks. Since I'd been so busy lately, I hadn't seen much of them—plus I was in full-blown avoidance mode due to dating Nick and not wanting them to know—but Dad's occasional texts told me the project was progressing well.

The sun shone brightly outside when I stepped out of the building, and the weather was pretty warm for this time of year, pushing fifty degrees. I heard water dripping from the trees as ice and snow melted. The ground was slushy and a gross brown, so I stuck to the sidewalks.

The trailer door was closed. I knocked—no answer.

Mom's car was right there, parked in front of the trailer. Maybe she was walking around the site. I knew I wasn't allowed to visit the site without a hard hat though. It was a hard and fast rule.

If the trailer was unlocked, I could snag one from there. She always kept a couple extra tucked away for visitors or anyone she spotted working without one. And it would be cool to see the progress being made anyway.

I tried the doorknob. It wasn't locked, so I opened the door to a darkened trailer. When I flicked the switch, I saw the feet of a form lying on the end of the couch in the back. Was someone taking a nap? Hm, looked like my mom's shoes on the floor.

I tiptoed over with a grin. Touched her shoulder. "Ooh, someone's gonna be in trouble for napping on the job."

I didn't get a response.

I shook her shoulder harder. "Mom? Hey, wake up."

There was a groggy groan, and then she tilted her head to look at me. Her eyes were glassy, and she gave a dopey smile. She looked a bit feverish. "Megan. Hey."

"Are you sick? Do I need to take you to a doctor?"

She sat up and her head flopped a bit as she shifted to a sitting position on the couch. With a sloppy wave of her hand she said, "No, no, I'm fine." Her words were slurred as if she'd been drinking, but she didn't smell like booze.

I frowned. "Mom, did you take something? Is your back hurting?"

Her eyes closed and she leaned back to rest on the couch. Her head draped over the top. "I'm feelin' good right now," she said, then gave a slight giggle. "No pain, baby. No pain."

Anger, quick and sharp, rushed through me, threaded with fear. I stepped away from her and looked under the desk for her purse. A quick peek inside confirmed that bottle of pills I'd seen before was still there. Only it was empty now.

I held it up in front of her. "How much did you take?"

She opened her eyes, squinted. Dropped her head back. "I dunno. I'm fine. Go away."

"I'm not going away. You can't be like this at work, Mom. This is dangerous. What if something were to happen? What if you got caught?" Panic made my chest tighten.

I couldn't leave her here like this.

I dropped the empty pill bottle in her purse and fished out her car keys. "We're leaving." Should I take her to the ER? She didn't seem like she was overdosing. Just flying high as a kite.

Should I call Dad? Part of me wanted to, but the other part

thought I should wait for her to sober up and ask her what the hell was going on. First things first—I needed to get her home.

After slipping her feet into her shoes, I propped the trailer door open, then darted over and looped her arms over my neck. "Mom, you gotta help me," I grunted as I lifted her off the couch.

She staggered against me, and I had a flash of carrying my drunk friends out of parties. This was so jacked up. I shoved that thought aside and got her down the trailer stairs as carefully as possible, then loaded into the passenger seat of her car.

The drive to my parents' house was quiet. Mom had conked back out fast, her head lolling around in her seat. At every stoplight I checked her to make sure she wasn't showing signs of getting worse. So far it seemed okay and she was stable.

But there was no way I could just drop her off and leave her like this.

That tightness in my chest remained while I hauled her inside. Took her to her bedroom and tugged off her shoes. Marched to the living room and confiscated the bottles out of her purse. Then I spent the next half hour combing the whole house to find another half-dozen bottles stowed in various spots.

I was so sick I almost threw up. Mom was hiding pills? And I didn't recognize any of the people's names on the labels. Where had she gotten them from? Had she stolen them?

I propped all the bottles on the coffee table, made a fresh pot of coffee and grabbed my phone. I wasn't going to wait to talk to Mom before discussing this with my dad. He needed to know, now.

I dialed his number. On the second ring, he picked up.

"Hey, Megan," he said in his usual jovial voice.

"Dad," I began, swallowing. I sucked in a breath. "Can you come home? We need to talk right now."

"What's wrong?" In an instant, his voice grew sharp. "Are you okay?"

"I'm fine." Hot tears pressed at the backs of my eyes. I blinked. "It's Mom. I found some pills in her purse. . . ." I paused. "I think she has a problem. She was passed out on the couch in the trailer, and I brought her home. I don't know what to do." A sob ripped out of me.

In a clipped tone, he said, "I'm coming home right now. Stay there and keep an eye on her, please. I'll be there as soon as I can."

We hung up. I put my phone on the table beside the bottles of pills. My head throbbed at the temples.

Dad had sounded angry. But he hadn't sounded surprised. Like he'd known about this. Like I was the last person to really figure it out. And that realization ate away at my stomach like acid.

Chapter 15

"Anything in particular you wanna watch?" Nick asked me. "I have some movies on demand too."

I settled closer into the crook of his arm and rested my head on his shoulder, watching as he clicked the remote and loaded it to a movie channel. His dog, Gloria, was settled at the bottom of the couch, totally conked out. "I don't care. I just want to relax." I'd done a long shift at the sandwich shop today, and the Sunday postchurch crowd had been a bit chaotic. But since I needed the extra work hours, I took it without complaining.

My feet throbbed. I kicked one leg to cross my other thigh and massaged the tender sole through my sock. Flexed my toes and sighed as I stretched the aching muscles.

My phone buzzed. I took it out and saw a message from Nadia. *Girl, you still alive?? Haven't seen your face in ages. Where you been?*

I texted back, *Just busy, sorry! We should catch up soon.* For a moment I felt a twinge of guilt for not hanging out with her and my other friends as much. But why would I go to some generic party when I could be alone with Nick? No comparison.

Nick settled on a recent thriller release, then put the remote down and grabbed my foot with his free hand. His thumb pressed right into the arch, and I released a long groan.

"That's perfect, thank you," I managed to say as I stuffed my phone in my pocket.

"I worked at a restaurant for a while through college. I remember those days. Long hours on your feet."

"What did you do there?"

"Waited tables, mostly." He moved up to the pads of my feet and stretched, pressed. His other hand caressed the curve of my shoulder.

"Ever had any terrible jobs?" My voice sounded breathless due to the feel of his hands on me. "When I was in high school, I babysat these demon kids down the road. They did everything they could to make those hours miserable. At least their parents paid me well."

"Hm." He paused, then shifted me so I was stretched out on the couch with my back against the arm and both feet in his lap. I shot him a grateful smile. "Not that I can think of. I was too busy with school to have a job, for the most part."

"Oh, I forgot. You skipped ahead of all the other kids your age. How did that feel? Was it odd, being so young in comparison to everyone else?"

He scrunched his face up in thought. A shot rang out on the all-but-forgotten TV, and a feminine voice screamed. "I got used to it. Was teased a lot of course, especially since I didn't hit puberty until around when I graduated from high school. I was what they call a 'late bloomer.' "

I eyed the manly scruff on his face, the bold slashes of his cheekbones. "Really? That doesn't seem likely."

He crooked a grin, gave a casual shrug. "It was a while ago, so it doesn't bug me anymore. But I used to will it to happen sometimes. For a long time, I just wanted to fit in instead of standing out so much. It was obvious I wasn't one of them, and I didn't have a lot of friends growing up. Not a lot of people in my class wanted to hang with someone so much younger than them. And the people my own age were too busy hanging with others in their classes."

My heart lurched in sympathy. I couldn't imagine feeling like such an outsider. I'd always had lots of friends. And my parents had encouraged me to develop my social life as much as my academic one.

At the thought of the two of them, my good mood slipped away. I hadn't talked to either of them in the last few days. I was afraid to, in a way. Which was so cowardly of me, but I just couldn't. Nor had I told anyone—including Nick—about my mom, and this was all eating away at my chest.

It was one thing when a friend was having such dark personal issues, like Casey and her tragic past with her family. I was there to counsel in those situations, or just to commiserate with a hug and ice cream. Another situation altogether when it was my own mom.

Secretly, I was embarrassed about it, and then ashamed that I felt so embarrassed, and all these feelings were making me pull away from my parents. Our family had always been a "normal" one. We never had issues like this. To say I was left fumbling for the right way to deal with it was an understatement.

"Hey, you okay?" Nick's brow furrowed. "Your mood changed. What's wrong?"

I forced a smile. Shoulda known he could read my face. I never was much good at hiding what I felt. "Nothing. I'm fine. It's fine." Or I was trying to be anyway. When Dad had gotten home that afternoon, he'd told me he'd deal with the issue. I was trying to put my trust in that.

"So there *is* something wrong," Nick countered.

"I'd rather not get into it right now. I'd like to enjoy the evening before I go into midterms next week." Which were also freaking me out, because for once in my academic life, I wasn't as prepared as I should be.

His face flicked a brief flare of emotion before it smoothed out again. My pulse kicked up in response. I knew *exactly* what he'd been thinking—spending this much time with him the last few weeks had helped me learn to read the nuances in his emotions as well.

My comment on midterms had reminded him that I was a student. *His* student, to be exact, going to take *his* midterm next week. That emotion had been from his conscience battering at him over our dating.

I angled my head and studied him. "Is this going to keep happening, Nick?"

He blinked. "Is what?"

With a sigh, I removed my feet from his lap and tucked them under me. "Every time I bring up school things, are you going to have that . . . surge of regret or fear or whatever it is that makes you freak out?"

His face darkened. "That's not fair. This isn't easy for me."

"Like it's easy for me? I'm lying about us to everyone I know. I'm holding on to this big secret, and you're faking like you're 'fine' when you're obviously not."

"That's not the only secret you're keeping," he shot back, an obvious reference to my unnamed stress regarding my mom.

I clenched my jaw. Struggled to keep my breathing even. I didn't want to fight with him. "I'm sorry. I'm just not ready to talk about it right now. I'm still trying to sort it all out." Frustration poured into my voice, mingled with hurt and fear. "I'm feeling a bit overwhelmed and stressed at the moment, and things aren't quite going the right way."

His eyes softened and he leaned toward me. Wrapped me in his arms. "I'm sorry. I'm pushing you, and it isn't fair. I don't like to be pushed either. I just . . . I hate to see you so obviously upset and not be able to do anything about it."

I rested my head on his shoulder and tried to shake off my unease. His hands made lazy, soothing strokes on my back. "Can we let all of this go tonight? I wasn't trying to start a fight or anything with you."

I felt his nod. "Should I restart the movie?"

"Nah. I'm sure we can figure out what's going on," I said with a forced laugh. I pulled away from him and turned to sit beside him. Cupped his hand and let my fingers rub along the lengths of his.

The conversation fell away. Nick got caught up in the movie, but I couldn't focus. My stomach was a knot of tension, and I kept thinking about our brief argument. I had to be honest with myself. There was dissatisfaction brewing in me, growing larger and larger every day . . . not with the relationship, but with all the secrecy around it.

And it was definitely beginning to impact me.

I got to watch Casey and Daniel together, so happy, so in love. Not caring who saw. And I had to watch my mom change to a person I didn't even recognize, one who stole pills from people and got high in the middle of the day while at work. In the meantime, I was forced to pretend my life was normal, regular. I couldn't let on that my whole world was tilting on its axis.

What had Dr. Morrow called it? A mix of bad stress and good stress. Both impacted us.

Two major situations happening to me right now, eating away at me. And I felt powerless to deal with them, unable to do more than roll with the punches. Maybe I should take a closer look at the coping mechanisms chapter to see if anything in there could help me. Of course, I wasn't going to write my homework assignment on them.

But right now, I was growing desperate enough to try anything. This prolonged distracted state was impacting me more than I wanted to admit. I hadn't studied much for midterms, nor could I muster any enthusiasm to do so. Every time I cracked open the books, my brain would wander, and I'd close them in frustration. I hadn't started my psych homework yet, either, which was due early Tuesday morning.

And I couldn't talk to Nick about any of that. Because he was a prof, and I knew what he'd do—he'd send me home. Wouldn't see me outside of class, would cut almost all personal contact, which would only increase my anxiety. Frankly, I also didn't want him parenting me like that. It was so hard to maintain a relationship that felt equal when I was frequently reminded it wasn't.

Nick held all the cards, had all the power.

Which left me here, all of this emotion and frustration and anxiety boiling over in me with no outlet in the discernible future. Trying to keep everything together and not let this chew me into pieces.

The movie ended, and Nick did a subtle glance at his watch. He shot me a smile. "Well, we should probably end the evening. Morning comes bright and early." So many words not being said, hanging heavy in the air between us.

I squeezed his hand and tried to act casual, like I wasn't all mixed up inside. "I'll see you tomorrow."

His kiss was potent, powerful, but it wasn't enough to fully release me from all my thoughts. I gathered my stuff, patted Gloria on the head and left.

"Since I'm sure you guys want to know where you stand in our class so far, I went ahead and graded the midterm exams last night," Nick told our class on Wednesday morning. His gaze brushed over me, and I saw his brow furrow a touch. My stomach dropped. Shit. That didn't look good. "If you want to discuss your grade, I'll be in my office this afternoon. Just drop by and see me."

Wordlessly he handed back the exams.

Kelly turned to the last page of her pack of papers and gave a heavy sigh of relief. "Oh, thank God. B-minus. I was sweating bullets." She wiped her brow with exaggeration.

Nick reached my aisle and handed me back my paper, no discernible expression on his face. Double shit.

My hands trembled as I flipped through the pages and saw notes in the margins. The last page showed a score of D. He'd also written a note:

Come to my office after class. We need to talk about this.

I groaned. Oh God, it was worse than I'd feared. Monday morning, when I'd faced the test, I'd known I wasn't going to ace it. Peeking at the first page had made me realize I should have fought past my stupid feelings and forced myself to study harder. But I hadn't realized I'd screwed up this badly.

My eyes burned.

"How did you do?" Kelly whispered to me.

I shook my head.

She made a small sound and reached over to pat my back. "I'm sorry. You should go talk to him about it."

"I will," I managed to choke out.

I'd never done this poorly on an exam before. My parents were going to be pissed. Nick was probably pissed too. Well, they could all get in line, because I was pissed at myself.

I tried so hard to push aside those feelings and listen to Nick as he walked through each question, giving the right answers. I wrote them down so I'd know for the final, since it would be cumulative.

After a half hour, he let our class go early. Dallas turned to say something to me, but the look on my face must have warned him off, because he immediately whipped back around and left without saying a word.

"Go talk to him," Kelly said. "He's a good teacher. I'm sure he'll work with you on it. And it's just one grade—it isn't going to kill your GPA. I know you can pull this up before the semester is over."

I hugged her. The words did give me a little bit of comfort. She was right; I'd done well until now, so it wouldn't tank me. And I hadn't failed. But I was bitterly disappointed in myself anyway.

A couple of students lingered behind to set up appointment times with him. I fiddled with my stuff and didn't leave my seat until the room emptied out, except for him and me.

He finally looked at me, and there was so much concern in his eyes that it made mine flood with tears. "Megan. What happened?"

I burst into sobs, cupping my hand over my mouth. Everything was spilling out of me and I couldn't hold it in anymore.

"Hey, hey, shh," he said as he rushed up the aisle. He maintained a respectful distance from me, but the warring emotions on his face showed me he wanted to come closer. But he couldn't.

Because of the damned circumstances.

"Let's go to my office," he said. "You're not busy right now, are you?"

I shook my head. Gathered my stuff and followed him out of the room. I kept my gaze on the ground until we made it to his office. He locked the door behind us.

I dropped into the seat in front of his desk, clutching the exam.

"Megan," he began in a stern voice. Stopped and seemed to rethink it, because he continued in a softer tone, "I don't know what's going on here. Why you're suddenly so stressed out. Why you did so poorly on this test. But we have to talk about this. Because if . . . our being together is distracting you—"

"It's my mom," I blurted out. Shit. I rubbed my brow. I hadn't realized I was going to just word-vomit it out like that, but I couldn't stop now.

I had to tell someone.

Nick stayed silent, giving me the space to continue at my own pace.

I sucked in a shaky breath. It took me a few stops and starts but I got the whole story out. My eyes stayed fixed on his desk; I was afraid to look at him and see what he was thinking right now. "We haven't talked in a week. I finally left my dad a message to see what was going on, but he hasn't returned it yet. And what can I do about it anyway?" I exhaled loudly.

He was quiet for a long moment. Then he got up and moved in front of the desk, a foot or so away from me. He leaned his backside against it. "Megan, you need to talk to your dad again. *Immediately*." Tension threaded in his voice and drew my attention to his dark eyes. "If your mom comes back to work here, there's a safety liability. Not to mention if the president gets wind of it . . ."

He didn't have to finish the sentence. I knew what he was saying. The heavy weight in my chest grew heavier. My parents would get fired from the job.

Probably even sued over it. I couldn't imagine it was legal for her to show up under the influence of drugs.

In which case, I'd have to leave the school. No Smythe-Davis graduate school education for me. There was no way I could continue going here when my mom had messed up so royally. My reputation would be damaged in the aftermath.

This whole time, I'd been worried about the relationship with Nick doing me in when it could be this shit with my mom that struck the death blow on my future at Smythe-Davis. Unreal.

I dropped the paper at my feet and rested my head in my hands. "This is so messed up."

He went down on his knees and cupped my cheeks, tilting my face up. His gaze poured with empathy. "I'm so sorry this is happening to you, but thank you for trusting me with it. I'm going to stay quiet about this for now and give you a chance to handle it. But . . ." He cleared his throat and his eyes skittered away. "I can't sit on it for long, Megan. I have an obligation as an employee of the school to ensure the safety of everyone on campus."

I nodded miserably. The sensation of his thumbs stroking my cheeks couldn't ease the burden in my heart.

Somehow I had to convince my dad to fire my mom from the one thing she loved most, other than her family—her work. It was the right thing to do, the only way to save the business, and maybe even save her. Because if things were this bad, she needed to go into an outpatient program or something.

But God, this might be the hardest thing I've ever had to do. I knew she was going to be furious with me.

How furious, I had no idea.

Chapter 16

"This party needs more ice cream," Amanda declared as she scraped the bottom of her ice-cream bowl. "Okay, not really, because I'm stupid full right now. In fact, I might never eat again."

Kelly laughed and put her mostly empty bowl on the coffee table. She tucked her feet under her legs. "I'm glad to see you guys don't skimp on the good stuff."

"Only the best for our guests." Casey was in a chair, a pillow over her stomach, the stereo's remote control in hand. She got a mix loaded up with ambient music. "Give it to me straight, guys. What do you think of this song?"

We paused and listened for a couple of minutes. I nodded my head to the rhythm. Casey was so talented. I should try something artistic, as well. How long had it been since I'd pursued anything other than academics? Far too long.

"This is gorgeous," Amanda breathed. She shifted in her seat and tilted her head. "Did you make this?"

Casey nodded, pride clear on her face. "I've been working on it for a couple of weeks now. Something wasn't quite clicking, but it came together for me last night. So I stayed up late to finish it."

The two of them continued talking about how she made music.

Kelly, who was on the end of the couch closest to my chair, leaned over. "So did you talk to Muramoto after class? About your midterm grade?"

I nodded. "While I can't redo it, he did say my other homework scores were strong enough that this wouldn't impact my overall grade too strongly. I just have to bust ass and do amazing on the final."

This afternoon, I'd lingered in his office for a while after confessing about my mom. We'd worked in silence, me studying for tomorrow's exam in algebraic number theory and him grading papers. Somehow he'd sensed I didn't want to be alone and had graciously shared his space with me.

I wasn't sure why I hadn't thought of doing that before—us working together. For some reason, I'd been able to push aside my anxieties and finally focus on the books. Maybe it was his quiet, soothing presence. Or how he'd given me space to voice my concerns about my mother.

Whatever it was, it worked.

Kelly gave me a comforting smile. "Well, I'm glad. I know you were upset. It *was* a hard test, so don't feel too bad. I'm pretty sure Dallas bombed it even worse than you did. He looked like he was going to cry when he left the room."

"I'm sure that sucked." I did feel a bit bad for the guy, even if I didn't like him like that.

"So has he tried to ask you out again?" Kelly asked me.

"Has who?" Casey said, peering at our side of the living room with interest.

"That guy I went out with before Valentine's Day," I told her. "When I came home early."

She shook her head. "Oh, the bad date, right? I'm assuming he's not the guy you're seeing right now, then."

My heart froze and I stiffened. "What do you mean?" I hadn't told a soul about seeing Nick. Had she guessed? Seen something?

Casey gave a laugh. "You've been MIA from our apartment for a few weeks now, and I can tell it's not because you're going to parties. Like I wouldn't notice you weren't around? It gets quiet when I'm here by myself. . . ."

Kelly's brow quirked. "Whoa, dish it, girl. Who are you seeing? Have I met him? What's he like? Does he go to our school?"

My brain scrabbled for the right approach to this. I should play it cool, act like it wasn't a big deal. Obviously I wasn't going to get far by pretending there wasn't anyone. I just needed to downplay it all.

I waved my hand, affecting an air of nonchalance I hoped was convincing. "Just some guy I met at a party off campus. He's a good way to kill time when I'm bored." Oh, it hurt my heart to say that, but I didn't have much of a choice.

Casey didn't seem convinced. "Been bored a lot lately, huh?"

My cheeks burned. "He's quite entertaining."

"What's his name?" Kelly asked.

"Brett," I made up. "And no, he isn't a student at our school or anything." In that much I could at least be true.

Of course, my phone chose that moment to chime on the end table; I'd set it there since I didn't have pockets in my yoga pants. I knew without a doubt in my mind it was Nick.

It was so hard to not snatch the phone up; my hand shook with the effort to make my movements smooth. If anyone saw his name on my phone, the gig was up. I should change his name in there tonight, just in case.

I tucked the phone under my thigh without looking at it.

"Aren't you gonna see what Brett wrote you?" Kelly teased. "Do you have pictures of him? Can I see?"

My lungs squeezed. "No pics," I forced out. "It's not like that."

Casey's eyes lingered on mine for a long moment. Then she turned her attention to the stereo remote and clicked forward a couple of songs. "Okay, if Megan wants to talk about Brett, she will. What do you guys want to listen to? I have a massive music collection, so hit me with some requests."

I shot her a grateful smile as the conversation turned away from me and on to our favorite bands. I cleared our empty ice-cream bowls and lingered in the kitchen to wash them. My stupid hands were trembling from the near brush of confrontation. The phone was pressed in the waistband of my pants, out of sight and on vibrate.

Why hadn't I pieced together a cover story before now?

Because arrogantly, I'd assumed no one would care what I was doing. I didn't hold myself accountable to others for the most part—I was an adult, and I did what I wanted. But I should have known Casey would notice.

She was a quiet person in general, though opening up more and more every day. She saw things others didn't see. I needed to be more careful around her, or else I was going to slip up.

After I finished washing the bowls and spoons, I dried my hands and checked the text.

I hope you're having a good evening. Just wanted to say hi and I was thinking about you.

This guy had worked his way into my heart with devastating speed. I was so falling for him, and there was no way for me to stop it. And if I was being honest with myself, I didn't want to stop it.

All the secrecy, all the anxiety, was worth every second of being close to him, even if it was chewing away at me more and more each day. Because I knew there was an end date in sight. I just had to hang in there until then.

I was thinking about you too, I wrote back.

My phone buzzed a moment later. *Hopefully good things. ;-)*

All good things. What are you up to?

Going to a dinner tonight to celebrate a colleague's retirement at the end of the semester. Should be fun. But not really. :-P

I laughed under my breath. *Don't forget to wear your tweed jacket. You wanna make sure you fit in with the other uptight profs. . . .*

A moment later, I got a pic back of Nick with a pipe clenched in his mouth.

Where did you get that pipe? And please tell me you're taking it w/you tonight.

My dad gave it to me as a gift when I got my doctorate. I haven't used it yet—not sure why he thought I'd want a pipe.

Uh, because they're awesome?? I wrote back. Not that I'd used one before, but they seemed distinguished anyway.

I won't be getting home until 10 or so tonight. Wish I could see you. My house is so quiet without you here.

My heart softened. An echo of what Casey had said to me earlier about the empty apartment, but with a different connotation altogether.

I missed him too. I just saw him this afternoon, but I wanted to see him again. It was so tempting to show up at his place, but I didn't want to be a creeper. Not to mention smothering him would only make him grow tired of me.

I typed, *Let's do something fun this weekend. Maybe we can drive out of town for the day. Go to Pittsburgh? Columbus? Detroit? What do ya say?*

I say I'm in. Night, Megan.

I smiled, tucked the phone away and dried the dishes, my heart soaring as I listened to the girls talking and giggling in the living room.

"Order up!" the fry cook called out.

I shuffled over to the kitchen window and took the two

plates, loaded with sandwiches and fries. When I put them on the table, the customers gave me a grateful smile. "Let me know if you guys need anything else," I said. "Enjoy!"

They began to dig in with gusto. I stepped away and busied myself with straightening up around the shop for the next twenty minutes. Almost off my shift for the day—and it was Friday afternoon too, which meant I had a relaxing evening ahead with no homework on the horizon, nothing to make me feel stressed out.

And tomorrow, Nick and I were driving to Detroit for a day of exploring. I was so excited to have the opportunity to walk around with him, holding his hand, kissing him . . . not having to worry that we'd get busted by someone we know.

A chance to see what an open relationship would feel like with him.

When my shift was done, I tucked away my apron, gathered my purse and left. I dug into the pocket on the side and felt for my phone. Tugged it out, ready to send Nick a message saying hi.

I saw I had a voice mail.

From my mom.

My stomach clenched so tight, I thought I was going to throw up. There could be only one reason she'd called me. Yesterday I'd spent an hour on the phone with my dad, discussing at length what had happened with Mom. The research I'd done online about pill abuse and its slippery slope that often led to other drugs being abused.

When I'd dropped on him that he had to let her go from the job site, he'd sighed heavily and said he knew. He had an engineer friend he could approach and ask to take over. I could hear the pain in his voice, and I knew this had to be causing him no small amount of agony.

Apparently it had happened.

My hands shook so hard, it was difficult to navigate my way

to the voice mail. The message was a terse "Call me, Megan. Immediately." That was it.

I spent the whole walk home trying not to drown in anxiety. She sounded angry.

I waited until I got inside the apartment and in my room before I called her back. She picked up immediately.

"Seriously? I cannot believe you." Mom started in on me without even saying hello. I couldn't remember the last time I'd heard this much anger pouring from her voice. It nearly singed me through the phone line. "How dare you go behind my back with your father like this. You are a child—"

"Excuse me?" I interrupted. Anger made my hands tremble now, not fear. "Last time I checked, I was an adult. Not a child. And I'm free to do whatever I think is right. How dare *you* show up to work drugged out of your mind! Do you even realize how wrong that is, how you could have endangered yourself, other contractors, even students? Yet you're blasting me about your mistakes? What if you'd been caught? What if you'd caused someone to get hurt? Did you ever think about that?" The words rushed out of me, fast and loud.

"You have no idea what's going on," she shot back. "You made a snap decision without taking the time to evaluate what the consequences were."

"So fill me in. Why did you have a bunch of hidden pills around your house, Mom? Why are you taking medication that isn't in your own name? I'd really like answers." My voice wobbled with emotion.

"Do you realize I've been fired? By your father—who's *my own husband*? And he replaced me with some idiot who doesn't know anything about this project. I've put countless hours into the plans, only to have it yanked away without even a discussion. Total bullshit." The fact that she was busting out curse words meant she was good and worked up. "Instead of talking to me about it, you colluded with him, and you've caused serious damage, both to my career and to my marriage. I hope you're proud of yourself."

That last comment stung. I blinked back a rush of tears. "Actually? I am. Because I see a woman who needs help and won't admit it. And at least I did something about it."

There was silence for so long, I thought maybe she'd hung up or put the phone down and walked away.

"Mom," I continued in a quieter tone. It was hard to keep my voice even when I was feeling so ragey, so upset. "You're stronger than this. I don't understand it at all."

"I don't have a problem. You have no idea what you're talking about. And I don't have to justify my actions to you or anyone." She sounded mulish as she spoke.

I sighed. What could I say in response? She was determined to shut down everything I said. "I just need you to listen to me, to talk to me. Without getting defensive. Please." I pressed the heel of my other hand to my brow, where a headache was starting to form.

The coldness in her voice chilled me. "You crossed a line, Megan. I'm furious with you. I can't believe you'd betray me like this. I don't know if I can ever forgive you for what you've done to me."

The line clicked, and the call ended.

Chapter 17

I moved with a singular focus. Crammed my phone in my purse. Dug my keys out and rezipped my coat, which had been hanging open. Locked the apartment behind me and just . . . walked. No destination in mind.

The air was bracing, and the weak sun did little to penetrate the cold. A late winter snap was setting in, and the temperature felt like it had dropped several degrees even since I'd gone inside earlier.

I welcomed the cold, focused on its bite on my cheeks. A creeping numbness had edged its way into my bones, spread through my veins and muscles. In all the arguments I'd had with my parents, not one had ever gone down like that.

I'd never been so thoroughly blasted by my mother or had her tell me she didn't think she could forgive me for what I'd done. Was she right? Should I have talked to her first?

But I had, kinda. I'd asked her before, back in the trailer, why she had those pills. And she'd fed me some story that most likely wasn't true; it was possible the ear infection thing had been a total lie. She was hiding pills all over the house. She had to know what she was doing was wrong.

I wasn't at fault here. I knew that, logically. But the guilt and anger and fear still shocked me so hard I could barely feel anything. It was like all my emotions had collided into one blinding blast that left me shell-shocked.

I proceeded at a steady pace toward the math building. I didn't pay much attention to my surroundings. Didn't hear student conversations. All I heard was my mom's bitter voice, echoing in my head.

I swept inside the building, turned down the hall on autopilot toward Nick's office. I wasn't sure if he was still on campus, but if he was, I wanted to see him. Needed to have his arms around me and crack away the cold that had penetrated my bones. The numbness had spread so deeply in me that I couldn't seem to care about anything right now. Not about people seeing me walk toward his office and what they might think. The secrecy around him and our relationship didn't seem to matter, not in this moment. Who gave a shit? My mom was messed up and she hated me now, and I couldn't get her scornful words out of my head.

Nick was the only one who could do that for me.

My fist shook just a touch when I knocked on his door. When it opened, I just stood there in the doorway, staring at him.

The smile that had been on his face when he realized it was me slid away immediately. "Megan, you okay? Come in."

I entered, and he closed and locked the door behind us. My legs gave out and I collapsed into his guest seat. He leaned against his desk, not saying anything, just keeping that steady gaze fixed on me.

"My dad took my mom off the dorm room project," I started. My lungs were so tight, it hurt to draw in a breath, and my back bowed with tension. "She called me, angry. Lashed out at me for what I did to her job and her marriage with my dad. Then she said she didn't think she could ever forgive me." At that last part, my voice broke. In the warmth of his sunlight I was beginning to thaw, just a touch. The pain seeped in the cracks.

His eyes softened in sympathy. He reached a hand over and took my icy fingers in his. "I'm so sorry."

The fact that he didn't immediately try to tell me everything would be okay, or that I did the right thing even if it hurt at the moment, filled me with a small rush of relief. We both knew it was right; he didn't feel the need to rub it in, vocalize it.

My throat felt raw and sore. He moved toward me at the same time I stood, and our arms wrapped around each other. A rush of tears flew out of my eyes, streaming down my cheeks, drenching his dress shirt. He didn't care, just kept those strong arms encasing me, those soft lips pressing gentle kisses to my forehead.

I didn't know how long we stood there. I just knew that minute by minute, that dreadful ache in my heart started to fade. In its place was this man who took the pain away. I would focus on him, on this, and shut out my mom's voice for now.

Nick leaned his head closer to my ear and whispered, "You are one of the strongest, most intelligent women I've ever met. We'll get through this."

We. As in, not just me alone.

I peeled off my coat and tossed it on the chair behind me. Wrapped my arms around him again, our bodies pressed together, my heart throbbing almost painfully. "I don't feel strong right now, especially since I just cried all over you."

"Strength doesn't mean doing everything alone," he replied in a smooth voice. "It can also mean knowing when you need help. Even if it's just another person to talk to."

I nodded, stared up into his eyes. The little flecks of black in the dark brown irises I had grown to know so well. The slight lines that fanned out on the outsides. The light dusting of facial hair that emerged as day transitioned to night.

Now my throat tightened for a different reason, and my heart pounded. Tears flecked the ends of my eyelashes, and I reached up to wipe them away.

His thumb came up to stroke my jaw. The gesture made my heart flare. The thumb swept across my lower lip, and I sighed, parted my mouth slightly.

I didn't want to be sad or hurt anymore. I wanted to feel good. With him. Right now. Damn the consequences. Damn the risks.

"My mom's brother is an alcoholic," he said suddenly. His breaths mirrored mine, shallow and uneven. His eyes turned down a bit in the corners. "He's struggled with it for years, since I was a little kid. Hiding bottles all over the house, drinking when no one was around. Showing up to family dinners drunk. A few years ago, his wife ended up leaving him, taking their son with her."

"I just don't understand it," I told him as I shook my head. "Why?"

He shrugged. "If we're not addicted to something, I don't think we can ever understand. Every once in a while he surfaces in my life. Seems sober for a while, and I start to think it might be different. Then he goes on a bender, which makes him beat himself up and sends him deeper down the rabbit hole. Not to mention he's too stubborn to stay in a rehab facility when he actually does try to get help. He keeps checking himself out early, saying he's fine, but then he falls back into it again after a while. My family gets so mad." I heard the undertone of hurt in his voice and reached up to stroke the back of his neck. He closed his eyes, leaned into my touch. "Yanno, I don't ever talk about this with anyone because I don't want people to judge him, if that makes sense."

"Totally. I haven't told anyone about my mom. No one but you."

He looked at me and blinked. His lips pressed together. "I hope you know I'm not judging you. Or her. I'm glad your dad is there to support her and that he's taking this seriously, because I didn't want to go to the administrators about this. It's gonna be rough while she recovers, but if she's half as smart as the daughter she's raised, she'll take a step back and realize she's hurting the people around her, not to mention herself."

I couldn't help it; I leaned up on my toes and kissed him.

It was soft and unassuming at first, just a brushing of lips against each other. More of a gesture of mutual comforting than anything else. Then something shifted between us, a charge of electricity that crackled in the air.

I clenched his collar a fraction tighter and heard his sigh, the exhaled air softly caressing my mouth. Then he leaned in for another kiss. Nudged my lips open with a swipe of his tongue and tasted me.

All my tension and anxiety fell away as I gave in to the moment. Our arms wrapped around each other, bodies pressed together. Everything about him intoxicated me. I couldn't get enough.

"God, you drive me crazy, Megan," he rasped as he ran his tongue along my jaw. "But I don't want to take advantage of you when you're upset. We should stop." He started to pull away.

I gripped him tighter. "No, don't. Please." I knew I sounded pleading, but I didn't care. "I need you." I pressed a hard kiss to his mouth, willing him with everything in me to keep going. My body was almost shaking with desire. The pain had faded away, and all I could feel was the ache of my hunger for him.

Nick groaned; I could see the conflict on his face for just a moment before he gave a look that seemed close to surrender.

His voice was husky when he said, "Something about you is so tempting. I can't resist you. And I don't want to." He sucked my lower lip into his mouth, and I rubbed my breasts along his chest. Opened to him and dragged my fingers through his hair.

"Then don't," I whispered, letting my arousal show clearly in my voice, my face, my body. I didn't want him to push me away. I wanted him to remind me how to feel good.

We kissed for I wasn't sure how long, just losing ourselves in each other. His hands gripped my hips, kneaded the rounded flesh of my butt. I dropped a hand to cup his hardness, and his erection twinged beneath my exploring fingers.

Nick ripped his mouth away. "You're playing with fire, baby."

The words made me shiver. I fingered the zipper of his slacks, then lowered them. Slid my hand into the slit and stroked him with just his briefs separating our flesh. It wasn't enough. I fumbled with the pants button and undid it, exposing more of his length to me.

I could almost feel his pulse in my hand. His breathing became ragged, panting. He didn't speak, just stood there, fingers tight on my ass.

"I want you right now," I said in a harsh whisper. "Please."

The pulse on the side of his throat jumped. A dark gleam lit in his eyes. "We're in my office. Someone could knock on the door at any moment."

"We can be quiet," I promised. "No one will know." I turned back against the desk and spread my legs to nestle him between my thighs.

His body was hot and hard. He lifted my ass and dropped me on the edge of the desk. I wrapped my legs around him. "We shouldn't do this," he whispered in my ear before slicking his tongue along the flesh.

I arched into him and tugged his shirt out of his pants. "I don't care." I was almost blind with my hunger. Right now, I couldn't stop even if a tornado touched down on the building. I needed this. Needed Nick.

Apparently, that was enough to convince him, because before I knew it, my pants were opened and being pushed down to my ankles. I kicked my boots off, then my jeans and panties. The smoothly polished wooden desk was slightly cool beneath my ass. A frantic urgency had overtaken me. I had to have him inside me. Now.

When I went to shove his pants down, he dug into his back pocket, grabbed his wallet and whipped out a condom. That made me grin.

"Prepared for emergency situations, professor?" I said in a teasing tone.

His eyes grew dark as he stared at me. "I shouldn't be turned on by you saying that."

"And yet, you are. I want you, Dr. Muramoto." Oh, I was pushing every boundary in sight right now and I didn't give a shit. I wanted him half as turned on as I was, wanted to escape into the sheer, mind-numbing pleasure of having sex with Nick. This was so wrong, so amazingly, sexily wrong.

He growled and made quick work of ripping off his pants and boxer briefs, then his shirt. He stood there, beautifully naked before me, and I couldn't breathe. There was lust in his eyes . . . and more. Affection. Warmth.

Respect.

I saw it all on his face, and I realized right then that I was madly in love with this man.

I loved Nick Muramoto. I loved him so much, my heart hurt with the understanding of the depth of my feelings.

And I was scared to death to let him know. So I dropped my gaze to his bobbing erection, watched him roll the condom on. I took off my shirt, attempted to get my roller-coaster emotions under control.

We weren't at the point yet where I could tell him the depth of what I was feeling. But it didn't mean I couldn't secretly savor it.

Nick came back to me, pressed against me, and I scooted myself as close to the edge as I could without falling off. I leaned back, breasts thrust in the air, hands gripping the far end of the table, legs spread before him in invitation.

His breathing was so ragged, it undid me. "You're so damn gorgeous. I want to devour you."

"Yes," I whispered, careful to keep my voice hushed, though I longed to scream his name right now. "Please. Take me, Nick."

One smooth thrust, and he was inside me. Everything clicked into place in that single perfect moment. The raging roar of my emotions, the feeling of being completely filled by the man I loved beyond anyone else. His hands cupping my waist, his mouth nuzzling my breasts.

There was love and sensuality and desire spilling into us, and I savored it all.

He withdrew, then slipped back in. I could smell the rich scent of sex building, feel his muscles clenching beneath my hands. He groaned for a split second, then bit his lip.

"Stay quiet, Dr. Muramoto," I ground out into his ear.

His body grew even tighter, his thrusting more ragged. Each stroke uncurled that delicious sensation in my belly.

"You're a bad girl, Megan," he said, timing his words with his hard thrusts, and those words almost sent me over the edge. One hand reached up to caress my breasts, drawing the tight tip into a hard bead.

"Right there," I panted. It was so hard to keep my voice down. I was so close. "Don't stop."

"I'm not stopping until you come." He slammed hard, and the friction made me dig my heels into his ass.

I dropped a hand between us to stroke my tender flesh.

"Give it to me, Megan." He sounded so dark and quiet and

sexy that my whole body clenched with throbbing need. "I can smell how turned on you are. You're going to come so hard."

I bit his shoulder to silence my words as my orgasm ripped through me. Because right when I came, I almost cried out, *I love you.*

As my orgasm ebbed, Nick's thrusts grew more insistent. I wrapped my sweat-slicked body against him, pressed kisses to his mouth. I could tell from the way he moved and breathed that he was close. So deliciously close. After a minute he stiffened, jerked, his hot breaths pouring between my lips.

My heart was so full I was about to burst. I was overwhelmed, panting hard.

"Megan." There was so much reverence in the way he said my name that I shivered. "Thank you. That felt so good." I could feel him still pulsing in me.

"It did for me too." My throat was tight, bogged down with all the words I wanted to say. *Don't do it,* I warned myself. I wasn't going to rush this. Our relationship was going so well, and one slipup could change everything. I needed this to stay stable, given all the shit happening with my mom.

Nick pulled out, cleaned up the condom, then discarded it. I hopped off the desk with a hushed giggle, and we donned our clothes again. I knew my hair was messy, my cheeks flushed, and I didn't care in the least.

"You bit my shoulder hard," he murmured. "Not that I'm complaining. It felt good. Just surprised me."

"Well, it was a good one," I retorted with a shrug.

His eyes turned serious. "You okay though? Really? I didn't intend for us to have sex as a diversion to talking about what's bothering you."

"I didn't believe you did." I caressed his cheeks and let my feelings pour from my eyes. No, I couldn't say it yet, but I couldn't quite hide it either. "But feeling close to you really helped. I'm not quite so upset anymore." I was surprised to realize it was true. The deep, dull ache was still there, but the immediate sting had faded away. I would talk to my dad about what happened; surely he'd have good advice on what we should do. But I wasn't in this alone.

"Good." He wrapped me in his arms and rested his cheek against my forehead. "It killed me to see you so sad."

Eventually, I pulled out of his arms. "I should let you go back to work. After all, we're going to be together all day tomorrow."

A dimple popped out in his cheek. "I'm looking forward to it."

I donned my coat and boots. Stood on my tiptoes and pressed another kiss to his mouth. "I'll see you tomorrow morning." I unlocked and opened his door, unable to fight back the tiny smile on my face.

My heart was light and free as I stepped into the hall. Then stopped and froze in horror.

Kelly was standing right in front of me, eyes growing wide as she took in my messy hair, flushed cheeks. The sex signs were right there, loud and clear. And given the shocked look on her face, she saw it all.

Chapter 18

I gripped Kelly's arm and pulled her away from the door, tugging it closed behind me. I could sense the storm coming and didn't want Nick hearing it. *Shit, shit, shit.* My mind scrambled in desperation for the right words to say.

"Megan." Her exhale was loud, disbelief and horror clear in her voice. "Please tell me I'm not seeing what I think I'm seeing." She jerked her arm out of my grasp.

I bit my lower lip. My heart hammered so hard against my chest that I thought I might faint. "What are you doing here?"

"Don't you remember? I told you earlier this week that I made an appointment with Dr. Muramoto to discuss our next assignment." Her jaw was so tight, I could almost hear her teeth clenching. The disappointment in her eyes gutted me. "There is no Brett, is there?"

I took a few moments to drag in slow, steadying breaths. "Can we please go somewhere else to talk? I don't want to do this here."

Kelly gave me a stiff nod and followed me down the hall. I saw an empty classroom and walked in, flicking the light switch and closing the door behind us. We each took a seat at a desk. Her back was stiff and straight as she thunked her books on the desk surface.

My lungs were painfully tight. I gripped the end of the desk and said, "You can't talk to anyone about what I'm going to tell you."

She scoffed, a bitter sound, but I saw the flare of pain in her eyes. "Who would I tell? And why? I thought we were friends."

"I'm sorry. It's not personal, I promise. I just . . ." My eyes began to burn, and I tightened my clench on the desk edge. The agony about my mother rushed back and smothered me, mingled with the guilt over keeping secrets from my friends. Not to mention guilt at what I was about to confess to her, despite Nick warning me we had to keep quiet. "I'm in such a mess right now, and everything's so confusing and mixed up."

I heard her give a soft sigh but kept my attention on the fake wood pattern of the desk. "Megan, *what is going on?*"

I spilled the beans. I couldn't hold it in anymore. I told her about how Nick had been at the dance club that night. How I'd been drawn to him even though he'd tried to fight his feelings too. And the words kept coming out—I confessed about my mom's problem. The fact that all of this had been eating away at me little by little until I'd gotten in a fight with her this afternoon and came here to see Nick.

"I'm in love with him," I whispered past a tight throat. "I haven't told him that yet because I know it's crazy fast, but this feeling won't go away. The intensity of what I have in my heart doesn't care about the number of days, only about the quality of our time together. Every moment with him makes my heart happy."

I lifted my chin and made myself face her. This wasn't me—hiding my feelings, being afraid of them. I wasn't ashamed of it, though I did feel bad for lying to everyone.

"No, there's no Brett," I confirmed. "There's only me and Nick and this thing between us."

"Why didn't you just wait until school was over and you weren't his student anymore?" She didn't sound overly judgmental, though she was serious.

"Don't you think I tried?" I gave a mirthless laugh. "But I couldn't fight it. And I didn't want to. Why should I wait, just because someone else has determined I'm not allowed to have feelings for him? That's stupid."

Kelly's face grew tight, and she crossed her arms over her chest. "Did you ever think there's a reason the school implemented those rules? It isn't to punish you. It's to keep you from being taken advantage of."

"There's no way in hell Nick would do that to me," I retorted hotly.

"You're basing this off knowing him for, what, a couple of months? Do you realize how that sounds?"

I stood. My blood was almost boiling in my veins. "I don't need to justify anything I feel or do to you or any other damn person here. You wanted to know the truth, so I told you." But now I wished I hadn't. *Stupid, Megan!* I chided myself. What if she told someone on me? So much for my earlier bravado.

She held up her hands. "Whoa, wait. Okay, I'm sorry. My last comment was harsh, and I didn't mean it to sound like that. But I'm just saying all of this because I care about you. Because I'm worried. You have a big heart, and I don't want to see you hurt." Her eyes grew hooded and she bit her lower lip, looked away from me. "I've been where you are. Well, not exactly, but close enough. And it went so wrong." Those last words sounded like they'd been choked out of her.

I pushed aside my frustration and perched on the edge of the desk. "What do you mean?"

With halting words, Kelly said, "When I was in Chicago, I worked a part-time job while in school. My boss was an older man, married but unhappy with his wife. He and I grew close, started talking. Just friendship at first. But it became more."

"Nick isn't married," I pointed out. "Nor is he in a relationship."

She sighed and tucked a strand of hair behind her ear. "I know. Just bear with me here. I fell in love with the man—or thought I did. I was spending all of my free time with him. Dreaming about him. Wondering when he would leave his wife for me. But he kept saying we couldn't be together immediately. That we needed to wait until the time was right. I trusted him, believed it would happen."

A twist of uneasiness settled in my stomach. Nick and I had plans like that—that we could freely date once I wasn't in school anymore. But that was different than this, wasn't it?

"Eventually the man began to get controlling over my time. He'd get upset when I wasn't available during his free time. He started stalking me, driving by my apartment to see if my car was there. He showed up outside of one of my classes too. I got freaked out and tried to break up with him, but he told me he wasn't letting me go. That we were meant to be together." Her hands were clenched so tightly in her lap that her knuckles were white. I could hear the shake in her voice. She blinked rapidly, like she was fighting off tears. "So after one particularly bad incident, I left—the campus, the guy, my whole life. Just moved out one day without telling him where I went."

"Oh God, Kelly," I breathed. I reached over and rested my hand on hers. "That's so messed up. I'm sorry."

She gave me a watery smile. Sniffled twice. "Thanks. Hey, at least I got out before it got worse, right?"

"Honey," I started in a careful voice, "I'm proud of you for leaving him. That was totally the right call. But Nick isn't like that. Not all men are controlling."

She flipped her upper hand over and cupped my fingers in a chilly grip. "Older men have different expectations of girls who are younger than them. I just don't want you to be surprised or get hurt."

"I promise to be careful," I said. "I'm going into this with my eyes wide open. I'm too stubborn to not protect my heart." But even as I said it, I knew my heart was so far gone to him that there was no going back. I just had to hope everything would be okay with us. "Nick respects me, cares about me. He supports my goals."

Her eyes still looked concerned, but she just bit her lip and nodded.

"I don't expect you to be on board with it, and that's okay. But you can still be my friend, can't you?"

"Of course," she gasped as she reached up and hugged me. "You're my best friend, Megan. Because of your kindness and you welcoming me into your circle, I've made this place my home. Most of my friends back in Chicago have pretty much stopped talking to me since I no longer live there. Thank you." Her last words were whispered.

I started crying and hugged her tighter. The raggedness in her voice broke my heart. "I'm here for you," I promised. "I *never* abandon my friends."

"I'm glad it was me outside the door and not someone else who'd seen it. Please . . . just be careful." She pulled back and looked at me through tear-dotted lashes.

She was right. My desire to flee the pain of my mom's anger had made me rush headfirst into something that could have turned out disastrous. Shame swirled in my gut. This wasn't me—this girl who let her emotions run away with her. I had to get myself under control.

"I will, I promise. You be careful too." I frowned. "So this guy has no idea where you are, right? You're safe?"

"Haven't heard a single word from him since I moved here," she said. She straightened and sniffed again, seeming to pull herself together. "But if I do, I'll call you and maybe we can break his kneecaps or something."

"I know you're joking about that, but I keep a baseball bat under my bed," I said.

Her jaw dropped and she barked out a laugh.

"What?" I gave a casual shrug, glad to have the conversation turned to safer ground. "A girl has to be careful. I'm ready to beat the shit outta anyone who tries to mess with me."

Kelly gave me the first genuine smile I'd seen on her face since we'd run into each other in the hallway. "You know what? Somehow I have a feeling I shouldn't be worrying about your heart. You can take care of yourself, can't you, Megan?"

"Damn straight I can," I declared with a bold grin I wasn't quite feeling yet. "Let's get a beer somewhere tonight. I could use a drink."

"How do you feel about pistachios?" Nick asked me as he drove a little too fast for my comfort through downtown Detroit on Saturday evening. He hadn't been lying about being a speed demon, but he was careful and drove safely. We'd spent the day driving around the downtown area, taking pictures, visiting the local art museum, browsing in shops, even enjoying lunch at a brewery. Now I was stuffed and happy. It had been a great day, one I'd desperately needed with him. Being away from campus, away from the drama around my mom, had relieved a good portion of stress, even if just for a while. Here, I could pretend we were a regular couple. And it felt so good to sink into that fantasy.

"Here's where I insert a bad pun about being nutty over them," I replied drolly.

He took a quick glance at me. "And here's where I insert an insertion joke," he said with a bold wink.

I slugged his upper arm, and he laughed. "You're a dog," I said. "So what's the deal with pistachios?"

He turned the car right. "There's a small shop nearby that sells the best I've ever had. They have other stuff too. We'll swing by there before leaving for home, because I need to buy more."

"You're driving," I said. "So let's go."

A few minutes later we pulled into a spot on the street. We got out of the car and headed into the brick building on the corner. Nick made a beeline for the pistachios section, and I followed him, chuckling under my breath.

"But why *pistachios?*" I pressed him. "What makes them so special out of all the food in the world?"

He grabbed two huge bags of them and turned to me. "My dad and I would sneak and eat them all the time when I was a kid. We knew that if Mom busted us, we'd be in trouble for ruining our appetites." His cheeks curved with his goofy grin, and he gave a casual shrug. "I know that sounds silly, but it was our secret. We still buy bags for each other for birthdays. Mom has no idea why opening those gifts makes us laugh so hard."

"That's sweet," I said as I stepped closer and kissed his lips.

I envied the easy relationship he had with his folks. Could mine be repaired again with my mom? Even my communication with Dad was strained at this point, after a few terse text messages exchanged yesterday evening. I loathed feeling like this, because we were normally a close-knit family. We'd never had issues like this before. It was eating away at me, little by little, minute by minute. Lurking in the back of my mind, never quite letting me fully escape into the happiness of today.

"So have you heard from your mom?" he asked me, his eyes flooded with concern. He must have seen something in my face.

I shook my head, determined to not let on that my heart still bore a sharp ache from yesterday's argument with her. "Nope, but that's okay. I think we both need time to cool off." Last night, while talking with Kelly at a local bar, I'd decided I was going to give her a few days and then reach out to her.

She was my mom. Yeah, she was pissed, but I believed she

loved me. I just needed to reach that part of her heart, the part not angry . . . or shut off by the medication. It was still there, even if buried.

All I could do was hope she'd talk to me soon and not hold on to this grudge.

"I think you're probably right," he said as he nodded. He shifted the bags to the crook of one arm and took my hand with the other, and we walked toward the chocolate-covered nuts area. "So . . . would you like to meet my parents when the semester is over? Maybe for dinner?"

The air froze in my lungs. Here it was, Nick telling me he wanted to keep this going. Like a real relationship. I swallowed and said, "I'd love to. Yes."

Nick gave me a shy smile. "I think they'll like you." He squeezed my hand, and I found my pulse surging from the now-familiar warmth in his strong fingers. He lifted my hand to his mouth and kissed each knuckle. "I've wanted to tell them about you, you know. But I want to keep my promise to you, that I'll keep quiet until we can be out in the open. Though it's been hard at times, I admit."

My heart shrank a bit in a flare of guilt. I'd already blabbed to Kelly, but she'd sworn to not tell anyone. I had to trust her on that.

"What's wrong?" he asked, eyes narrowing.

I slapped a smile on my face. "Oh. Nothing. I'm just looking forward to the semester being over."

He gave me an easy grin. "Me too. Okay, let's pick out some snacks for the ride home." We found chocolate-covered peanuts and grabbed those too, then Nick purchased the goods and we settled back in the car.

I fought so hard to ignore that thud of shame in my heart. I'd told our secret, whereas he'd kept it. Would he be mad if he found out? Should I be honest with him? Or would it just create unnecessary drama? I wrestled with the dilemma for a full minute.

In the end, I decided to stay silent. God knew I had enough drama in my life right now. And Kelly understood the delicate nature of the situation. She'd keep mum. Besides, in two months, everything would be different. The secret wouldn't matter then.

Nick started the car and then turned to the backseat, a mysterious glint in his eyes. "Before we go, I have something for you."

I blinked. "What? Like, a present?"

He gave me a small gift box. I opened it to find a pair of delicately crafted wire earrings with purple drop beads. They were classy and gorgeous.

I looked up at him, the question in my eyes.

"Because I wanted to," he answered smoothly. "Because I saw them and thought they'd look stunning against your skin." He reached over and stroked my earlobe, and a shiver danced across my whole body.

"I love you." The words flew out of my mouth before I could stop them. I froze in horror and stared at him.

His eyes were huge. He just stared back.

"Oh God, I hadn't meant to say that," I added with a stilted laugh. My cheeks burned hot and I wanted to jump out of the car and hide. I made myself sit there though. "Okay, I mean, I *wanted* to say that, but I hadn't meant to do that here, like this, when—"

Then his mouth was on mine, his hand clamped to the back of my neck. I gasped, and he slipped his tongue between my lips. I drank him in, dropped the earring box in my lap, clutched his shoulders and drowned in this emotion.

My feelings were out there now, and he hadn't freaked out or pulled away. My heart fluttered like a caged bird.

His other hand slid to my waist and stroked expertly through my dressy shirt, and my skin tingled everywhere he touched. I felt the lines of his shoulder and arm muscles, memorized his body with my fingertips. Imprinted his flavor in my mouth. Etched his clean soap scent in my nostrils.

Every sense was on high, overloading with Nick.

When he pulled back from me, his pupils were large and intense, fixed on me. "Megan." Adoration poured from his voice, from his eyes. My pulse throbbed harder in response. "You're the most beautiful, intelligent woman I've ever met. I can't get enough of you. I can't stop thinking about you, wanting you. You make me feel . . . alive."

It was ridiculous, how my body flared with heat at those words. I loved him so much, and I could feel the strength in his emotions too. Was it love? I didn't know, but I did know it was strong. It was intense.

It was real.

My hands shook as I took the earrings out of the box and looped them in my ears. "When I wear these, I'll think of you." Their weight was light, barely there.

"I hope you do." He skated his thumb across my cheek, across my lower lip. "And I'll be thinking of you too."

Chapter 19

"I can't focus," I declared as I threw my pen into the seam of my textbook. I was unable to stop thinking about my mom, about the growing chasm of silence stretching between us. Despite what I'd told myself before—that I'd give her a few days to calm down before trying to reach out—I couldn't help but feel sick and distraught over the situation, and worried about how she was.

Should I ignore my dad's advice and drive over to check on her? Or should I respect her wishes for distance and wait until she was more receptive? I just didn't know, and it tore me up. Not to mention I still hurt over the cruel things she'd said to me. Making myself vulnerable to her again would take real courage.

I also couldn't stop thinking about Nick. The man who occupied my dreams, who'd stolen my heart. I sat back at the kitchen table and rubbed my fingertips along my aching eyelids. Then I slid my hands over and touched my earrings.

"Those are pretty," Casey said softly. "Did Brett give them

to you? Are . . . are you having anxiety about it or something? Like how serious it's getting between you guys?"

I blinked. "What makes you say that?"

"You've touched the earrings, like, a hundred times in the last hour. Plus, your eyes are glazed over and you haven't changed the page in your book in forever, nor have you written in your notebook. The obvious deduction is you're distracted."

Casey was way too astute for her own good. Even though she didn't know about the situation with my mom, or about Nick, she could tell I wasn't myself. My stomach lurched. It was on the tip of my tongue to perpetuate the lie I'd started before. But for some reason, I just couldn't do it. My emotions were too volatile to come up with a pat story. The stuff with my mom was so raw still. Plus I was kinda basking in the glow of yesterday's events with Nick. Of the generous gift he'd given me. How I'd told him I loved him.

No, he hadn't said it back. But I knew it wasn't fair to expect that, just because I'd said it.

I dropped my hands in my lap and straightened my spine. I'd already told Kelly the truth. Would it hurt to tell Casey too? I knew she'd keep my secrets—hell, she'd been keeping a whopper of a secret about her life for months before opening up to me.

If there was anyone I could trust, could confide in, it was her. I decided to start with the Nick situation first.

"There is no Brett," I told her in a quiet tone.

I watched her face frown in confusion. Then fall.

"Oh. I see."

My throat tightened, and I reached over and swigged my Diet Coke. "I'm sorry I lied to you. I panicked. So I made him up. I was trying to keep the guy I like secret, and I got put on the spot and . . ." I shrugged.

She gave a brittle smile, and I saw the moment she retreated back into her shell. "I'm sorry. I shouldn't have pried. It's totally none of my business."

"No, no, no." I reached over and took her hand. "Don't do that, please. Don't pull away like that. This is *my* screwup, not yours." I sucked in a shaky breath. "I'm seeing my professor—the one who came to The Mask that night—and I don't want him to get in trouble. We decided to keep it quiet."

She stared at me in shock for a few seconds, blinking a few times. "Oh."

"Yeah." I huffed a sigh and squeezed her fingers, then released them. Fiddled with my pen cap to give my hands something to do.

"Is it serious? Or are you two casually dating?"

With that, I barked out a laugh. "He's not a booty call, if that's what you mean."

Her lips pursed in a smarmy grin, and she rolled her eyes. "Sorry. Just being delicate. No judgment either way."

"I told him I loved him," I said; speaking it aloud to someone made it feel even more concrete.

"Oh," she breathed, clapping a hand over her mouth. "Wow."

"Yeah."

We sat there in silence for a moment, the weight of my words heavy in the air between us. Though we'd only become roommates less than a year ago, we'd grown close over the last few months. Casey knew me.

I'd dated a number of guys. Casey had even met a few of them. They'd been fun, exciting, casual. But none of them had come close to tugging at my heart the way Nick did. He was special. He was different.

He made me want to think long term, think serious.

A nervous laugh burst out of me. "I never thought I'd be *that* girl. The one who fell for her professor. Total cliché, right?"

"You mean as clichéd as a girl who pushes everyone away

until one guy comes into her life who breaks down her walls?" she retorted with an arched brow, a crooked grin on her face.

"Fair enough." I tipped my head in concession to her point. Basically the story of how she and Daniel had ended up together, though of course a bit more complicated than just that. "Tell me honestly. Am I crazy here? I'm basically just treading water now, waiting until the semester is over and we can be together out in public."

"Crazy? Absolutely not. I think you're intelligent enough to be able to tell what is right for you and what's not, correct?"

Pride warmed my heart. I nodded. "But not everyone feels that way. I know we'll be judged for it. That others will think badly of him for dating me—not just because of the age gap, but because he's my teacher."

"As your friend, I trust that you know what's best for you. You've always given me such savvy advice, even when I was scared about opening up and telling you what I was thinking, what was going on in my life." Her eyes turned stern, resolute. "If this guy is the one for you, then screw what others might say. They're flat-out idiots, and they don't deserve one minute of your time or concern."

My jaw dropped in surprise. I'd never seen her that vocally expressive about something before.

She tilted her chin and eyed me. "If I'd followed plain-old logic instead of letting my heart guide me, I wouldn't be with Daniel right now. And he's the best thing that's ever happened to me—except for you and my family, of course. Sometimes you have to silence the noise around you to listen to what your heart is whispering."

My eyes flooded with tears, and I gulped. Stood and moved around the table to give her a hug. "You get it," I said as I gripped her tight.

She gripped me right back. "I'm so happy for you, Megan. You have a right to find love wherever you see fit. If this man is it for you, then run with it." She pulled back and peered at me, and I saw a few tears in her eyes as well. With a weak sniffle, she gave a self-conscious chuckle. "Of course, since you are still in his class, you should be careful."

I nodded. "Definitely. I don't want him to get in trouble." Once again I cursed myself for how rash and irresponsible I'd been on Friday afternoon. Thank God Kelly had been the one to find us. If it had been anyone else, it could have turned into a total disaster.

"Do you think it could impact your grad school plans?" she asked.

I sighed as my stomach sank. The question I'd been avoiding. "I don't know. But we'll be a lot closer to being peers at that point. He won't be my prof then either. I have to think that if we're discreet and don't flaunt it everywhere, it'll probably be okay." God, I hoped.

I moved back into my seat and took a deep breath. Then I tentatively explained the situation with my mom. Surprisingly, it didn't hurt as badly this time, nor did I feel that sting of pride the way I had before. After all, Casey understood about messed-up family situations. I knew she'd be the last person in the world to judge me on it.

She responded just as I'd thought she would—with empathy and support. She vowed to help me out however she could and made me promise to let her know what she could do.

"And thanks for telling me the truth," Casey added. "About all of this. I know it wasn't easy, and I appreciate it."

I gave her a brash grin, trying to shake off my earlier melancholy. "Look how close we're getting. If we keep this up, you'll be dumping Daniel to stay with me in this majestic apartment." I swept my arm around the room.

She shrugged. "Well, you *are* pretty damn hot. . . ."

My jaw dropped again. "You sassy wench." It was amazing to see how much Casey had changed and evolved from the quiet, withdrawn girl from last semester. This one was light, free, happier than I'd ever seen her. "Okay, we'd better get back to studying. I can't bomb anything else this semester, or I'll have to kick my own ass."

"Can't have that." Casey softly smiled at me and went back to studying.

I did the same, though I couldn't help the bittersweet tinge in my heart when I realized how lonely I'd be in this apartment when she moved out.

"Extra mayo," I recited back to the teen boy at my table. "Got it."

He eyed my nametag. "Thanks . . . Megan," he said as he drawled my name. He gave me such a flirty, broad wink that I couldn't help but laugh. "I'm Allen. So . . . what do you think of younger men?"

His friend across the table just sat there with a smirk on his face. These two couldn't have been more than sixteen. Players in training.

"I think I don't wanna end up in jail," I told him with a chuckle. "But you're kinda cute. Ease up on the game, and you'll be good to go with the ladies." I walked off to place their order.

I got their sodas and brought them over, putting them on the table and taking off before the teen decided to get even flirtier. The door dinged, and I saw Nick stroll through.

My heart fluttered in excitement. When our eyes met, a slow smile creased his face. He moved to the table in the back corner.

"I got the new customer," I told my coworker Dorinda, who gave me a quirky grin with a knowing look on her face.

"He's cute," she said to my departing back as I sauntered over to Nick. I resisted the urge to shoot her a mock glare over my shoulder.

"Hey," I told him, setting down a rolled napkin bearing a

knife and fork. I handed him a menu. "What can I get you to start?"

His mouth parted slightly, and those eyes almost caressed me as his gaze slid down my uniform, then back up. A subtle look, but potent and sexual nonetheless.

The Detroit road trip—and my confession of love, I imagined—had changed things between us. Dropped all the emotional walls, left us open and connected. Our texts and emails and even looks were loaded with intimacy now.

"How about a coffee?" he murmured.

"Can do." It was almost embarrassing how breathless I sounded. "I'll be back over in a few minutes to get your order."

God, it was so hard to pretend there wasn't a relationship here when all I wanted to do was jump in his lap and kiss him senseless, no matter who saw us. Class this morning had been the same way, an hour of pent-up arousal building in me, watching Nick engage with students, his brilliant mind at work. He was so smart, so sexy, I wanted the world to know he was mine.

Thankfully, Kelly hadn't ribbed me about it in class. She seemed to sense the need to play dumb, so there were no side glances, no little teasing comments to me. It had made me even more grateful for her friendship. And more reassured in her promised silence.

I got Nick's coffee and poured him a cup. Popped one creamer on the dish and brought it to him.

He grinned as he dumped the creamer in. "You remembered."

"I'm a good server," I said with a cocky wink. Like I could forget anything about him anyway. Our conversations were branded in my head.

"Okay, I'll take a cheeseburger and fries." He waved to a pile of papers on the end of the table. "Have some grading to do and got bored in my office. Figured I'd take a chance and drop by here to see if you guys were open." But the look in his eyes spoke more than what he was saying.

He'd wanted to see *me*.

I nodded, swallowed. As I picked up the discarded creamer container, I brushed my fingers along his. A small gesture, all I could allow myself to do here, but I couldn't resist.

His Adam's apple worked in his throat, and his eyes grew dark and piercing for a moment. My skin tightened in response. I wanted to touch him again, touch him more, but I was at work and we were on campus. Total bad idea.

"I'll get your food ordered," I said in a throaty voice, then turned and walked away before I did something stupid.

I relayed the order to the cook and made myself check my other tables so I wouldn't keep staring at Nick. But there was an invisible string between us, and I was perpetually aware of his presence in the room, no matter where I was.

When I brought the teen boys' orders over, they did that awkward-guy chuckling, giving each other loaded looks.

"Uh, can I have some ketchup, Megan?" the teen asked. His throat had redness climbing up toward his cheeks.

I grabbed a bottle off an empty table and plopped it in front of him. Kept my smile friendly and polite. "Anything else for you guys?"

"How about your phone number?" the other asked. He suddenly jerked in his seat and reached down to rub his leg. "Ow. Why did you kick me, douche?"

"Why don't you shut your mouth?" his friend hissed back, eyes slit.

"Okayyy, I'll be back to check on you later." I left quickly, not wanting to be caught up in goofy teen boy drama.

Finally, Nick's order was up. I gripped his plate and brought it to him.

"Can I get ketchup too, Megan?" he asked in a low, teasing voice.

My lips quirked and I shot him a little glare. "Overheard that, did you?"

"Can't blame him for wanting your attention," he said as his gaze dropped to my lips.

I sucked the lower one in my mouth, and he groaned. I loved the way I turned him on without even touching him. It made me want to keep pushing the envelope, see how much I could arouse him until he exploded.

To break his careful control.

My nipples hardened at the possibilities, and I found myself arching toward him without realizing it. With a tiny jerk of my torso I swayed back, pressed my hands to my hips. "Can I get you anything else?"

He shook his head slowly, a sexy, crooked grin on his face. "I'm good, thank you."

Twenty minutes later, when I went back to Nick's table, his plate was empty and his napkin was balled up beside it.

"How much do I owe you?" he asked.

"It's on me." When he opened his mouth to protest, I continued, "Seriously, just say thank you and move on."

His laugh was hearty. "Then thank you, Megan. I enjoyed the meal very much." He stood and looked down at me. Leaned his head just a fraction and whispered, "Check the napkin."

With that, he left, the door announcing his departure.

The air that had been locked in my lungs due to our proximity whooshed out. I grabbed the napkin and tucked it in my apron. Hustling to the bathroom, I locked the door behind me, then smoothed the rumpled paper out. A code. Shoulda known.

With a wild grin on my face, I grabbed my pen and began working on it. This wasn't the same code we'd been using, so after a few minutes I had to stuff it back in my apron and finish my shift. In the meantime, my brain was working hard at trying to decipher his message.

I tested a few different patterns. The thing I'd learned about code breaking was that it required patience, diligence, thoroughness. In between serving customers, I tried substituting letters in multiple ways.

Then out of nowhere, the pattern just . . . clicked. The vowel substitutions were my first indicator I was on the right path. I almost dropped the plates I'd bused in excitement. Brought them to the kitchen, then whipped out the napkin and gave it a shot.

Come over tonight after work. Bring a toothbrush.

Oh God. My lungs squeezed so tight it was hard to inhale. Was he asking me to stay the night with him? This would be a big first for us. Funny how I wasn't afraid though—of falling for him, of trusting him, of giving him my heart.

How could I be afraid of something I wanted so badly I could taste it?

Chapter 20

On Wednesday morning, I rushed into class and dropped into my seat with a winded sigh. Thankfully, Nick wasn't there yet, so I wasn't technically "late."

"Oh shit, I overslept," I told Kelly with a breathless laugh. "I can't remember the last time I did that." I'd stayed up late last night working on a paper for my psych class. Since I'd been spending most of my free time with Nick during the school week, I'd spent yesterday doing nothing but schoolwork.

He must have been really busy too, because I hadn't heard from him all day yesterday. Which made me all the more eager to see his smiling face this morning.

"I'm so ready for spring break next week," she said. "This semester has been stupidly long."

Nick and I hadn't made any spring break plans. I was on the schedule to get some good work hours in at the sandwich shop. But I hoped he would be free and wanted to hang out some.

Maybe do another sleepover.

When I'd come home yesterday morning from a night of amazing, intimate sex on Monday night, I was floating on cloud nine. Nick was vital to my life now. I found myself thinking about him all the time. Wondering what he was doing. Wondering if he thought about me half as much.

I dug my notebook out and grabbed a pen, ready to take notes. But my mind wandered a little. Maybe I should ask him to do something with me for spring break. Leave some kind of a coded note for him.

My thoughts were interrupted when Nick came into the room, wearing a dark blue dress shirt and black dress pants. As usual, my breath hitched in my throat at the sight of him. God, he was ridiculously hot. I couldn't help but remember the feel of his hands clutching my hips Monday night as he drove into me, said my name over and over again.

Nick sorted out his stuff and cleared his throat, eyeing the classroom. His face was all lines of tension, and I noticed he didn't look at me.

My heart gave a funny twinge.

"Okay, let's get going on this chapter. Everyone read, right?" He gave a tight smile.

"Is he okay?" Kelly whispered so low I could barely hear her. "Did you two have a fight or something? He seems pissed off."

I shook my head, unable to speak. My heart jumped like a wild bird in my chest. What was going on? I stared at Nick, willing him to look at me. Anything to ease this ache settling in me.

Nothing.

The class period dragged on as I did my best to take notes and pretend I was like every other student in there . . . just eager to finish the week and move on to spring break. But I wasn't. No, my mind was going back through Monday night. Wondering if something had happened then that I hadn't recognized at the time.

He was the one who'd invited me to stay with him. Surely he wasn't pissed about it now, was he? Had I said or done something that had offended him?

Yesterday I'd been studying, too busy to talk with him. But he didn't seem like the kind of guy who'd hold a grudge for that. In fact, he hadn't reached out to me once.

The anxiety of not knowing was eating away at my stomach.

Nick finally dismissed us. I faltered for a moment, wondering if it would be too obvious if I rushed him at the front of the classroom. But before I could do more than rise out of my seat, he'd already gathered his stuff and left.

Pain, swift and sharp and hard, pierced my chest in an almost physical puncture. I blinked back the tears threatening to spill. I was confused, hurt, angry. What had I done to deserve being shut out like this?

My fingers shook as I gathered my stuff, coat draped over my forearm, and ran down the aisle, into the hall. But Nick wasn't there. I just stared into the crowd of students milling through the hallway.

"Hey, you okay?" Kelly said, coming up beside me. She rested her palm on my upper back and made smooth stroking motions.

"Yeah, I'm fine," I managed to say. I sniffed hard and stiffened my face so as not to show the agony coursing through me. I felt abandoned, shut out. This wasn't like him—he wasn't one to do something this harsh.

Was he?

Did I really know him as well as I thought?

"I don't wanna push you," she said gently. "But if you need to talk, just holler. I'm here for you."

I wrapped my arms around her and gave her a shaky hug. "Thanks. I don't know what's happening, but I will find out." When she left my side, I grabbed my phone and composed a text to him.

What is going on??

Then I made a halfhearted attempt to study for the next couple of hours until my second class of the day. The silence from my phone, tucked safely in my pocket, ate away at me until it was almost all I could think about.

But I refused to send him another message. He was the one pulling away, so he had damn well better explain what was going on. If this involved me or if it didn't . . . though I couldn't imagine why he'd freeze me so hard-core if I had nothing to do with the issue.

Of course, my brain wouldn't stop manufacturing scenarios.

That he'd realized he didn't love me the way I loved him and was struggling with how to end it before my heart was too broken.

That someone had told him party gossip about me that tainted the way he viewed me.

That someone had spotted us out together and he was avoiding me now.

That I really was just a piece of ass and nothing more.

I couldn't accept any of those possibilities though. Not until I heard the truth. Right now, all I had were the speculations of my confused, uninformed mind. But I wasn't going to beg him to tell me. Sheer stubborn pride wouldn't let me be reduced to that, no matter how much this was killing me.

My phone vibrated near the end of class. I made myself wait until it was over and I was on my way home before I checked it.

A text from him with four ominous words.

We need to talk.

I exhaled and looked up at the gray sky. The clouds loomed right overhead, filling the entire expanse above me. No sunshine. No break from the monotony.

He was going to break up with me. I could sense it. I didn't know what had happened between us, if it was me or him, but there was only one reason he'd text that to me.

It was hard to keep my hand trembles under control, but I managed to type, *I'll come by tonight.* I put my phone away, gripped my bag and walked home. My heart was cramping in nervous anticipation, but I wouldn't let myself give in to it.

* * *

I swiped my sweaty palms on my jeans and rang Nick's doorbell. A dog bark greeted me, and then the door opened, Gloria's head poking out first, tongue lolling. I bent down to pet her on the head, then rose and faced Nick.

He had a glass in one hand, half filled with a deep amber liquid. The collar of his shirt was undone. His eyes were hooded; I couldn't read him. "Come in," he said, then backed away and opened the door wider for me.

My pulse jackhammered in my throat and at my temples as I stepped inside and stripped off my coat. I hung it up and followed him into the living room. Perched on the edge of his tan couch.

"Can I get you a drink?" He sounded so polite, so formal, so distant. Was it really just two nights ago we were here on this very couch, writhing against each other with naked, sweat-slicked bodies? Now it was as if we were total strangers.

I shook my head and rested my hands in my lap. Sat there quietly, though it was so hard to do so. I knew the answers would have to come from him though.

Nick shrugged. "Suit yourself." He took a swig of his drink and then sat down in the chair adjacent to the couch. His long legs stretched out in front of him, crossed at the ankles. There was a slight smirk on his face—he was drunk, that much was obvious.

My jaw tightened at the devil-may-care flare in his eyes. Was he playing a game here? Was this funny to him? Because I sure as hell wasn't amused. I felt like I was being jerked around. "What is going on with you?" I finally blurted out.

He didn't move, just swirled the drink in the cup, eyes fixed on the sloshing liquid. "I got called into a meeting yesterday." His words were slow and purposeful. "With the dean and others on the tenure hiring committee."

I struggled to keep breathing evenly. My hands tightened on my knees.

"They knew about us." He took another big drink. Still wouldn't look at me, but his voice carried multiple layers of emotions. "They didn't have any physical proof that they could present to me when I asked them to, but my tenure track position is on the line anyway. I was explicitly told I'm being watched. And if I do anything that will sully my reputation—or that of the school—I can kiss it good-bye."

I took a moment to digest what he said. "Okay, that's terrible. I'm sorry. But . . . even if you don't get tenure, can't you just keep teaching—"

"If I don't get tenure, the school lets me go. I'll be canned." This was delivered matter-of-factly, but the impact still hit me like a knife in the gut.

He was going to lose his job over this thing with us.

"Are you serious? How is that even fair?"

"That's the risk you take when you look for a tenure-track job." He took another draw from the glass, then set it on the coffee table and leaned forward. Rested his forearms on his thighs. Finally he looked over at me, and I could see a hint of red in the whites of his eyes, the bleariness in his gaze. He'd definitely been drinking for a while.

Could I blame him though?

No wonder he'd been so weird in class earlier. He'd been stewing in this for two days now.

"I'm so sorry," I managed to say.

He glanced away. "This was my fault, not yours."

"We're both involved here, not just you. I carry equal blame." I crossed my arms over my chest and jutted my chin.

He gave a low snort and rolled his eyes. "And yet *I'm* carrying all of the consequences."

I froze. Anger washed over me in a sweeping tide. "Seriously? You're going to throw that in my face? You don't think this has complicated my life any? I mean, yeah, my job isn't at stake, but my reputation on campus is, not to mention my future at Smythe-Davis. Don't you think a student could come forward and complain to the college that I slept my way into a decent grade in your class, even if that wasn't true? Don't you think that would get me booted from the grad school program? This isn't just you."

I couldn't believe I had to even point that out to him.

Nick opened his mouth to say something, then clamped it shut. Nodded his head and raked his hands through his hair. The locks stood up in messy pieces. "Shit. I'm sorry. That wasn't right of me to say. This isn't just impacting me, I know." He huffed a heavy sigh and sank his face in his hands. His whole body was slumped, defeated.

I'd never seen him like this before, and it broke me, my anger falling away. My heart throbbed in pain, and I bit my lower lip. I wanted to reach out and touch him, but I was afraid.

After a moment, he shook his head and sat up in his chair. His eyes flashed with anger. "Who would have told about us, Megan?"

Oh God. Why hadn't I thought of that part? Someone had alerted the hiring crew, the dean. I'd mentioned it to only two people, Kelly and Casey. Surely neither one of them would have said a word. Would they?

My stomach flipped over, and I pressed a hand to my mouth. Guilt surged hot and hard in me. Was this my fault? Had one of them slipped up and mentioned something to the wrong person?

Would Kelly have gone behind my back and addressed her concerns with the dean? She had been worried about me. But she didn't seem any different today in class. It wasn't just an act, was it?

I hated that this made me doubt the people around me.

I would get to the bottom of this. Find out who had told. But in the meantime, I couldn't have him lose his livelihood over me. Getting canned for fraternization with a student would haunt him wherever he went. He'd be lucky to get part-time adjunct classes anywhere if that were to happen. I couldn't be responsible for his whole life being turned upside down.

I knew what I had to do. My lungs were painfully tight, but I managed to say, "We need to stop seeing each other."

He blinked, looked over at me. His eyes were ricocheting emotions left and right. I could almost see the thoughts crossing his mind. He swallowed, then turned his head away from me. A full minute of silence slipped by without either of us talking.

The weight of my words sagged in the air between us.

Okay, I was the one who'd suggested it, but the fact that he didn't disagree or even put up a fight made my chest sink in on itself. Pride was the only thing gluing me together at this point. I wasn't going to let him see how badly this hurt me.

I stood, grabbed my purse. "I gotta go."

"Wait." His hand snatched out to grip my forearm. His eyes were anguished as they locked on my face. "This feels . . ." He frowned and stood, peered down at me.

Tell me, I willed him. *Tell me this feels wrong, that you want me, that we can make this work somehow.* I knew it was ridiculous to hope for it, given the odds stacked against us, but I still wanted it. Because I was so in love with this man and I wanted to feel I was worth fighting for, even if the fight was harder than anything we'd expected to face.

But he didn't say a damn word, just let go of my arm and exhaled. His breath was warm and tinged with the sweet edge of liquor, and his eyes were dark and hooded. Anguished with what was being left unsaid.

And I could tell in that moment that I'd already started losing him. Or maybe I'd never had Nick to begin with—I didn't know anymore.

That gutted me more than anything. The fact that maybe all

along I'd been lying to myself about how important I was to him. I wasn't worth the wait, wasn't worth hunkering down and persisting for.

"You should be with your mom right now," he finally said in a gravelly tone. "She needs you." His eyes slid away from mine.

He was right; I knew that. But the truth of the matter hurt me anyway. I wanted Nick to need me too, and for him to be there for me while I tried to repair the damaged relationship with my mom. While I tried to make sure she got the help she needed.

The way people in love were supposed to support each other during those rough patches.

I had totally created a fantasy that could never exist, and reality was smacking me in the face.

I gave a stiff nod and turned. Grabbed my coat, ignoring Gloria, who'd lifted herself off the floor to follow me to the door, and left. Walked down the stairs and got in my car and drove to my apartment.

My heart was a solid piece of ice, brittle and cold and aching in my chest. My cries were lodged right behind it, but I refused to let them out. I kept blinking away the sting of tears and focused on driving home.

Only when I was safe in my room, listening to the soothing clacking of Casey's fingers as she typed away at her computer in her room, did I let the tears go and give in to the overwhelming sorrow.

Chapter 21

I scrubbed the deep pot until the mac-and-cheese bits were no longer clinging to the surface. From the living room, soft R&B played, and I tried to let the musical strains wrap around my ragged heart. A week had passed since I'd seen Nick. A week of total silence.

What was he doing? Was he thinking about me at all?

I spent so much time now trying to force him out of my thoughts, willing myself to not give him any extra space in my heart or my head. But it was *so* hard to do, because all of our intense conversations kept creeping back in. My gut told me that he had dropped walls for me too.

And stupid logic hammered steadily away at my emotionally battered noggin, saying it was easy enough for *me* to be upset and feel betrayed when *my* livelihood wasn't on the line. Nick had been faced with a tough decision. Given that this was his life, and I'd only been a part of it for, what, a couple of months? Of course he would choose work.

That was the sensible, smart thing to do. And sensible, smart Megan couldn't fault him for that.

But sensible, smart Megan hadn't had her soul snapped in half last week. That had been the raw, vulnerable side. The side no one else had seen or touched before him.

It was Wednesday of my spring break. I'd basically spent the last several days eating more food than I should, working long hours at Stackers and sleeping. Totally unlike me to not be out having fun. I wasn't one to live in a funk this long, but I couldn't seem to shake it off.

Casey and Daniel had left last weekend on an impromptu out-of-state road trip, so she wouldn't return to the apartment until Friday afternoon, in time to see her grandparents and do her shift at The Mask. So the place was quiet.

Before she'd gone, I'd asked her as evenly as possible if she'd said anything to anyone about me and Nick, and she'd flat out denied it. The truth was there in her eyes—she was innocent. I knew she wouldn't lie to me. But I tried to downplay my feelings about the situation and the breakup during our conversation so she wouldn't change her plans and stay here instead. Because that was the kind of friend she was.

No sense in both of us being this maudlin. I wanted her to go out and have fun. The irony struck me then—how we'd essentially switched places, with her being more social and me withdrawing.

I dried the pot and put it away, then wiped down the sink. Grabbed a Diet Coke and headed to the couch, then draped a blanket over my lap. My phone buzzed.

When I picked it up off the coffee table, the air locked in my tight lungs.

Mom.

"Hello?" I said tentatively.

"Megan, it's me." Her voice was slurring, and my stomach sank to my feet. She sounded like she was intoxicated. Or drugged up, more likely. "We need to talk."

God, those effing words were haunting me lately. I bit back my angry response to them so I wouldn't overreact before hearing what she had to say. "What do you want to talk about?"

I heard her rasping breaths on the phone, then some weird staticky shifting. "Megan, I . . . I need help." There was such weakness in her voice, such pleading that I couldn't help but react. My heart squeezed.

"Mom, did you take something?" I asked quietly.

"He hasn't . . . he hasn't talked to me for days." She gave a weak sniffle, and her voice broke. "I'm afraid he's gonna leave me. And it's all my fault."

"Dad?" Oh wow. I'd been sitting here, festering in my hurt over Nick, and I hadn't bothered to check on my parents in the last few days. Shame and guilt scratched at my skin. I was the worst daughter. "What's going on?"

"I'm losing it," she admitted in a ragged, slurred voice. "And I'm tired and I'm scared and I can't deal with this anymore." Her tired sigh sounded like it ached her bones. "Getting so sleepy, Megan."

I jumped up and gathered my keys. This wasn't a convo we should be having on the phone. I wanted to see her face, talk to her. "I'm on my way, okay? Just stay on the phone with me. Keep talking. Don't go to sleep."

The drive there seemed to take forever. While I drove, I rambled on the phone about anything and everything. What it was like working at Stackers. Which homework assignments I hated. How Casey and Daniel were moving in together. I had no idea whether she was paying attention; she didn't speak much, just made small noises and sniffles here and there, which let me know she was still awake. My head throbbed at my temples, and I was so scared I could barely see straight. But I got to the house—saw only Mom's car in the driveway—and pulled in.

I ran to the front door and went right inside. Saw her curled on the couch in a long T-shirt, her dark, thin legs tucked under her. I hung up the phone and went over to gingerly remove the phone from her grip under her cheek.

Mom tilted her tear-streaked face up to me. "Megan, you're here." She looked exhausted, with massive bags under her eyes. Her skin was ashen, and her hair was a frightening mess. Her eyes couldn't seem to focus, and she gazed around the room.

"Do I need to take you to the hospital?" I asked her as I pressed a hand to her forehead. Looked at her pupils to see how responsive she was. She didn't seem like she'd overdosed. More like when she'd been on the meds for pain. Seriously drowsy.

I wrestled with what to do.

Her head lolled a bit. "No, I only took a couple, I promise. Just because . . ." A fat tear streaked down the side of her face onto the couch, and I bit back my own tears of sorrow. I had to hold it together for her. "I think he's gonna leave me. We had a fight. I love him so much." She paused for a long moment, just drawing in shallow, slow breaths. "I don't wanna feel this pain anymore. I'm tired."

After shifting her so her head was resting on my thigh, I stroked her brow. "The meds won't take away that kind of hurt, Mom. Trust me." I had to swallow a few times to loosen the knot in my throat. "And Dad won't leave you. He loves you too. He's just upset, watching you damage yourself like this. You can't keep doing it."

"I'm not trying to." Her voice took on a stubborn edge. "But when the back pain started returning, I got scared. And the pills took it away." Her eyes fluttered shut, and she seemed to calm from my touches. Her breathing grew a bit steadier.

I scrutinized her for any changes, phone right at my side, ready to call an ambulance if she seemed to show any signs of overdose. Every ten minutes or so, I nudged her to see if she was responsive. Her little sighs and movements showed me she was.

My thighs ached from sitting in the same position, but I held still for the next couple of hours and tried to not shift a lot.

Somehow I sensed my mom needed sleep right now more than anything. The tension in my body unwound fraction by fraction as time ticked by.

Finally I saw her eyelids open. She blinked up at me, then sat up and scrubbed a hand over her face. Her whole body was hunched over.

"You okay?" I whispered.

When her shoulders started to shake, I wrapped my arms around her, and we both cried together. All the agonizing stings in my heart split wide open. Mom threw her arms around me and held me.

"I'm so sorry," she kept saying. I could hear the shame heavy in her voice, still thickened from drugs and sleep. "I was wrong, so wrong to push you away. I know you're trying to help."

I rested my chin on her shoulder. My eyes ached; my head throbbed. I rubbed her back, noting the rib bones were a touch more pronounced than usual. My poor mom. "I'm here for you. But I can't help you until you wanna help yourself."

I felt her nod. She sniffled and pulled away. Her eyes were still glassy, but she seemed more awake than before.

"I promise," she said as she gripped my hand. "I don't want to feel like this anymore."

As I looked in her eyes, I could see the sincerity in them. In this moment, she really was done with it—she wanted to get better. My mom was coming back to me, bit by bit. And I would do my part to ensure it stayed that way. "I'm moving back home for a couple of days while you sort out what you want to do," I added with a steely stare at her. "And *no* fighting me on this, because that's all there is to it. I've already decided."

Her face grew sad, and she stroked my cheek. "My stubborn Megan. So much like me." I heard the ache in her words, the embarrassment. I knew she was beating herself up over this. My mom had never been a weak woman, and I could tell she was mortified to have her vulnerabilities on full display. But the fact that we were talking about this openly gave me real hope for the first time in a while.

"We're family. That's what we do—we don't give up on each other," I whispered hotly and hugged her again. Tears flew to my sore eyes again, slid down my cheeks. But they were cleansing tears, ones that eased that dull throb in my chest.

When we pulled away that time, there was a lot of sniffling and self-conscious chuckles. She and I wiped our tears, squared our shoulders. We were Porter women, and we weren't going to dwell in this darkness anymore. Mom wouldn't let her demons eat away at her, and I wouldn't let my own hurt chew at me either.

This self-pitying wallowing I'd been indulging in was going to stop.

Now.

Every minute that passed, Mom got more alert and sober until she seemed more like her usual self, though a bit more fragile. A bit more skittish. But the high set of her chin was prominent, a hint to the strength still lingering in her, even if she didn't fully feel it right now.

Mom and I researched online what her best options were. She decided it was best if she did a stint of inpatient treatment, to help break her addiction, then pursue aggressive outpatient therapy to address the underlying problems. Obviously it was more than just her physical pain, but I could sense her hesitancy to get into the details with me. That was okay, though— as long as she worked it out with a therapist, that was what mattered. We made a few phone calls to get stuff set up for her.

When that was all taken care of, Mom and I walked into the bathroom, her bedroom, the kitchen, and she dug out new bottles she'd hidden away again after I'd found her old stash. We didn't speak, just flushed the pills down the toilet. Her hands trembled a bit, and I rubbed her back with soothing circles.

Back in the living room, I bent down to the side table and gave Mom her phone. "I think you should call Dad and tell him the steps you've taken. He needs to know."

She took the phone but didn't move to call him. "What if it isn't enough?" The tremulous edge in her words broke my heart. She was so afraid of him rejecting her. "I said some terrible things to him when we last spoke. I don't know if he'll forgive me."

"You have to be honest. Lay it all on the line and keep your promises so he can trust you again. If you do and that isn't enough, then he isn't worthy of you," I said bluntly.

"When did you get so smart?" She gave me a watery smile, her head tilting as she studied me in a new light.

I shrugged. "I dunno. Probably when I realized my mom was the best role model a girl could ever have."

She cupped her hand over her mouth to smother her sudden hiccupping sob. "I'm no role model. I'm weak and I messed up big time. I don't deserve your forgiveness," she managed to say. "Yours *or* his."

"We all make mistakes." I reached over and cupped the hand holding the phone. I hoped my sincerity showed in my eyes. "But what we do about those mistakes is what defines us."

She nodded, and I stood and headed to the kitchen to give her space to talk to Dad without me hovering. I heard her drag in a deep, shaky breath. Then she said, "It's me. I wanted to say I'm sorry and I've decided to get counseling." A pause. Then she sniffled. "Yes. I know. I agree, and it was wrong." Another pause that stretched on for a while. "Thank you. I was so afraid. . . . I love you too, honey." Her voice dropped then, and she murmured more quiet words of affection.

The relief that rushed into me was vivid and strong. I sat down at the table, dropped my head in my hands and let out all the lingering emotion rattling around in my chest with a deep, audible exhale. Then I washed off my face and sent Casey a text to call me when she got a chance.

Things weren't perfect here, but they were on the right track. Mom might have some setbacks, but Dad and I would be there to support her, remind her that she was stronger than her addiction. I could tell she didn't want to take the pills anymore though—it was a baby step, but a step nonetheless. And right now, that was what mattered. I'd totally take it.

I needed something positive to cling to in order to pull me out of my funk. Helping my mom was just the thing.

Right then, I had a sudden strong desire to call Nick and tell him about the breakthrough. I knew he'd be happy for us, that he'd wish for the best. He'd be proud of her, and of me, for what we'd accomplished today. But I had to let him go, and that meant not running to him with everything going on in my life.

The loss stung me again. I rubbed my upper chest and tried to nudge aside my own agony, but it wasn't so easy to shake off. The ache of missing him stole the air from my lungs. The way he'd wrap me in his arms and give me a safe space to talk and cry.

It would be a long time until I stopped craving him.

Chapter 22

I didn't want to be here. At all.

The realization hit me so hard, it was a wonder I didn't have a lump on my head. I leaned my back against the plaster wall and watched a bunch of people grind on each other, laughing, drinking beer and having a great time. It was Saturday, almost the last day of spring break, and everyone was partying it up.

To my far left was a gay couple wrapped around each other, giving sweet kisses and gentle murmurings. My heart squeezed in jealousy whenever I looked at them. God, I'd wanted to have that with Nick.

I stared at the mostly full beer cup in my hand. Beside me, Nadia was dishing on campus gossip—who was hooking up, who had cheated on whom and so on. I could barely pay any attention to her ramblings. She scanned the crowd with a hungry gleam in her eyes, obviously hoping to gather more news to talk about.

Nadia had been texting me the last day or two to ask if I'd come to this party, which was just off campus, giving me a heaping dose of guilt because I'd been ditching her lately. The guilt had worked. I'd been hesitant to go at first, because I knew my dad would be home alone this weekend. Mom had checked herself into the facility Thursday morning, giving us both big hugs and kisses and promising to keep us updated on her progress when she could.

My poor dad had kept it together until she'd gone inside. Then he'd collapsed in my arms and cried. I'd never seen him like that, so vulnerable, so filled with grief and relief at the same time.

We were both praying Mom would stick to it.

As crazy as it sounded, this thing with Mom had drawn us all closer together. The rest of Wednesday evening we'd spent a bunch of family time just talking about anything and everything. I had briefly mentioned that I'd broken it off with a guy I was seeing, not getting into specific details about Nick. They had expressed their sadness about it. We'd played board games, then watched movie marathons late into the evening. Anything to keep Mom distracted from her cravings.

Thankfully, the withdrawal symptoms hadn't had time to really sink in before she'd checked herself in to the facility. I knew from research that they had medication she could take to wean off the narcotics addiction. I prayed it helped.

On Wednesday evening, he and Mom had also called and told their brothers and sisters about her problem—at her insistence, since she knew she'd been acting weird around them lately and wanted to apologize and make amends. Everyone had been so supportive. My uncle, in an effort to help distract my dad, had even invited him over tonight for steak and cards. So this afternoon Dad had basically ordered me to get out of the house and enjoy the last weekend of spring break.

I'd finally caved to Nadia's texts, though I really hadn't wanted to. But if we were all going to move forward with our lives, I needed to take those steps too.

That meant getting myself back out there. Not for dating—

there was no way I was ready for that—but to reclaim my healthy social life. Step one of Operation Stop Being Such a Reclusive Hermit. A wild, crazy party had always drawn me out of my funk before. But it wasn't working this time.

"—unbelievable," Nadia was saying. She tossed a blond lock over her tanned shoulder. "And he didn't even call me to make sure I got home okay. Totally rude."

"Hm," I murmured, and forced myself to pay more attention to her. My brain was screaming for me to get out of here, but I couldn't. I'd roped Kelly into meeting me, and I couldn't ditch before she arrived.

I could understand now why Casey hated these kinds of things, why she'd dragged her feet on coming to parties with me. There was no resonance in them. No way to really talk to someone and get to know the person. It was booze-fueled hooking up. That used to be just fine with me, but it wasn't anymore.

A guy stumbled out of the kitchen and bumped into me, sloshing my beer on my shoes. I groaned and shook them off, the droplets flying everywhere.

"Oh, sorry about that, babe," he said, his bleary eyes locking on mine. He gave me a wide, drunk smile. "Lemme get you another drink." He was pretty cute, a Latino with broad shoulders and a trim body, but he wasn't lighting my fire.

No one lit me like Nick did. I smothered a sigh at the thought and shoved him out of my head.

"I'm good, thanks," I said politely. I didn't really want the beer anyway, but I made myself drink some. Maybe more beer would help me stop thinking of him. I told Nadia I was going to wipe off my shoes, then went into the kitchen. There was a couple making out against the fridge. I grabbed a paper towel, wet it in the sink, then swiped it across my flats. When I went back to Nadia, she'd already had herself wrapped around the drunk guy, their tongues in each other's throats.

Well, that was fast. I couldn't help but laugh. He didn't waste any time making his move when I'd turned him down. It hadn't even been five minutes.

I moved farther into the room, waving at people, keeping a polite smile on my face. Why couldn't I find happiness in this anymore? I'd always known there wasn't anything meaningful in these parties. They were nothing but fun. I flirted like it was my job, sometimes hooked up, got my drink on and danced my ass off.

But nothing about that sounded appealing to me right now.

Maybe this thing with Nick had changed me. And that wasn't necessarily bad—it just was what it was. Maybe it was okay that parties like this weren't my thing anymore. I still liked hanging out, but I could do it on a smaller scale with Kelly and Casey, without all the fakeness.

When Kelly came through the front door, I almost sagged in relief. I rushed to her side and gave her a big hug. "Thank God you're here," I yelled over the oppressive bass thunking through the house.

She eyed the crowd, her brow raised. "Pretty heated up tonight, aren't they?" She didn't sound enthused to be here either.

I looked around. Why was I staying? Because of obligation? To whom? I didn't owe anyone anything. A little of my old backbone made me straighten. "Do you wanna stay?"

"Honestly?" She gave me a hesitant smile. "Eh, I will if you want to."

I laughed. "That's a good non-answer."

"Sorry," she said with a toothy grin. "I love going out, but I'm usually a homebody. I like smaller get-togethers."

"I'm starting to understand why." I paused. "Let's get out of here."

"Really?" Her face lit up. "What do you want to do?"

"Anything. I don't even care." I tossed my beer in a nearby

garbage can, hooked my hand in the crook of her elbow and led her outside through the crowd. The cool night air pebbled my skin, and I sucked in my first breath of fresh air in an hour.

"I know a place where we can get great Indian food," she offered. "Where are you parked? I'll lead the way."

"That sounds perfect. I'm over there." I pointed down the street.

Kelly paused, and I saw the concern in her eyes as she looked at me. "Hey, you okay? You seem a bit . . . off. Not quite your usual bubbly self."

I drew in a breath through my nose. Though we'd previously talked a little about my mom's progress, I hadn't told her about the breakup with Nick yet, for a few different reasons. I was pretty sure she hadn't said anything to anyone; nothing in her body language gave evidence of guilt. But I needed to ask her, and this was a good time for it. "We can talk about it over food. Okay?"

She squeezed my hand. "Absolutely. Follow me, and I'll see you there."

The days slid by in torturously slow segments. Class, work, home. Class, work, home. Lather, rinse, repeat. It was *so* hard going to Nick's class on Monday after spring break and every day thereafter for the next few weeks. But with Kelly at my side, I made it.

That night at the Indian restaurant, I'd talked to her about our breakup. The sadness and pain in her eyes for me were real, and she swore she hadn't said anything to anyone. Each day in his class, she reached over and gave my hand a small squeeze before he came in. A gesture of comfort and support. She knew how much it hurt me to show up there every day with steel in my spine, pretending like my heart didn't crumble apart each time I saw him.

I sat in the back as usual, took notes, never spoke up to answer his questions. I was a ghost in a chair, and he didn't press me, didn't reach out to me at all. I barely looked at him too, because when I did, it ached. Beyond any pain I'd felt. Deep and searing. And it wasn't just my own personal hell that made me feel this way, but the emotion I saw in his eyes.

Nick looked like the light had been snuffed from his life. And it was killing me to see him this way. He was still as clean-cut and well styled as he ever had been, but that warmth wasn't there. I wasn't the only one to notice this. I heard a few students mumble around me about the change in Nick.

Was it because of the threat to his job?

Or was there any part of him that grieved us the way I did?

When our eyes connected, that soul-ripping sizzle ran through me, leaving a dull throb in its wake. Did he feel that too? Did he miss lying beside me in bed, our hands stroking each other's bare skin, our mouths spilling secrets we could only share in the dark intimacy of his room?

I couldn't have imagined how difficult this was going to be.

March slid into early April, and time kept moving forward, as it always did. The hole in my chest didn't quite heal, but somehow I learned to live with it. Grew used to it, even. I hung out with Casey, Amanda and Kelly sometimes. Visited my dad regularly. Mom left the facility and was in intensive outpatient therapy. I could see the difference in her already; she was a lot more emotional than she'd ever been.

And I thought about Nick all the damn time. He haunted me. I could feel his phantom kisses on my brow sometimes when I was lying in bed, thinking of him. I wanted so badly to just go to his house and beg him to not give up on me, on us. But he'd made his choice, despite the misery I'd see flashing on his face sometimes.

You couldn't make a man love you or want to be with you. A hard lesson, but one I'd now learned well. He might be unhappy, but he wasn't doing anything to reach out to me. Though in all fairness, I wasn't doing anything back. We didn't speak, our exchanges limited to brief seconds of eye contact. The silence between us was deafening, a chasm neither of us could—or would—cross.

Finally, it seemed the spring thaw was hitting us. Monday morning, with only three weeks left to go in the semester before finals, I roused myself and went to cryptography. The air was growing warmer by the day, and birds chirped. I noticed tiny buds forming on the trees, and the sight heartened me a bit.

When Nick arrived in class, he looked a bit rushed. Not as well put together, his chin scruffy with a five o'clock shadow. He plopped his papers down on the desk and went over to the chalkboard to scrawl the words *Digital Signature* in his usual assured handwriting.

He turned to face us, leaned back against the desk. His toe tapped on the ground as he said, "Today's chapter is on digital signatures. As you read in your text, when someone sends a message, we need to make sure that person was the actual sender of the message—and that the message maintained its original integrity and wasn't compromised in transit." He paused and scrubbed at the scruff on his chin. Flipped through his papers for a moment. "Hold on. I need to find my notes on it."

A strange feeling slithered into me. This wasn't at all like him. He seemed on edge, distracted. Nick could normally talk at length in our class without once looking at his notes. What was going on?

Students around me began to whisper in confusion. I heard snippets of "He seems weird. Is he okay?" and "I think our prof is having a breakdown." My heart sagged, and I bit my lip to keep from saying anything in response.

Then Nick just slammed his notebook closed and sighed, a world-weary sound that brought everyone to full silence. His eyes slammed into mine for the briefest of moments, and there was something intense pouring from him I couldn't quite understand. My stomach flipped. There was a message in his eyes, but I couldn't interpret it.

He glanced at his watch, scratched his jaw with his other hand. "I'm sorry, class, but I need to leave early today and handle a few matters. You're dismissed." Then he gathered his stuff and left behind a roomful of stunned students.

We all just sat there for a moment, and finally people started getting up and leaving. Kelly shot me a look filled with concern that I felt too.

I needed to go to him. Now.

I tucked my stuff in my bags, fingers fumbling to cram the books in as fast as I could.

"That was so weird," Kelly whispered. "Did you notice how shaken up he seemed? And he's never let us go early."

"I think I need to go see him." Every cell in my body vibrated with the need to do so. I wanted to be the one to comfort him through whatever was wrong.

"So it *is* true," a low voice said from my side.

I raised my head and met Dallas's hot gaze, filled with anxiety and some other emotion underlying. Something that looked dangerously close to guilt. My heart hammered, and I unclenched my jaw. "What?"

"You and Muramoto. You two were dating, weren't you? I mean, I already knew about it, but . . ." His words were thick and stuttered as they rolled off his tongue. His whole face was blood red, down to the tips of his ears.

Kelly gasped. "Dallas," she ground out, narrowing her eyes. "What did you do?"

He turned his eyes down to the ground, and right then I knew the answer with every bit of certainty. Somehow, Dallas had figured out my secret. He'd been the one to tell on me and Nick.

He'd been the one to break us up, to threaten Nick's livelihood.

Chapter 23

Anger hit me hard and swift, and I took a step down the aisle toward Dallas. "What the hell?" I barked out. My hands shook, and I clenched them at my sides. "My life is none of your concern. Who I choose to see, what I do, where I go is my business only. How dare you stick your nose in and gossip about me! I can't believe you." My heated words poured from my lips in a furious rush.

He swallowed and crossed his arms over his chest. His jaw jutted out, and his right eye twitched in the outer corner. Self-defense flared all over his face, in his body language. "I know you're mad, but it shouldn't be at me. *I'm* not the bad guy here." He stabbed a finger at his chest. "And if you step back and be logical, you'll agree." He dropped his voice, but he was still vitriolic. "Megan, I saw the way he looked at you, especially when you two thought no one else was around. Totally inappropriate for a man in his position—a disgusting abuse of his power."

I stood there and glared at him, deadly silent, stomach churning. I had no more words to voice the anger throbbing in me. My forehead cramped with a pending headache, but I ignored it. Kelly didn't speak either; she seemed stunned.

"Okay, yeah, maybe I was a little jealous too," Dallas continued with a defiant glare, but he fumbled his words as he kept talking, revealing his growing anxiety. Obviously he'd expected me to gush about how he was my hero for saving me from the predator professor. Right. "But I couldn't help it. I didn't understand why you liked him and not me, when I tried so hard to win you over. And you wouldn't give me another chance—"

"Who did you tell?" I finally ground out.

His face grew pale as the color washed away from his cheeks. His attention shot over my shoulder, and he cleared his throat. "It's all done now, so we should just move on. Trust me, you're better off."

"Since it's 'all done now,' I deserve to know how it happened." My words were deadly calm.

His Adam's apple bobbed, and he shot his gaze back to me. "Fine. I'm not ashamed of what I did—it was the right thing. I needed some advice on what I should do, so I told my aunt what I suspected. When she told me she was going to mention it to the dean's wife, who goes to church with her, I didn't protest." The righteous indignation pouring off him reeked as he slit his eyes. "*Someone* needed to intervene on your behalf and protect you, so I did."

"Oh, Dallas," Kelly said as she shook her head. She seemed to sense my new burst of anger at his last words and took a step closer to my side. "That was unbelievably caveman stupid of you."

"I can't believe I even need to say this," I said to him slowly, enunciating every word, "but this is the twenty-first century, and I'm a grown woman. I don't need or want a man dictating *anything* I should or shouldn't be doing. Those are my choices, not yours, not anyone else's." My voice dropped to a near growl as I shot him a glare that had him swallowing and backing away. "Stay the hell out of my life, Dallas. I mean it. I swear, if I so much as see you *looking* in my direction again, you will regret it." I knew I was being over the top, but I couldn't help it. I was so pissed off, I could barely see straight.

I flung my bag over my shoulder and stomped away. He called my name a couple of times, but I ignored the sexist jerk.

"Megan, wait, I'm sorry, just let me explain a bit better," he yelled right before I slammed the classroom door behind me and Kelly, right in his face.

Kelly walked with me down the hallway at a fast-paced clip, then drew me down a side hall. We tucked into an alcove, and she stood there quietly while I tried to push my rage back in.

"Dallas broke us up," I whispered a moment later in shock. "Because he was jealous and thought I should have given him another try. Because he thought he knew what was better for me than I do. What a petty asshole."

"I know," she soothed as she rubbed my upper arm. "I can't believe it either. What can I do to help?"

"I don't know." Despair leaked from my voice. "I don't even know what *I* can do."

"Have you talked to Dr. Muramoto at all since you stopped seeing him?"

I shook my head.

"He seemed very . . . upset today," she said. "Something might have happened. I think you should go see him. Do you think it's possible the school is firing him anyway, even though you guys aren't dating anymore?"

The sudden swell of concern in my belly pushed away the last of my anger. "Shit. Do you think that could happen?"

"I don't know." She thinned her lips. "But you should find out."

"I want to talk to him," I admitted. "But I'm scared he'll push me away. It's been so long since we've said a word to each other. What if he doesn't want to see me?" A month of living without him. A month of feeling empty inside. My heart longed to be filled with his soft laughs and easy smiles again.

"But what if he *does* and is afraid to reach out to you? After all, you're not exactly sending him any signals that you want to talk to him either. You look so cool and collected in class, and the only reason I see your deeper feelings is because I've been around you enough to recognize a few of your tells."

"I'm just trying to give him his space," I protested, though of course I'd thought the same thing she had. It had been insanely hard, but I had kept myself closed off so as not to give away my personal agony over our breakup. To not make him feel guilty—or reveal my weakness. Maybe he'd read that as my losing interest.

Or maybe he simply thought he was doing me a favor by staying away.

I just didn't know. And I wouldn't unless I confronted him. Which meant I needed to be brave.

"So why don't you show him just what he's missing? What can it hurt?"

It was a good question. With my heart thudding, I nodded. If my mom could go through all of this to get on the right track, I could go see Nick.

She bussed my cheek. "Be brave, Megan. If you care about him this much, let him know. He might be struggling with this just as much as you are, wondering how you feel, if you miss him too. Guys are vulnerable and emotional, but they don't always know how to show it." She paused. "I know I wasn't supportive of this at first, but seeing you this sad, this lonely, even when you try to put on a brave smile and keep champing through the days . . . it's breaking my heart for you. I just want you happy, lady. And if he makes you happy, go get him."

"You don't think it makes me desperate? Chasing after him like that?" I was stalling because I was afraid. If he rejected me, I wasn't sure how I would ever stop hurting from it.

"Doesn't love make us all a little desperate?" Her smile was filled with understanding, even a little longing of her own. "If I had what you guys did, I'd be running him down until he got tired of me."

I chuckled. My heart lightened a touch with hope. Maybe she was right. It was worth seeing him. And if it was over, then I'd pick up the pieces and move on. But I hadn't given up on my mom through all those rough spots, and I shouldn't give up that easily on us.

If he could possibly love me too, as much as I loved him, then we would find a way to work.

I'd walked away from Nick when he'd agonized with this huge decision. I knew it had tortured him, but instead of talking out options on what we could do, I'd just turned and run, too hurt by what I'd viewed as his dismissal. My chest tightened.

Kelly gave me a quick nod, then left me there with my thoughts. I gathered myself and my courage for another moment, smoothed my shaking hands over the thin fabric covering my stomach, then walked toward Nick's office.

Knocked on the door.

No one answered.

"Dr. Muramoto?" I said tentatively. I didn't see a light coming from the slit at the bottom of his door. Was he not in his office?

I took out my phone and texted him. *Can we talk?*

Should I stay here and see if he'd come by, or leave? Indecision warred in me, and I struggled with what to do.

After a few minutes of no response and no sign of him anywhere nearby, I tucked my ragged heart back in my chest and left his office door. With heavy steps I walked out of the math building. Went to Coffee Baby and halfheartedly tried to study, then trudged to my last class for the day. I didn't hear a word that was said as the teacher droned on and on. All my attention was focused on my silent phone.

I knew he'd gotten my message; my phone told me it had been received right after I'd sent it hours ago, so he'd seen it. But he hadn't written me back.

I guess it was really over.

Sadness hit me in a fresh wave, and I blinked back my emotions. I filed out of the room behind all the other students. Exited the building into the afternoon sunshine and headed to my apartment.

When I reached my apartment building, I paused. Nick was in my parking lot, leaning against his car, arms crossed in front of his chest and lean legs crossed at the ankles. That familiar pose I loved so much. Those gorgeous dark eyes of his were fixed on mine.

My whole body slammed with awareness as I drank him in. Unlike earlier this morning, he didn't seem scattered or distracted anymore. I could sense his attention hot on me, and my skin tightened in response. He was freshly shaved, wearing a new outfit.

"Megan," he murmured as I neared him. I tried my best to fight back my body's response to his proximity. I could smell him—his scent wafting in the soft spring air. "Can we go somewhere and talk?"

Suddenly my eyes began to burn. I felt confused and lost and totally exposed, as if my insides were visible for everyone to see. Why was he here now when he couldn't bother to respond to my text earlier? Not even a quick message to say he wanted to speak with me too? That he would meet me here?

I didn't know if it was petty for me to be upset about that, but I was. I felt out of control, uneasy, my earlier bravado long gone. My brain was scrambled with all the words I wanted to say.

"What for?" I asked him outright.

"I have some things I need to tell you and they're long over-due." His voice was low and steady, but he didn't sound very sure of himself. There was hesitation in his eyes, like he was weighing his words as carefully as possible before speaking. Another glimpse of his vulnerabilities; I wasn't the only one on unsteady ground here. My nervousness faded just a touch. "Just a little of your time, please. I'll bring you right home afterward if you want. I promise."

"We could talk in my apartment," I found myself offering. I wasn't sure I could bear to sit in a cozy car beside him without wanting to touch him. In my apartment I could put space between us.

He paused, then nodded.

My hands shook as I opened the door. I knew Casey wouldn't be in yet, since she'd told me she was working on a big paper all afternoon in the library. I flicked on the light switch.

"This is my apartment," I said lamely. Duh, of course it was. My nerves were making me dumb, apparently. But Nick hadn't been here yet, and I felt beyond awkward.

He stepped in and headed to the couch. Seemed to pause before sitting down, resting one ankle on the knee of the other leg.

I took the chair adjacent, even though my body cried out to rest in the crook of his arm.

Nick was silent for a good minute or two. Silence stretched out between us.

"Is everything okay?" I finally asked, unable to stand the quiet anymore. "You seemed . . . off in class. Is that what you came here to talk about?"

He thinned his lips and nodded, and my heart sank. The look in his eyes wasn't happy or hopeful. Nick hadn't come here to tell me he missed me, or that he wanted me back.

I steeled myself and tangled my fingers together in my lap. Drew in a slow breath and waited for him to start.

"I quit my job," he finally said.

I blinked. "What?" That was so not what I'd expected him to say.

Nick dropped his foot to the floor and leaned toward me, his face inscrutable. "At the end of this semester, I'm done with Smythe-Davis. I put in a call with a grad school buddy to get adjunct work at a nearby college this summer. Plus another sent me a lead on a potential full-time teaching position in the fall. No guarantees, but it looks promising."

"But . . . I don't understand." Why would he quit? What if he didn't get tenure track with another college? "The school dropped everything against you after we stopped seeing each other, didn't they? Are you still in trouble with them?"

Nick rose from the couch, then crouched down at my feet, on his knees. He cupped my hands in his, and that warmth I had craved daily seared my skin, slipped into my veins. His eyes were wide open, and I could see the nervous hope all over his face, tinged with a number of other emotions. My pulse kicked.

"Watching you walk out my door and not stopping you was the single stupidest thing I've ever done in my life. And I have regretted it every damn day. I've seen you in class and have been torn apart by self-loathing at my weakness. It killed me not to talk to you, not to kiss you or smell your skin or hear you laughing. You gave me your heart, and I didn't value it. I'm so sorry for that."

I sucked in a ragged draw of air and bit my lower lip. Hearing those words come from him eased a bit of that raw ache that had taken up permanent residence in my heart. His thumbs stroked the thin flesh of my fingers, sending goose bumps across my arms. He was so close to me, so close, and my whole body just wanted to lean into him.

"Time has given me perspective," he continued in a husky voice. "And I couldn't go one more day in this hollow existence without at least trying to win you again. Am I alone in this, Megan? Have you stopped loving me?"

I shook my head as tears flooded my eyes and streamed down my cheeks, unchecked. I wanted to speak, but my throat was so tight and painful I wasn't sure I could. The hurt and anger and loneliness was fading fast now, replaced with a light buoyancy I hadn't felt in so long.

"I know this seems fast and probably a little crazy, but for once I wanted to follow what my heart told me, not my head. I've spent my whole life aggressively pursuing my life plan without deviation—finishing school, getting a dependable job, buying a house, right on schedule. Then you showed up. . . ." He paused and shot me that familiar crooked grin. His teeth flashed. "And all those plans went right to hell. Because all I wanted was you."

I couldn't hold back anymore. I flung my arms around his neck and slammed against his torso, sliding down to my knees between his thighs. We sat there for a few minutes, touching, exploring, refamiliarizing ourselves with each other. His body was hot beneath my fingers. I felt like I'd been cold until now.

I ran my hands over his muscled nape, his shoulder blades, as he pressed kisses to my tear-streaked cheeks. "I missed you, Nick," I managed to say. "So much."

"Every night for the last month, I've reread all of our messages, relived each moment I spent with you," he breathed against my skin. The warm puffs sent shivers along my flesh. I arched against him, rubbed my breasts to his pecs. He lifted me until we stood, then wrapped his arms around me. "It's been hell, being without you. You haunted my bed, my house, all of my previous solitary spaces. And seeing you on campus was a special kind of torture. My life has been missing that spark you brought into it."

It was everything I wanted to hear. But something kept me from being able to fall into it completely. Guilt over the total upheaval of his life. He was willing to give so much; I could do the same for him.

I pulled back and said, "Nick, I don't mind keeping quiet about us if you want to withdraw your resignation." I'd just have to be extra careful with him on campus so no one else would figure it out. "Or I'll apply to another college for grad school so you can stay, if you're worried about that. I know how important this job is to you—"

"My life is more than a job," he interrupted. His mouth swept a row of soft, soul-rending kisses along my jaw. "I know that now. I can teach anywhere. I want us to have a fair chance, to not have to hide you anymore like you're a dirty secret. You deserve more than that. And so do I." He paused and peered down at me; those infinite, intense eyes looked right into my heart, into all the nooks and crannies of my brain, into every little part of me. "I know this is happening a bit fast, but Megan, my gut tells me if I let you go, I'll spend the rest of my life regretting it. Can we try again? We can take it as slow as you want, but I want another chance. I'll prove to you that I'm worth the effort. I won't hurt you again, I swear."

My answer was simple. I closed my eyes, breathed his name and pressed my lips to his.

Chapter 24

When our lips touched, all the pent-up tension seemed to evaporate from Nick's body. He tugged me deeper into his embrace, then slanted his mouth over mine. Deepened the kiss in a sensual lick of his tongue that had me shivering with need.

"I've missed tasting you," he panted against my mouth.

That made me throb. My belly tightened, and my pulse fluttered in my core. "Me too," I said in a breathy voice. I pulled away long enough to take his hand and lead him into my room.

He followed without a sound. The door shushed closed behind us. Then he was on me again, his hands everywhere, his mouth tasting and nipping and licking. My fingers clawed his shirt apart, fumbled at his pants, and then we were both standing there in our underwear.

His arousal was hard and heavy between us. Nick darted a hand to my naked waist and tugged me to him. Our bodies were flushed with warmth, our mutual heat feeding into each other. "Do you feel how much I want you? Do you have any idea what you do to me?"

With a quirked smile, I reached down and palmed his erection through the thin fabric of his boxers. He groaned, and I felt him twitch against my hand.

"I missed this," I said as I skated my tongue along the line of his collarbone. He shuddered under my ministrations. I pushed down his boxers and let him spring free, then cupped the globes of his ass.

His hands locked on my wrists, and he shoved me away, then pushed me onto my bed. Laid me down and pressed his body against me. His hands slid all over my skin, from ankle to calf, from knee to thigh, up my belly, skating along the edge of my breast. Again. Again.

After a few minutes of that, I was squirming for more. My breasts were ripe and full, nipples aching. I was clenched in need for him.

"Please," I begged him.

He gave me a wicked smile and leaned to my ear. "Please what, Megan?" His tongue and teeth played with my earlobe, the shell, and I shook.

"Please, I need you inside me." I wanted to get him to go faster, so I decided to push the button. "Make love to me, Dr. Muramoto."

That did it. My bra and panties were ripped off and discarded on the side, and I heard the plastic of a condom crackle as he sheathed himself. Nick stroked me between my thighs and my flesh swelled and grew impossibly damp.

"You're so ready for me, aren't you, Megan." He aligned himself on top of me, his strong knees pressing my thighs apart. We were close, so close. I held my breath and waited for him to enter me. "Tell me how much you missed me."

I lifted my legs and wrapped them around his waist, tilting my pelvis so he could enter me easily. My hands cupped his shoulders and I looked right into his eyes. "I missed you more than you'll ever know, Nick."

"I love you." With those words spilling from him, Nick entered me, and I gasped, my core full, my heart full. He withdrew, thrust again. "I love you, Megan. I love you so damn much it hurts."

"Yes, Nick," I murmured, the strokes along my walls bringing that delicious surge to my belly. I squeezed him with my lower muscles, and he groaned, pressed his mouth to the curve of my breast.

One of his hands reached up to caress my cheek as he thrust faster. My orgasm was building, building, and my body began to tingle in anticipation.

"I love you," I told him with all the bald honesty that was in my heart. I loved this man, who had given up something important to be with me. How could I not? My chest filled with everything I was feeling as my heart spilled over.

Nick drove harder, his moves becoming more erratic. He dropped his other hand to flick my tender flesh between us, and I groaned, pressed against those expert fingers. "I need your orgasm, Megan. Give it to me, baby. Please."

"I'm so close," I panted. Part of me wanted to close my eyes and savor the other sensory feelings—his mouth sucking my flesh, his fingers rubbing frantically, the throb of his heartbeat against my chest, the mingled scents of our sex. But I needed to see his eyes when I came.

Right there.

Right there.

He must have read it on my face, because his eyes slid into a confident smile and his finger rubbed the perfect spot.

I exploded. My whole body flew apart in a torrent of sensations, and I shuddered and cried out. "God, yes, yes!" I was a riot of feeling, a maelstrom of need. Nick's body was the only thing anchoring me to the ground.

As the orgasm ebbed, I gave a satisfied sigh and arched against him. My nipples hardened more from each brush of skin. I used my core muscles to squeeze him, and I felt Nick's body stiffen with his growing need.

"Your turn," I breathed into his ear.

He growled, filled me to the hilt and paused. I ground our pelvises together; Nick closed his eyes. "That's going to make me come," he managed to say.

I cupped his face and stole his breath with a deep kiss. I let all of my feelings pour out into him. Nick's eyes flew open and locked on mine, our mouths tangled together; he was as deep inside me as a person can get—both in my body and in my heart.

He stiffened, groaned into my open mouth, and I felt his body jerk as he orgasmed, still staring at me. Those eyes gave me everything that was in him. Those eyes promised Nick's heart belonged to me, Nick's body belonged to me, that he wasn't going to let me go.

It was the most intense moment in my entire life.

Nick collapsed, withdrew and rolled onto his side, pulling me against his sweat-tinged skin. My pulse ricocheted and echoed the frantic gasps of my breaths. His head rested on the pillow as our exhales mingled in the scant inches of space between our mouths.

"That was . . . unbelievably intense," he said as he quickly discarded the condom, then resumed his position at my side. "I've never done that before—had my eyes open when I came."

"Me neither." I was like our souls had touched. I knew that sounded cheesy, but there was no other explanation for the way it had made me feel. My heart tightened and I sniffled.

His eyes turned sad, his hand brushing the curve of my hip. "Are you upset?"

I shook my head and fought back the tears that threatened to come out. "No, I'm just so . . . happy. So overwhelmed by how happy I am. I thought we were done."

Nick brushed a sweet kiss to my brow. "Not by far, Megan."

He loved me. He'd told me he loved me. I was pretty sure my chest might explode from everything I was feeling right now.

As we lay there, luxuriating in coming down from the sexual high, we got caught up on the last month. Nick hadn't done much outside of work, though he said Gloria hurt her hip and was slowing down. "I think she has glaucoma too." He sighed. "My old girl's getting older. And she's pissed at me that you're not there."

I laughed. "How do you know this?"

"Because she keeps going to the front door, waiting for you to show up. Every night. When I call her from the door, she grumbles under her breath and refuses to sleep near me. She misses you almost as much as I do."

Okay, that made me tear up. I squeezed his upper arm and struggled to regain control of myself. I didn't want to dissolve into tears, not now. "I miss her too," I managed to choke out.

"How's . . . your family?" he asked gingerly.

I knew what he was really asking. "Everything's going well." I filled him in on Mom's breakthrough, her inpatient therapy, her intense outpatient counseling. "She says she still has cravings, but she's taking it day by day."

"I can't tell you how happy that makes me. And I'm sorry I wasn't there for you during that." Shame echoed in his words.

"None of that," I chastised as I leaned over and took his mouth in another intimate kiss. "If we're going to move forward, let's let it go."

Our talk meandered more; I wasn't sure how much time had passed until I heard the front door open. Nick sat up and looked at me in alarm.

"It's Casey, my roommate," I said. "Totally fine." Her bedroom door closed a moment later.

He scrubbed a hand along his jaw as he jumped out of bed

and tossed on his clothes. "No, that's not it. Gotta hurry. Time got away from me."

"Where do you need to go?" I sat up and draped the sheet over my naked body.

He eyed my form and his eyes turned inky dark, filled with sensual hunger. "You'd better put some clothes on, or I might end up staying all night here in bed."

I dropped the sheet and gave him the cockiest smile I could. "Is that such a bad thing?"

He groaned and dropped his gaze. "Any other day, no. But we're gonna be late if we don't get going." He finished buttoning his shirt and tossed me my clothes.

"Wait, where are we headed?"

"It's a surprise." He leaned down, kissed my lips, then slipped into his shoes.

I tugged my clothes on, and Nick and I left my room, donned our jackets, then exited the apartment. He ushered me to his car, and we practically peeled out of the parking lot on squealing tires.

"Hold on to your panties, Megan," he said with a sexy, wicked smile.

"God, I forgot what a crazy driver you are," I said breathlessly, then laughed. I clenched the handle as Nick wove the car to the highway. Before long, the downtown Cleveland skyline was in front of us. The setting sun was dipping west into Lake Erie, bringing a warm, clear night in its wake.

Had he made us dinner reservations? I bit my lip to fight the girly sigh that threatened to escape. I hadn't expected anything like that. The preparation he'd put into coming to me today made me feel special. Important.

I reached over and touched his thigh, felt the muscles bunch under my fingers.

Nick got off at an exit and navigated through traffic. He found a parking spot on the street and whipped into it. Shut the car off and practically dragged me out of the car. "Come on, come on," he said in a breathless tone.

I couldn't help but laugh. "They won't start without us," I mumbled. We speed-walked down the sidewalk, turning toward Public Square. Crowds and clusters of people bunched together as we wove our way through and around them.

We crossed the intersection and walked into the small park area, right in the center of Public Square. Spindly trees thrust into the sky around me, tiny buds on the tips of the branches promising that true spring was right around the corner. A stiff breeze danced through the park.

Nick took me to a bench and sat us down, then wrapped his arm around my shoulder to draw me into his heat. I sighed and sank into his arms. Okay, so we weren't rushing off to a dinner reservation, but that was fine. I wasn't starving anyway.

Nick glanced at his watch. There was a strange tension on his face that left me confused.

"Everything okay?" I asked him.

"I've been busy today," he replied lightly. "After I left your class, I had to go offer up my resignation. Then I ran back to my house to pick something up." He dug into his jacket pocket and gave me a small box.

My heart thudded in surprise. "What is this?"

He handed it to me, and my fingers shook as I took it. When I opened it, I saw a small circular disc on a delicate silver chain. A necklace.

On the disc was etched a series of letters.

A laugh poured from my mouth as I clapped my free hand to it. "Oh my God, did you really?" I said, a grin splitting my face almost in two. "You put a code on a piece of jewelry for me?" I studied the letters; it was the simple code we'd first used in our earliest email exchanges.

I quickly translated, and tears filled my eyes. I looked up at him, not bothering to wipe them away. "It's beautiful."

His smile was shy. "I actually got this for you before the stuff happened with work. It has been sitting on my bedside table for a month now. Reminding me what an asshole I was for how things had gone down." He paused, his eyes glowing with all the feelings he let shine through. "I knew back then how I felt about you. I'm just sorry it took me this long to say the words. I was scared, and I thought that letting you leave was the best thing for both of us. That I was being noble, honorable. But nothing made me happy without you there to share it with."

I looked down at the pendant. *Love You Megan.* A simple endearment that etched its way into me like a tattoo. My fingers dug the necklace out of the box as I draped it around my neck and fastened it. I touched the smooth, polished surface. "I don't know how to thank you for this. It's the best gift anyone's ever given me." My heart was roaring with so many things, I wasn't sure I'd ever get it back to a normal size again. It barely fit beneath my rib cage right now.

He gave a secret smile. "I'm glad you like it. When I was out today, I ran another errand too." In the dimming twilight his face warmed with that grin I loved so much. "That's why I didn't text you back, actually. I was busy arranging this."

"Arranging what?" I glanced around. I was pretty sure the park was an open space that didn't need reservations.

Another quick glance at his wristwatch, then he pointed up to Terminal Tower. "Watch."

A few seconds later, the lights just below the golden dome at the very top exploded with color. Red and green chasing lights danced around the building. A couple of kids in the park stopped and pointed.

"Ooh!" one little girl hollered as she tugged on her mom's hand. "Look, up at the building! How pretty, Mommy!"

My heart leaped to my throat, and I turned, teary-eyed, to face this man I loved so very much. "Nick," I whispered through a tightly pinched throat. "I can't . . . I can't believe you. . . ."

"They're red and green, right?" he said with a self-conscious laugh. "I can't tell, but the guy told me he'd make sure to do it. My friend's uncle manages the Terminal Tower. I called in a favor."

"They are the most beautiful Christmas lights I've ever seen." Tears eked out my eyes in a steady stream. I took his hand and moved it to my upper chest, right at my heart. Let him feel the strong, unsteady beat of my pulse. "My heart belongs to you, Nick. I'm never gonna forget this day."

He slid that hand to my neck and drew me to those sexy lips for a kiss. I lost myself in him, willingly gave in to everything I was feeling. All my worries had evaporated. All my pain and sadness was forgotten, scattered like flower petals in a breeze.

When he leaned back, he said, "Would you like to go inside for a tour? We can go all the way up to the top, even into the dome, which is over fifty stories up."

I glanced back over at the red and green lights, which changed to a different blinking pattern. A giggle escaped. "Wow, no way. I've always wanted to see up there." The skyline had to be unbelievable.

"I'll move heaven and earth to make you happy, Megan," he said, the sincerity in his voice ripping my gaze away from Terminal Tower to his eyes. He stood and offered me his hand. "Ready?"

I nodded and tugged him to me for one more kiss, then said with a half smile against his mouth, "I'm as ready as I'll ever be."

Acknowledgments

I wouldn't be here without my family and friends. I'm blessed to be surrounded by so many supportive people.

Peter and all the fab folks at Kensington, thanks for your help in shaping this book and getting it out there to the world. I'm excited that I got to tell Megan's story.

Courtney, you kick ass. Thanks for being an Agent Extraordinaire.

And thank you, readers—I'm so grateful that you took the time to read me, to write me and let me know how much you love my work. I value you so much.

Don't miss Casey's story in
Scratch,
available now!

The most painful scars are the ones you never see.

In her DJ booth at a Cleveland dance club, Casey feels a sense of connection that's the closest she ever gets to normal. On her college campus, she's reserved, practical—all too aware of the disaster that can result when you trust the wrong person. But inexplicably, Daniel refuses to pay attention to the walls she's put up. Like Casey, he's a senior. In every other way, he's her opposite.

Sexy, open, effortlessly charming, Daniel is willing to take chances and show his feelings. For some reason Casey can't fathom, he's intent on drawing her out of her bubble and back into a world that's messy and unpredictable. He doesn't know about the deep scars that pucker her stomach—or the deeper secret behind them. Since the violent night when everything changed, Casey has never let anyone get close enough to hurt her again. Now, she might be tempted to try.

Chapter 1

"Do you have that one new song by Dogface Thirty?" The girl tilted her overly tanned face and gave me a patronizing smile as she hollered up at me, one high-heeled toe tapping on the steps leading up to my booth. "I'm sure you've heard it. You know, where he says in the chorus, 'I wanna bounce your big—' "

"Yeah, I got it," I interrupted with a polite smile in return. I hated that song and its misogynistic, stupid lyrics, but that didn't matter. "I'll cue it up to play as soon as I can fit it in."

"You really should. People want to hear that one, and sooner rather than later. Oh, and here." She dug into her purse, flipped through a massive wad of cash, peeled off and tossed a single dollar bill on the corner of my equipment. Then she waggled her fingers and walked away, swaying hips encased in the tightest, shortest skirt I'd seen so far tonight.

"Thanks so much," I said to her retreating figure, fighting the urge to roll my eyes about her cheap tip. Oh, well—she didn't have to give me anything at all, so I guess it was better than nothing.

She either didn't hear me or didn't care about the edge of sarcasm in my tone, having disappeared back into the sweaty, raving crowd, which was currently tangled and dancing en masse to the deep, thrumming bass blasting out of my speakers.

I popped my headphones back on and transitioned to the next song, a dub-step that recently came out and was hitting the indie charts big-time. While a few of the club's patrons were full of themselves, like the lovely Oompa-Loompa chick, most of them were awesome and enjoyed my varied music mix. They would shimmy up to my table, drinks in hand and smiles on their faces, and toss me a ten just for playing a song they love. Being here made my weekend nights fly by.

And I had to admit, there was something hypnotic and empowering about being the person to bring dancers to a fevered pitch. Whenever I deejayed here and fed the crowd's craving for good music, we connected in a way. Something I didn't allow myself on campus or anywhere else. Up here I could watch them without actually being a part of their chaos.

I took a swig of the dregs of my lemon water, fanning my plain blue tank top to cool the streams of sweat slipping down my torso. Gently, so my shirt wouldn't pull out of my waistband and show my stomach scars. The Mask, one of the Cleveland area's most popular dance clubs, typically heated up fast due to being packed, but tonight it was warmer than normal. Only an hour into my gig and I was already dying in these clothes. Perhaps if my outfit were smaller and sheerer, like the other girls', I wouldn't be sweating like this. No way in hell was that gonna happen, though.

Justin, one of the bartenders, strolled over to me bearing a fresh glass of lemon water. "Here ya go, Casey," he said with a friendly smile. His red-tipped hair was styled to perfection, and he wore a slim-fitted black tee and skinny jeans. Smart guy, playing up his trim body—women came on to him all the time.

He was gay, but had no problem flirting with anyone to get a bigger tip.

"Oh, you're psychic," I replied, tugging out an ice cube and rubbing it across the back of my neck. My hair was pulled up, but the thick tips of my ponytail clung to my wet skin. "It's extra hot in here tonight."

"Sal said the air conditioner is on the fritz." He snorted. "Let's see how long it takes him to get it fixed."

"Probably never." I chuckled. "He'll make more money off these people by keeping them sweaty and thirsty. Clever man."

When I'd answered the ad in the paper three months ago looking for a part-time DJ in an up-and-coming dance club close to my campus, Sal had instantly struck me as a savvy business-man. Short, squat and completely unapologetic for his brashness, Sal had taken one look at me, rubbed a thick hand over his bald head and said, "*You're* a DJ? Ain't you a bit young, sweet-heart?"

Yeah, I looked younger than a freshly minted twenty-one-year-old, which made it hard for people to take me seriously. But when I'd assisted my older cousin John two years ago as he deejayed a distant relative's wedding, I was instantly hooked. I saved up my spare money for several months to buy my own refurbed equipment and music and started working with him regularly, doing parties and other gigs.

William had seen Sal's ad and encouraged me to give it a shot, though with the way Sal's eyebrow had crooked at me, I knew he was skeptical. So I'd looked Sal straight in the eyes and said, "I have an amazing music collection and I own my own equipment. I'm reliable, hardworking and I know music. If you want this club to be a success, fast, I can help you."

I had no idea where that had come from. Desperation? False bravado? I didn't know, but I wanted this job for some reason. Needed it. Enough to blow smoke up his ass and make myself sound amazing.

Sal had stared at me for a long moment, then laughed, clapping me on the back. "You ain't too bad, kid. We'll give it a trial run, see how it goes."

Three months later, I was still here.

A group of young women, wearing nothing more than tiny, stretchy dresses and wide smiles, stumbled into the club, arms thrust in the air and whooping loudly. They looked trashed already, and it was barely eleven. I hoped they wouldn't cause any drama. One girl had on a tiara and a sash—either she was getting married soon or it was her birthday. Odds were, one of her friends would come over and insist I *had* to put on an overplayed booty-grinding song just for her. Since they typically tipped the best, I accommodated their wishes as quickly as I could.

Justin came back over, a mysterious grin on his face and a light beer in his hand. He put the beer on my side table. "This is for you."

I squinted at him. "Uh, thanks, but you know I don't drink." Never while I was working and rarely any other time, even my nights off when I was at home. Drunk people lost control, said and did things they regretted.

"It's not from me." He nodded his head toward the bar. "One of the guys there bought it for you."

Someone had bought me a drink? I scanned the bar, looking over the crowd. So many people packed in there that I couldn't tell who it could be.

"Well, it was nice of you to deliver it personally," I said, giving him a wry smile.

He grinned back, winking boldly. "I wanted to see your reaction."

I knew why. No one ever bought me drinks. I didn't dress sexily, didn't flaunt my stuff or make myself front and center at the club. The music spoke for me, and I was happy that way.

But someone had noticed me anyway.

"He's *really* cute, too, by the way. If you don't want him, I do." Justin sauntered back toward the bar, waggling his fingers over his shoulder.

My heart thudded. I was flattered and uncomfortable at the same time. Who was my mysterious benefactor? Should I acknowledge it? Would it be rude to not do so?

My hand shook just a bit as I lifted the beer and nodded my head toward the bar. I couldn't see the guy, but I figured he could see me and my thanks. Then I took a tiny drink to be polite and put it back down on the table.

The next couple of hours flew by. Despite the growing heat, the club was packed and extra feisty tonight. A couple of girls in my business finance class had taken a break from the dance floor and came up to me to say hi, beer bottles in hand. I'd given them a polite smile in return and told them to let me know if there was anything they wanted to hear.

Break time. I needed a stretch and some fresh air, stat. I set up the mix CD to play through, gave a wave to Justin to let him know I was taking my break and slipped out the back door near my DJ booth. The air outside wasn't that much cooler than in The Mask, but a refreshing breeze slipped down the alley. I leaned against the warm brick, lemon water in hand, and sighed happily, taking a sip of my drink.

Normally the alley had a few smokers milling around and a couple of drunk people making out hot and heavy—not bothering to hide the sounds of their horniness—but no one was here right now, which gave me a moment of much-needed quiet. I took a deep breath and rolled my stiff neck.

Then a deep voice from about twenty feet away in a pitch-black part of the alley broke the silence. "Uh, is this spot taken?"

At the guy's voice, I nearly jumped out of my skin, sloshing my water all over my arm. I slipped my free hand to my back pocket and patted my pocketknife to make sure it was still there. I'd never had to use it, of course, but better safe than sorry—especially since no one else was around. "Who's there?" I was proud of the way my voice sounded smooth and confident, despite the tremor in my hands.

A tall, black-haired guy in faded jeans and a white T-shirt came out from the darkness, holding his hands up in front of him as a universal sign of nonaggression. I recognized him—he was in my philosophy class. Couldn't remember his name, but his green eyes struck me just as hard now as the day I'd first seen him in class two weeks ago. He'd cracked a couple of philosophical jokes with our professor that went over everyone else's heads, and they'd laughed for almost a minute, to the point of her practically wiping away an amused tear.

His odd sense of humor hadn't put off any girls, though—he'd already attracted two in our class who sat on either side and flirted nonstop. I sat right behind him, and despite my best efforts had noticed how broad his shoulders were, how nicely a T-shirt hugged his lean torso. I'd also noticed how piercing a girl's giggle could really get when she was in serious man-hunting mode.

The guy had a wry grin on his face as he stepped closer, stopping about ten feet from me. He ran a hand over his mess of black hair, and I could see the muscles in his arms flexing. "Sorry, didn't mean to scare you. It's hot as hell in there, and I ducked back here to cool off."

"Hot as hell out here too," I said cautiously, eyeing him. My upper lip beaded with moisture. I forced my shoulders to relax. He wasn't acting odd or anything, but I'd keep a close eye on him anyway.

He glanced at my water glass, the spilled liquid drying rapidly on my skin. "Sorry, I'd have sent something else to you if I'd known you weren't a beer fan."

My heart thudded in surprise. *He'd* sent me the drink? "Uh, thanks. But why buy me something at all?" I blurted out. God, I sounded so awkward. And unappreciative. I didn't want to give him the wrong idea about me, but I didn't need to be rude either. Grandma would have given me the evil eye for being so ungracious.

He crooked his head and a slow smile spread across his face. "Why not?"

I raised one eyebrow at him and pursed my lips, not really sure how to reply. Master flirter, I was not.

"You're Casey, right? We're in philosophy together," he said, tucking his hands into his back pockets and rocking back and forth on his feet. "I sit right in front of you, as a matter of fact."

I nodded, trying to ignore the way my heart rate kicked up a notch. So he'd noticed me too. For some reason, that realization made small tingles cascade across my flushed, damp skin.

"I've never met a DJ before. How do you pick what music to play?" he asked suddenly, sliding over to lean on the brick wall, facing me but not moving any closer. He crossed his arms in front of his chest as he studied me.

"Um, I . . . do a mix of stuff I dig and stuff the crowd wants to hear. Mostly top-played songs that everyone knows, but also some B-sides and indie hits," I replied, feeling a bit too off-kilter to sound intelligent. The way he was staring at me openly, yet giving me patient space, threw me off.

Sure, I'd been hit on before—pretty much any woman with working female parts would get picked up in a bar by some guy at some point—but after a couple of minutes of clumsy conversation, the guys backed off, realizing I wasn't going to be an easy lay. This guy was different, though. He ignored my awkwardness, keeping his mood casual, nonthreatening.

My body relaxed a touch more.

"I liked that one song where the bass line was echoed by the keyboard, back and forth like a duel," he said. "Haven't heard it on the radio before."

My throat tightened for a second and my cheeks burned hot

in a strange flush of pleasure. I knew exactly which one he was talking about.

It was my song.

This week I'd done something I hadn't dared try before. I slipped in one of my own compositions, a piece I'd worked on for weeks in my spare time. I'd loaded up another dance song just in case I needed to change it out due to poor crowd reception. But no one had seemed put off—they'd simply shifted their dance around the tempo and continued the musical foreplay on the floor.

The guy shoved off the wall and gave me a friendly nod. I noticed the well-worn Converse on his feet, and for some reason that made me smile. I had a pair of Chucks, too, stashed in my closet, in a neat row beside my other shoes. "I'd better head back in before my friends think I got my ass kicked in the alley or something," he said with a laugh.

I licked my lips. Sweat dribbled down my back, tickling my skin. "Uh, I have to also. Thanks again for the beer," I added.

He gave me that slow, wide grin again that flashed his bright teeth. Something about that smile made my breath hitch in my throat. Justin was right—this guy was *really* hot. Hot and unnerving. I didn't know what to make of him at all.

He turned around to leave.

"What's your name again?" I said to his back, embarrassed I had to ask but needing to know.

He paused his step and looked over his shoulder. "It's Daniel. See you in class on Monday, Casey." He stepped back into the dark, swallowed whole in the pitch-black early September night.

I took my half-empty glass and made my way back to my DJ booth. For the rest of the night, it took all my willpower to not look over at him with his group of friends by the bar.

In spite of my better judgment, I couldn't get him out of my mind.